Praise for Amanda Robson

'A fabulous rollercoaster of a read – I was obsessed by this book'
B A Paris, author of *Behind Closed Doors*

'Fast-moving, compulsive reading'
Jane Corry, author of *My Husband's Wife*

'An addictive, compelling read, full of tension'
Karen Hamilton, author of *The Perfect Girlfriend*

'Compelling and thoroughly addictive'
Katerina Diamond, author of *The Teacher*

'Characters you will love to hate and an ending that will make your jaw drop'
Jenny Blackhurst, author of *How I Lost You*

'A taut thriller full of page-turning suspense'
Emma Flint, author of *Little Deaths*

'Expertly injects menace into the domestic'
Holly Seddon, author of *Try Not to Breathe*

'No one does toxic relationships quite like Amanda Robson'
Sam Carrington, author of *Bad Sister*

'Twisty, taut, vibrant and addictive. The queen of the page-turner'
Caroline England, author of *My Husband's Lies*

After graduating, Amanda Robson worked in medical research at The London School of Hygiene and Tropical Medicine, and at the Poisons Unit at Guy's Hospital where she became a co-author of a book on cyanide poisoning. Amanda attended the Faber novel writing course and writes full-time. Her debut novel, *Obsession*, became a #1 ebook bestseller in 2017. She is also the author of three more domestic suspense novels: *Guilt*, *Envy* and *My Darling*.

Also by Amanda Robson

Obsession
Guilt
Envy

AMANDA ROBSON

my darling

avon.

Published by AVON
A division of HarperCollins*Publishers* Ltd
1 London Bridge Street
London SE1 9GF

www.harpercollins.co.uk

A Paperback Original 2020

First published in Great Britain by HarperCollins*Publishers* 2020

Copyright © Amanda Robson 2020

Amanda Robson asserts the moral right to
be identified as the author of this work.

A catalogue copy of this book is available from the British Library.

ISBN: 978-0-00-840340-9

20 21 22 LSC 10 9 8 7 6 5 4 3 2 1

Typeset in Bembo by Palimpsest Book Production Ltd, Falkirk, Stirlingshire

For more information visit: www.harpercollins.co.uk/green

To my family

1

Emma

After my last relationship, I was looking for love in all the wrong places. Until I began to use Tinder. Until I found you, Alastair, and swiped right. It's hard to find the perfect man. Men can be so controlling at times.

2

Jade

We move into our new house, Fairlawns. A large Victorian detached, near the river in Henley-on-Thames. Top-end comfort. Top-end price. Arriving in our Porsche, just as the removal men are entering the house with our walnut dining table, I look up and see a man and a woman standing at the side window of the house next door, staring down at us.

The woman is seriously tarty. Long blonde hair, bleached, not natural. Smelling of Botox. Not wearing very much clothing. Her short house coat does not leave much to the imagination. Very much your sort of thing, Tomas. Not a woman, but a stereotype. As I watch her looking down on us, I determine you will not get away with it again. *Don't even try it*, I tell you with my eyes.

3

Alastair

'Spill the beans, what are they like? Save me from getting out of bed,' you say.

'The man is a serious looker – like Jason Donovan in his prime, with darker hair and darker eyes.'

'I'll look forward to meeting him then.'

'Watch it, Emma. You know I can't cope when you admire other men,' I joke.

'And is there a woman?'

'Yes. Big-boned. Neat-featured.' I pause and continue staring out of the window. 'Four removal men. Furniture coming out now. Expensive furniture.'

'How do you know it's expensive? Can you see the price tag?'

My stomach tightens, because money is an issue between us. Dentists earn far more than forensic scientists. Especially dentists who have inherited a lot of money. Top career. Expanding your dental practice to inject Botox and facial fillers, it all adds up. Whereas I'm always struggling. A child and a difficult ex-wife to support means any unexpected extra expense is a mountain to climb.

'A walnut dressing table.'

'Brown furniture isn't as expensive as it used to be.'

'It's still expensive to me.' I pause. 'OK then, what about this? A fancy sofa. Candelabra. A racing bike.' I press my face against the window. 'A large box marked "Silver".'

'You sound as if you've got the binoculars out,' you say, slipping out of bed, pulling your silk dressing gown across your naked shoulders and coming to join me.

Your cat Casper yowls from the bed. He doesn't like it when you leave him. He follows you everywhere. Sure enough, seconds later, this special animal who looks like a cross between a baby polar bear and a tiger – stripy face and tail, fur like white candy-floss – leaps off the bed to join you, rubbing his head and body against your ankles. Smiling, you lean down to stroke him. You dote on him. I know he's some unusual pedigree breed that you insist on not allowing out, but don't you think that keeping a cat inside is a little cruel, however highly strung and dependent he is?

You put your hand in mine. I pull you towards me and kiss you. You taste silky. Like strawberries and cream. My erection stirs and I want you again. Even though I know you're too good for me, every time I have you I want you again.

4

Jade

I walk around our new home. Almost everything is in place after the move. I set out towards the Stereotype's house, to invite her and her partner over for supper. Time to get to know her. Time to see what I'm dealing with.

5

Emma

Dinner parties have never been my thing; trapped around a table making small talk. But my new neighbour Jade coerced me into accepting her invitation. With a nod of the head. With the solidity of her face. So at 8 p.m. on Friday evening, I find myself standing with you, Alastair, on Jade and Tomas' doorstep, clutching a bottle of red wine and twelve yellow roses. The door opens. Jade. A big woman. Nearly six foot tall. Short dark hair. The 'make-up-is-a-sin' type.

'Do come in,' she beams.

We step inside a hallway of mirrors and lights. I hand her the roses and wine.

'You shouldn't have,' she says, voice so hard I almost guess she means it.

She leaves them on a glass dresser as we follow her along the hallway. Through the dining room. The table is laid for supper. Silver mats. Silver goblets. Heavy silver cutlery. A centrepiece of shiny black orchids. We arrive in a large sitting room containing toffee-coloured sofas draped with cowhide, which scream against the period of the house. Why did they choose a Victorian house when they own furniture like this? Jade's husband is standing by a cocktail bar built of oak, with brass cupboard handles. I've only ever seen anything like this in 1970s sitcoms.

'What can I get you?' Tomas asks. His eyes sparkle at me. 'We've got everything. Beer. Cocktails. Bubbles.'

'Bubbles, please.'

'And you, sir?' he asks, turning to you.

'Beer please, mate.'

Jade is standing by Tomas' side, back straight, hands by her side. She is wearing a simple black cotton shift with a belt. Too plain. Too simple. Clothing suitable for a funeral. Not much fun for a Friday night supper.

Tomas fixes our drinks and we sit down. Couples together on opposing sofas.

'You look pretty organised. How are you settling in?' I ask.

'I can't function if things are out of place. I'm a bit OCD. Aren't I, darling?'

Tomas stirs uneasily. 'Isn't everybody? No one likes their house to be a mess.'

'Where did you move from?' you ask.

'Hampton Hill.'

'And what made you choose the Thames Valley?'

'Why do you ask that?' She leans forward and pushes her eyes into mine. 'Are we the new neighbours from hell, or something?'

I shake my head. 'No. No. I just wondered whether it was a job thing?'

'The job conversation always feels like pulling teeth.'

'That's an apt thing to say to me, because I'm a dentist,' I say, trying to keep things light.

She shrugs. 'OK. So now, thanks to you, we do the job thing.'

I stiffen inside. I didn't mean to offend her. You glance across at me. He puts his beer on the table in front of him, leans back and folds his arms.

'It's fine with me. I'm a forensic scientist. I'm happy to tell you what I do. What's wrong with talking about work?'

'It's good with me, too,' Tomas smiles. 'I work in the City, as a hedge fund manager.'

Jade gives her husband a look, to scold him for joining in.

Not wanting her to get away with this, 'What do you do?' I ask.

7

A saccharine smile. 'Since you're wanting to judge people by their jobs, why don't you try to guess?'

'Are you an estate agent?'

She shakes her head.

'Travel agent perhaps?'

'No.'

'Teacher?'

Her head continues to shake.

Frustrated by this silly game, 'Circus acrobat?' I suggest.

She laughs. I sigh inside with relief. At least she has a sense of humour. 'No. I'm retired. But I used to be in forensics too,' she replies.

'What sort of forensics?' Alastair asks.

'An academic. Professor of Forensics at the University of West London.'

'So why did you quit?' he pushes.

She hesitates. 'It's difficult to feel fully involved in crime when you're based at a university. So distant from the cut and thrust of the police.'

'So why didn't you move to my side?'

'Too boring and repetitive.' A slow, strangled smile. 'In this life nothing is ever perfect.' There's a pause. 'And I would like perfect.'

'Wouldn't we all,' Alastair replies. 'But I have to say, I get a lot of satisfaction from my job.'

'Each to their own.'

She turns to me. 'Come on, Emma. Enough small talk. Come and help me with the starter.'

I stand up and follow her from the room. Out through the dining room, across the hallway. Into a smart, shiny kitchen with white cupboards and a black granite top. A large arrangement of black and white orchids adorning the central station. The type of orchids that look as if they are plastic, but if you squeeze their stems they bleed. She opens the stainless-steel larder fridge, takes out four dishes of prawn cocktail and bangs them onto a tray.

'It's ready. I don't need your help, I just wanted an excuse to talk to you in private.' She leans towards me, across the kitchen counter. 'I want to warn you that my husband Tomas has a wandering eye.'

'What do you mean? Are you trying to tell me that he's unfaithful?'

She sighs. 'He'd be upset if he knew I was talking about him behind his back.' She shrugs. 'But, yes. He has a penchant for having affairs.'

I stand looking into Jade's sad face, unsure of what to say.

She blinks and shifts her weight from side to side. 'Come on, let's go back and join the men. Make yourself useful – carry the tray.'

6

Emma

'What do you make of our new neighbours?' I ask you, later that night, as we lie entwined in my king-sized bed.

'Tomas seems all right,' you reply. 'But Jade's a strange one – disparaging about my job. Unenthusiastic about her own.' You pause. 'A glass-half-empty type to be wary of.'

I snuggle up closer. 'When I was on my own with her in the kitchen, she said Tomas has "a penchant for having affairs".'

'Strange thing to tell your neighbour the first time you meet.' You kiss my neck. 'I reckon she's a clusterfuck.'

I giggle. 'Clusterfuck. I like that. But maybe it's a bit unfair. Lots of people are glass-half-empty about their jobs.'

You laugh, 'But not many people are so disparaging about their husband to a complete stranger.' You roll away from me and slide into your sleeping position. 'Living so close to her, I guess you'll soon find out what she's like.'

7

Alastair

Driving home from the lab after a boring day. Hanging around in scrubs for too long, waiting for some evidence that required urgent analysis to arrive. So urgent the police hadn't found time to bag it. By the time it came it was 5 p.m., so I stayed a few extra hours to make a start, but I'll have to finish off tomorrow. The salary I'm on is not enough to justify pushing the boat out and staying all night. Perhaps I would if they promoted me.

Stuck at the lights, longing to get a beer. Longing for a chat with Mother. Hoping Stephen is in bed. I fancy a quiet time. Supper, beer, TV, chat with Mum.

I park on the street outside the Italian restaurant and open the door beside it, which leads upstairs to our flat. As usual the scent of toasting mozzarella and basil assaults my nostrils, making me feel hungry as I climb up. As soon as I step inside my home, Mum scuttles into the hallway.

'Heather is here. In the sitting room. Waiting to speak to you,' she whispers. 'Stephen's in bed.' My heart sinks. Heather, my ex-wife. Another clusterfuck. 'Now you're here, I'll leave you in peace and go and relax in my room,' Mum continues.

She pads along the narrow corridor rubbing her back. Sixty years old, hunched, as if she was eighty. Why won't Heather take responsibility for our son? What's wrong with her? Mum disappears into her cramped bedroom. I've made it as nice as I can, with a small TV, and big cushions, to make her bed double up as a sofa. I wish I could afford a nanny. Mum needs a break. If I could, I'd send her on an exotic holiday, to Mauritius, or the Caribbean.

Sighing inside, I open the door to the lounge. Heather is sitting on the sofa, glued to *Love Island*. As soon as she sees me she turns the volume down, but leaves the picture on. A group of women with pouty lips and extravagant figures are sitting by a swimming pool drinking cocktails; an orangey-brown mixture decorated with pink umbrella cocktail sticks. And laughing. A male Adonis walks towards them, beer in hand, and their eyes fix on his pecs. I try to ignore the screen and look at Heather, but I become glued to his pecs too. I really should work out more.

'We need to chat,' Heather says, forcing me to drag myself away from the on-screen overdose of oestrogen and testosterone.

'OK then. But let's turn the TV off.'

'I can watch and chat,' she snarls, her upper lip curving upwards like a horse's.

'Well, I can't. So if you want to talk to me, you need to turn it off.'

She waves the remote at the screen, remaining transfixed as it closes down, then turns to look at me. Her hair is a mess, and she's gained quite a bit of weight. I thought newly divorced women tended to smarten up. With Heather, divorce has had the opposite effect. What is going on with her?

'What do you want to talk about?' I ask, hovering in the door-way. I haven't had a civil conversation with her since the day she left me.

'I need more money. I can't cope.'

I shake my head. 'I don't have any more to give you.'

'Yes you do. You've shacked up with that wealthy bint.'

'If you mean Emma, I've only just met her. And I haven't shacked up with her. As you may have noticed, I live here with our son Stephen, who you've abandoned. Hardly the lap of luxury, is it? A flat above an Italian restaurant. If I'd taken better advice I'd still be in the family home.'

She shrugs her shoulders. 'Well, I'm not in the family home either. The Robinsons who bought it off us are.' She hesitates. 'You know I'm living with a girlfriend for now, while I decide what to do.'

I frown, exasperated. 'I know you're living with Shelly. But that's your choice. You got your share of the house sale.' I pause. 'What have you done with it? Why are you asking me for more money?'

'That's a no-brainer, isn't it? You know I'm out of work at the moment.'

'Get a job. Any job. It was your choice to stop your teacher training.'

She sighs. 'I was finding it too stressful, after everything that had happened between us.'

'Life is stressful,' I say, really losing patience now. 'You need to get a grip.'

'Always so empathetic, aren't you?'

'Look, Heather, you only have Stephen every other weekend. I'm already bearing the brunt of the expense. I don't see what's unreasonable about suggesting you get a job.'

'You're selfish, Alastair. You even went to Paris for the weekend.'

How does she know that? I didn't even tell Stephen where I was going for my birthday treat with you, Emma. You must have put a picture on Facebook and Heather must have seen it.

'Alastair, I need you to cough up, please.'

I shake my head. 'I'm sorry, I just can't afford to, Heather.'

'I don't believe you.'

'Try. Just try and get more money out of me,' I hiss.

8

Emma

On Tuesday evening as soon as I pull into my drive, Tomas scurries towards my front door. I park the car and step out.

He looks pale and worried. 'Is everything all right?' I ask.

'I've got toothache. It's killing me. I was hoping you could take a quick look.'

Not what I wanted after a long day at work, but how can I refuse to help?

'Come in then, I'll find my equipment.'

I open the front door. He follows me into the house, through the hallway into the kitchen. I reach for the spare dental tools I keep in the dresser, in case of an emergency. I pull out my bag, unzip it and take out my sterilised tools: a probe and a mirror stick.

'Let's get you comfy in the sitting room.'

He follows me through.

'Please sit in the leather chair.' He does as I ask. 'Open wide,' I instruct, leaning over him. I examine each tooth carefully and sigh inside. Poor man. His mouth is in such a mess.

'The gum by your lower right molars is red and inflamed. It looks like a pretty painful infection. I'll write you a private prescription for some antibiotics.' I find my prescription pad in the drawer by the telephone and prescribe metronidazole. 'No alcohol while you take these tablets. I'm giving you a five-day course. But if you don't see a substantial improvement in a few days' time, come and see me in the surgery.'

His soft brown eyes melt into mine. 'I'm terribly grateful, thanks.'

9

Alastair

Heather's voice grumbles down the intercom. 'Who is it?'

'Alastair. I need to speak to you.'

'Come on up.'

The intercom buzzes and I push the door to open it. Up the staircase to the fourth floor. To Shelly's flat. Shelly. My least favourite friend of Heather's. Bridesmaid at our wedding. Shallow. Artificial. Always looking to find a rich husband, rating boyfriends' attraction by the value of the car that they drive. Well, she hasn't found one yet, otherwise she wouldn't be living in this dump of a flat. Lord only knows why Heather has decided to live here with her, when I have given her half of everything I have, even though I have custody of our son.

Flat 4B. I knock on the door and Heather opens it. She is wearing a navy Juicy Couture tracksuit which clings to her heavy thighs. Her hair needs brushing.

'I suppose you'd better come in,' she says with a snarl.

I wince. Her breath smells acidic and I know she's been drinking. I follow her into a small, dark sitting room, with a brown faux-leather sofa and a russet carpet. She picks up a bottle of beer and takes a swig.

'Can I get you anything? Coke? Dope? Beer?' she asks with a sneer.

'No thanks.'

'Only joking about the drugs.'

Does she really expect me to believe that, when her life is in such disarray and she has no money? We sit on the plastic sofa. She turns to me. 'To what do I owe this pleasure?' she asks.

'Where's Shelly?'

She shrugs. 'What's that got to do with anything?'

'I just want to know whether we're alone. Whether this conversation is private.'

She pushes her hair back from her forehead. 'Shelly's out.'

'Good.' I take a deep breath. 'I need you to stop texting me asking for money. There's no way you're getting any more money out of me.'

She raises her eyebrows. 'No way? And how do you figure that?'

'I've done nothing wrong – I've paid my dues.'

She puts her head back and laughs. 'Do you think your precious Emma will believe that?'

I breathe calmly. In. Out. 'Of course she'll believe me. She knows I've always done everything I can to look after both you and Stephen.'

A wry smile. 'All truth is relative.'

'So you're a relativist now, are you?'

'At least I'm not a bullshitter. I bet you don't even understand what relativism is.'

'I didn't come here to discuss philosophy – I came to tell you I'm not reading any more of your texts. And, I don't have any spare cash.'

'The collapse of our relationship has ruined my life, Alastair. You deserve to pay up more than you already have.'

I shake my head. 'I don't know where you've got that from, Heather. You're just being irrational.'

'Don't you dare call me irrational after the way you've treated me,' she almost spits.

'But it was *you* who left *me*.'

Anger burning inside me, I stand up and leave. As I walk away

17

my heart bleeds for the way she has treated me. The way she has abandoned Stephen. I need to protect him. To give him all my love. My love stretches without bounds to Emma. To Stephen. To my mother. But Heather? I shudder inside. How did I ever let her pull me in?

10

Emma

After slinging my Mercedes across my parking slot, I stop for a few minutes to admire the gardens that surround my dental practice. The perfectly manicured lawn caressed by cascading willow. Snowdrops dangling their delicate teardrop heads. First crocuses trumpeting bold colour across the grass.

However well my life is going, however much your company gives me a high over the weekend, Alastair, pulling into work on a Monday morning always fills me with a sense of peace. The surgery is the one place in the world where I have total control. I bought this practice when my relationship with Colin ended, four years ago. It gave me purpose; kept my life moving forwards after my loss.

I say good morning to my receptionist as I walk past. Andrea Smith. Auburn hair. Handpicked. Intelligent. Bursting with helpful ideas and common sense. Attractive, but not attractive enough to put me in the shadow. I smile at her. She smiles back hesitantly. Her smile for me is always hesitant. She knows if she smiles too hard I will criticise her teeth. I criticise everyone's teeth from the Queen to Victoria Beckham. Dentists prefer looking at mouths of perfection.

I walk through the waiting room – no patients yet – stopping for a minute to admire the new leather sofas. The fish tank; neon tetra, danios, guppies and platies. The piles of perfectly arranged glossies. Into my consulting room where Tania is waiting for me, removing instruments from the steriliser, laying them neatly on a tray.

'Good weekend?' she asks.

I nod. 'And you?'

'Not bad.'

Tania. My dental and aesthetic assistant. A plump girl of twenty-two, with mousy hair, a mousy face and mud-coloured eyes. So young she still has spots. Young. Sweet. Gentle. Her mousiness disappears when she smiles. Perfect teeth. The Hollywood kind.

The internal telephone rings. I pick up.

'Hello again, Andrea.'

'Hi Emma.' A pause. 'Just to say you have an emergency patient coming in first thing. Tomas Covington. Pain in his back teeth.'

Tania looks up from laying out the instruments. She flashes her film-star smile. The internal phone rings again in warning, and Tomas is here. Entering my consulting room. City suit. Suave. Sophisticated. White shirt. Red tie. Hair smoothed back. Closely shaved.

'Hello, Tomas. Sorry to hear you're in pain again.'

He winces a little. 'It seems to be getting worse. I've been taking co-codamol.'

'Sit in the chair and I'll take a look.'

He slides into my chair. I have to adjust it as he is so tall. I put a bib around his neck and his eyes catch mine. Warm brown eyes, dappled with pain.

'Which tooth hurts?'

He pats the rear part of his lower right jawbone. 'This whole area.'

'Open wide.'

He puts his head back and obeys. I press my probe on his lower right rear tooth. He jerks in distress.

'The root of your back molar is infected. I'll drill a root canal through your tooth, remove the infected debris and deaden the nerve now. The pain will stop. But your tooth will die so you'll need a crown.'

'Work your magic. Do what you must.'

I inject his gum with anaesthetic. When his mouth is numb I drill through his tooth and deaden the nerve. I apply a dressing coated in antibiotic to kill the infection.

When I have finished, he rinses his mouth out with the glass of pink antiseptic I hand him. He slips out of his chair and stands looking at me gratefully.

'The pain is gone. Thank you so much.'

'It's not over yet. You need to come back in a few weeks' time for your crown to be fitted.'

'Thank you so much, Emma.' He turns to leave. As he reaches the doorway he looks back. 'Why don't you and Alastair come to our place on Saturday evening and have a drink with us? I'm sure Jade would like to thank you, too.'

'That's very kind, but surely it's our turn?' I pause. 'I insist you come to mine.'

11

Jade

I'm standing beneath the willow tree, watching you. Looking through the surgery window. You are looking into her eyes. She is lovely, isn't she – in a predictable skinny blonde way? As soon as I saw her, I knew she was your type. Lots of men's type. Men are like lemmings; they all follow the same thing. No individual taste.

Memories

My earliest memory was before the violence started. A time when I felt free. Running along a beach, holding my mother's hand. Sun on my back. Sand between my toes. Where was my father then? Was he back at the holiday cottage working? Waiting for us to come back?

The memory flashes across my mind and fades. I can't hold it or place it. It never stays for long.

12

Emma

Following my invitation at the surgery, Tomas, Jade and Alastair are at mine for drinks and nibbles. We are all standing around the fireplace making small talk. Alastair is looking suave. Pink shirt. White jeans. Tomas' kindly brown eyes shimmer towards his wife. Jade hovers next to him wearing a baggy dress with small flowers on the fabric. A modern replica of Laura Ashley that doesn't quite work. The dull brown flattens her complexion. She is quite pretty really, but she doesn't know how to dress.

I disappear into the kitchen to take my M&S canapés out of the oven. When I reappear, carrying hot mini quiches and luxury sausage rolls, Tomas and Jade are sitting next to one another, on the sofa opposite the fireplace. Alastair has settled in the winged chair by the TV. Silence floats awkwardly as I walk across the room, laden with protein and carbohydrate.

Jade watches Tomas like a hawk as he leans towards me and takes a sausage roll. I move the plate in her direction. She stiffens and shakes her head.

'No, thanks. I'm watching my figure.'

'You have a lovely figure,' Tomas says, patting her thigh.

She turns her head towards him. 'Do you expect me to believe you?'

'As I meant it, I do, yes.'

She shrugs her shoulders. 'Men never mean what they say.'

Alastair looks as if he is about to object. I glare across at him and grimace to silence him. The word 'clusterfuck' resonates in my head.

13

Alastair

Tomas and Clusterfuck are here in your house, Emma, invading my weekend privacy. I cannot warm to the Clusterfuck. Even her scratchy voice annoys me.

My favourite way to spend Saturday night is snuggled on the sofa with you, drinking red wine and watching Netflix. Inhaling the scent of your perfume, your body heat, your sweet, sweet breath. But tonight I sit eating sausage rolls and drinking Champagne watching the Clusterfuck guard Tomas like a mother hen. I look at her and see feathers and beaks and dowdiness. You stand next to her holding a plate of canapés, and shine. I want your guests to go home. I need my Saturday fix of you, alone. *Tell them, Emma.* Put down the tray of canapés and tell them to go.

'Are you all right?' the Clusterfuck rasps, looking across at me and frowning. 'Are we so boring? You look as if you're in a total daydream. On another planet.'

Her voice scrapes across my mind.

'Sorry. I was thinking about work.'

'Swabs and latex. So much more interesting than us?'

'No, no. Not at all,' I mutter. I look at her and smile. A wide forced smile. The Clusterfuck is so annoying that smiling at her has to be forced.

She leans forwards and rests her elbows on her knees. 'Was it an interesting case, taking your attention?'

'You know we're not allowed to talk about individual cases.'

'Not allowed to, but people do.'

I sigh inside. Why is she pushing this? 'They'll lose their jobs if they get caught.'

She pouts her lips. The conversation is getting worse. 'So, you're a man who toes the line, are you?'

Trying to flirt now. Flirting that doesn't work. 'As much as I need to. As much as anyone else.'

I look across at Emma dressed in blue silk clinging to all the right places. And suddenly, from nowhere, I'm back on the day my ex-wife Heather left. Off to a nightclub in Brighton with her best friend Shelly. Both looking cheesy in matching onesies. Black onesies with orange flowers on. Whatever made them pick those? She rang me, from the nightclub, to tell me our marriage was over. I could hear a man's voice in the background. Drum and bass music pounded down the line. I could hear the shrill tones of Shelly's laugh.

Life has moved on. I have a much more attractive partner now. Emma, you are pure class.

14

Jade

Sitting in your drawing room looking across at you Emma, oh jewel of middle-class suburbia. Stereotypically beautiful. Multi-toned highlights. Gym-enhanced figure. Long legs. Designer clothing.

If I spend more time with you, will some of your effervescence rub off on me? Shoulder to shoulder. Face to face. Let me get to know you. Teach me your tricks.

I stand up. 'I need the bathroom, where is it?' I ask.

'There's one off the hallway,' you answer nonchalantly, keeping your gaze fixed on my husband.

I sidle away unnoticed and irrelevant, but I do not visit the bathroom. I go upstairs and open door after door until I find the master bedroom. Girly and frilly with gold bedding. So girly and frilly it makes me feel sick.

15

Emma

It's Sunday evening. Jade is standing on my doorstep, smiling at me.

'Hi,' she says.

'Hi,' I repeat.

'It was so lovely having you in for drinks. But I'd like some girl time without the men.' There is a pause. 'We can talk about them, then.' She laughs, a small jittery laugh.

I grit my teeth. I like being with men, not talking about them. And we had drinks together only last night. This is claustrophobic. Too friendly, too soon.

'Would you like to come over for coffee one morning?' she continues.

I put my head on one side and smile at her. 'But . . . but . . . I work full time.'

'What if I pop into the surgery tomorrow and take you out for lunch?'

'Well . . . I usually have a quick sandwich and do paperwork at lunch.'

'There's a sandwich bar a few minutes away. I promise to only keep you twenty minutes.' She pauses. 'Pretty please.'

Pretty please? Insipid playground talk harking back to the

seventies. I feel like putting my fingers down my throat to let her know the phrase makes me want to vomit.

But she flashes another steely smile at me and I find myself saying yes.

16

Alastair

I'm sitting in my lab taking swabs from a crowbar suspected of being used to smash a garage window by a car thief. It was found on the ground at the crime scene. So many swabs. So many changes of pairs of gloves. Twenty-nine of each so far. I'll be so glad when I've finished. Maybe Jade has a point: you require patience beyond compare to do this job. No one warns you when you apply. TV glamorising our work in crime dramas has a lot to answer for. Swabs finally complete, I place them on the collection tray, and step out of my lab into the changing area.

As I open my locker, pleased to be changing back into my normal clothes, my iPhone buzzes. A text. I grab it. Heather.

I'm going to warn Emma about you.

Leave me alone you creep, I reply.

Don't say that to me. I'm the mother of your child.

I know she won't do anything. She has threatened me like this before and nothing has come of it. I take off my scrubs and hang them up. As I pull on my jeans, I shudder inside remembering the girl I first met at school. Sixteen years old, so different from the woman she has become. What happened to the girl I met? The shiny girl with swinging chestnut hair? The girl who swept me along with her bold attitude? She says our relationship breakdown is my fault and bandies about words like 'coercive control'. But anyone with any sense must realise we just met too young and grew apart. It wasn't my fault she started to sleep around and smoke dope.

17

Emma

It's Monday lunchtime and Jade is here, stepping into my consulting room, wearing a stripy trouser suit. Her short hair is shorter than ever, too short to be fashionable. She must have had it cut this morning by a butcher not a hairdresser.

I put the tools I have just finished using into a tray for Tania to sterilise in the autoclave later, grab my coat and walk towards her. 'I've not got long.'

She shrugs. 'You told me and I'm not bothered. I'm used to being fitted in.'

'What do you mean?' I ask.

A grimace. 'Well, you know. Busy husband and all that.'

We walk through my waiting room, nodding at Andrea as we pass. Outside. Into a sharp, cold day, breath condensing in the air in front of us.

'How long have you been feeling abandoned?'

'Ever since I met him.' Her voice is bitter.

In the sandwich bar, a solid wall of heat pushes against us. The hiss and steam of the coffee machine drowns our conversation. We raise our voices above the background noise to order two cappuccinos and two club sandwiches. Then we sidle towards a table at the back of the shop, as far away from the cacophony as possible.

We wait for our lunch to arrive, huddled at a small wobbly table, knees touching.

'Tell me about your relationship with Alastair,' Jade asks.

'We've only just met. On Tinder, a few months ago. We're busy in the week with our careers, so we just hook up at weekends.'

'Tomas and I met on Tinder too. I'm not sure Tinder is all it's cracked up to be.'

'What do you mean?'

'I think it encourages promiscuity.' She sighs. 'Do you feel tempted to use it to roam?'

I shake my head. 'No. And I don't think roaming is a good idea. I'm starting a new relationship. I want to make it work.'

'I know Tomas visited you on the twentieth and twenty-fifty of February.' Jade gives me a slow, stretched smile. 'How convenient to have such troublesome teeth, when you have a beautiful dentist.' She leans across the table so that her breath touches my face. I lean back.

'I'm flattered that you think I'm beautiful, Jade, but I can assure you, there is nothing between Tomas and me. He needs a crown. It's my job to help.'

The sandwiches and coffee arrive. Suddenly not hungry, I look down at the food. Not wanting to put up with any more of Jade's company, I make a show of looking at my watch, and stand up.

'Sorry, I didn't realise what the time was. I need to get back to work.'

18

Jade

I know you've slept with my husband. I can tell from the way you narrow your eyes when you talk about him. You feel guilty, don't you? Too guilty to stay and eat lunch with me.

Memories

My earliest memory of the violence is when I was six years old. The day after my birthday. Walking down the stairs to look for my mother, when I woke up in the morning. A sunny morning, sun streaming through the landing window. Usually I called for her and she came to me. Held me in her arms for a hug. But that morning, I called and she didn't come, so I went to look for her.

I heard her scream.

I crept down the stairs. She was in the lounge, shouting at someone. The door was open. I hid behind it and peered through the gap. My mother was on the floor and my father was kicking her. Her legs, her arms, her back. She was curled up trying to shield her face.

I ran back upstairs and hid in the wardrobe in the spare room. Body and mind trembling.

19

Jade

'How's it going, Jade?' my psychiatrist, Siobhan, asks, leaning back in her chair, flicking her glossy red hair.

'Not good. I'm sure Tomas is at it again. With a dentist this time.'

'Have you discussed this with him?' She pauses. 'Do you want to come and see me together?'

I sigh. 'I have asked him. And, as usual, he denies it.'

Siobhan shakes her head and frowns. I watch her tapered nails tapping together.

'We've been through this, so many times. You know he loves you. You know you perceive this situation incorrectly because of your paranoia. I know it's difficult for you because of your illness, but you need to trust him.'

I shake my head. 'I can't. I just can't.' I take a deep breath. 'And you're not helping. You're making me feel bullied and bulldozed into accepting things. Things no woman should have to accept.'

I want to be alone. To scream and cry. To stand on a mountaintop and holler.

Siobhan's eyes widen in sympathy. 'I think you need another course of CBT. And I'm going to up your dose of Valium.' There is a pause. 'But please, come and see me with Tomas. You always seem so much better after the therapy sessions he is involved in. Try and accept it, Jade. He supports you so much.'

20

Emma

The internal telephone chirrups into my consulting room. I pick up.

'Your next patient is here. Tomas Covington,' Andrea announces.

'Send him in,' I instruct.

A few minutes later he is stepping towards me. 'Hello, Emma. Thanks for fitting me in.'

'My pleasure. Let me take your coat and briefcase.' I put them on the chair in the corner. 'Do sit down, make yourself comfy.'

'Isn't that a contradiction in terms, when I'm about to have my tooth ground to a stub to anchor a crown?'

'It should be fine when the anaesthetic kicks in.' I pause. 'How has your mouth been?'

'The pain has gone. I love you for that.'

'I know you're only joking, but I don't think Jade would appreciate what you just said.'

His face crumples. 'No. I'm sorry; you're right.'

'It's just that whenever I see her it's clear she's very suspicious of us both.' There is a pause. 'She implied that you only needed dental work so that you could see me. So, I'm feeling sensitive.'

He raises his eyebrows. 'She must be joking. Who'd want root canal treatment, however hot the dentist?'

'Exactly. Even if the dentist was Brad Pitt or Leonardo

38

DiCaprio, I'd rather have my teeth intact.' I shake my head. 'OK, OK. Come on, sit in the chair, try and relax. I'm taking the mould for your crown today and will then fit the temporary one. You'll need to come back to have the permanent one fitted in a few weeks, when it's ready.'

Tomas does as I ask, as Tania puts on classical music. *Swan Lake* by Tchaikovsky slices into the room as I make up the anaesthetic.

'Open wide,' I instruct.

He puts his head back and stretches his mouth. I inject his gum.

'OK. You can relax now while you wait for the anaesthetic to work.' He closes his mouth and his eyes. He lies in the chair, almost asleep. I stand looking at him. At his sculptured face. Is Jade hard on him because he is charming and beautiful? Or is he as unreliable as she says? For a second I'm back watching her face spitting towards me, telling me the dates of his visits.

Tania and I busy ourselves preparing for the procedure. We work together like a well-oiled machine, as we have been crowning teeth for so long. Tania readies the drill for me. I arrange the mould. As the anaesthetic begins to work I make an impression of Tomas' teeth with dental putty. He is a very obliging patient, still and uncomplaining.

Shaping the tooth ready for the crown is the tricky bit. Slowly, carefully, I grind the remainder of the dead tooth to a square peg. Bits of bone and spittle flying everywhere. Now that I'm peering down his throat, Tomas does not seem quite as attractive as before.

Nearly there. I put cord around the base of the tooth, to expose it and make sure we get a good fit. Tania prepares the temporary crown, shooting the acrylic into the mould of his tooth. She keeps a spot out on a tray so that we can see how it sets. Then the most uncomfortable part for him. Clamping the mould with the temporary crown into his mouth and making sure he doesn't move while it sets.

A perfect patient, still as stone.

It's done. I remove the clamp. Then I check the bite and drill it back a little.

'All done,' I announce. 'You can rinse.'

21

Jade

You are back at Willow Bank Dental Surgery. I stand outside and watch you slip out of the chair, pull on your coat and hold her body against yours before you leave. Not again Tomas. Please don't do it to me again. I've tried taking more Valium, but it is not a magic pill. Taking Valium has not changed the situation. I know you are in love with someone else.

Memories

Trembling like a leaf in the woody darkness of the wardrobe. Back pressed against the door. Surrounded by dust and fear. By air that tasted musty. By coats we never wore, flapping in my face. Trying to close my mind to the sound of Mother's piercing screams. Then the screaming stopped.

Footsteps. Clumping up the stairs. My father was calling my name. I could hear him padding across the landing. I moved to the back of the wardrobe, closed my eyes and rolled into a ball. I wanted to go away. I wanted to be anywhere but there. My heart was thumping like a piston in my chest. Blood pulsated and thrashed against my eardrums. I was fighting for air, breathing quickly.

Slowly, slowly, the wardrobe door creaked open. I opened my eyes. My father was peering in. Eyes spitting. Red-faced with anger. My heart beat faster. Faster than I had ever felt it.

'Get out of there,' he yelled. 'Now.'

I scrambled out on all fours and stood up in front of him. Heart still racing. Ears still buzzing.

'Your mother has fallen in the sitting room. Go downstairs and help her.'

22

Jade

'Thank you for coming to lunch again, Emma.'

You smile your angelic smile; saccharine and artificial. 'My pleasure. What did you want to talk about?'

Noise swirls around the coffee bar. I push through the background chatter.

'Tomas,' I announce.

You sit up. Your face straightens. Trying to cover up your feelings, aren't you, Emma? You shake your head.

'Are you worried about him?' you ask.

'I'm worried about myself, in fact.' I pause. 'I want to make Tomas love me, like he loves you, Emma.'

You splutter into your coffee cup. You compose yourself and lean across the table towards me.

'Don't be ridiculous.' Your voice is rising in pitch. 'He doesn't love me, Jade,' you continue. 'I hardly know you both. We've all only just met. I'm his dentist. You're his wife. It's you he's in love with.'

'I knew, from the first moment I saw you, that you two would be together. You are his type. Most men's type. A template. A stereotype.'

23

Emma

A man I hardly know – who has made no advances towards me
– in love with me? And I'm a stereotype? Why did such a clusterfuck have to move next door to me? I stand up to leave.

Memories

I raced downstairs, and pushed the living room door open. My mother was lying on the floor, curled in a ball, holding her stomach, groaning softly. I stepped towards her and bent down.

'What can I do to help?'

She opened her eyes. 'Where is he?' she asked.

'Upstairs.'

She grimaced and sat up, still holding her stomach.

'He'll be all right now. His temper is over.'

I sat next to her on the floor. She put her arm around me. She smelt of blood and fear.

24

Alastair

I'm in the Henley Pizza Express with Stephen, for our Thursday night treat. Sitting at a table by the window. Stephen's eyes shine with anticipation as he orders the American Hot and dough balls. As he sips a pint of Coke.

'Daddy, Daddy,' he asks. 'Can I see a photo of your girlfriend Emma?'

I pull my iPhone out of my pocket and tap to unlock it. Emma's golden face shines from my screen. I hand my phone across to him and he grabs it eagerly and sits staring at it, engrossed. He lifts his head.

'She's pretty, isn't she? She looks like Dr Who.'

I frown, confused for a second.

'Dr Who?'

Then I realise how out of touch I am. Dr Who is no longer a man, but a very striking female actor.

'Well, yes. Although I think Emma is even prettier than Dr Who when you actually see her.'

'Wow, Daddy. When do I get to do that?'

My body tightens. 'Soon. Soon,' I say, wanting that to be true. But, so far, Emma has not shown any enthusiasm to meet my son.

'Do you love her, Daddy?'

Fortunately for me, he is distracted by the arrival of the starters. Anything I say will doubtless go straight back to Heather, so I need to be guarded at all times. An acrimonious divorce is a constant battle that rattles on for years. Despite the fact she left me, Heather seems disproportionally jealous of anyone I have the audacity to be friendly with. Let alone Emma, who I sleep with.

Stephen wolfs his dough balls. I pick at my Caesar salad, wincing every time I hit on an anchovy.

He looks across at me. 'Are you a bad man, Daddy?'

I splutter into my beer. 'Of course not. What a strange thing to say.'

'Mummy says you are.'

'Look, Stephen, sometimes when a couple split up, they say things about each other that aren't true, because they're upset and angry.'

'Do you tell lies about Mummy then?'

I shake my head. 'Of course not.'

'Then why does she tell lies about you?'

I tap my fingers on the table, nervously. 'Stephen, I can assure you I'm not a bad man. You know that really, don't you?'

He looks at me wide-eyed and nods his head. 'Mummy must have been joking.'

The waitress arrives with our pizzas. Stephen starts to tuck into his greedily. As if he hasn't eaten for a week. Melted cheese drips down his chin.

'But it didn't seem funny. She sounded as if she really meant it,' he says.

'Your mother is always cross about something.'

He wipes the cheese from his chin with his napkin. 'No she isn't, Daddy. I have a lot of fun with Mummy and Shelly.'

I try to stop my lip curling in distaste at the thought of fun with Shelly and Mummy. I suspect they take drugs and go picking up men together. Drinking heavily. Crossing boundaries.

'What sort of fun?' I push, not sure I want to hear the answer. Knowing I must find out.

'Laughing, singing, playing games.'

And suddenly I see Heather, as she was when I first met her. In a pub with a group of friends. Sharing a joke, head back laughing. It was the sense of fun that pulled me towards her. Fun without responsibility. Fun that went too far with other men instead of me, so far that she left.

25

Jade

Siobhan has Tomas on her side, and together they have forced me into a joint counselling session. We are sitting in her office, in a triangle of high-backed armchairs. Tomas is sitting too close to me. I can't bear to look at him, so I look at the oatmeal carpet. At the magnolia walls. The room smells of vanilla and cinnamon. Siobhan must hope that the reed diffusers she uses will affect my psyche.

I do not look at Tomas, but I know he is leaning back in his chair, in a daydream, thinking of you, Emma. And you are probably thinking of him as well. He is good-looking. Too good-looking. Overwhelming and enticing. A face that never changes. Always beautiful. Never tired. Never groggy.

Siobhan tosses her exuberant hair. 'Shall we make a start?'

I nod my head.

'Yes,' Tomas says and his resonant voice spreads like honey across the room.

Siobhan looks across at him and smiles. Tomas always makes women smile. She leans forwards.

'You start, Tomas. What would you like to say to Jade?'

'I love you Jade. Always have. Always will.'

The words trip off his tongue. So casual. So complacent. How many times do I have to listen to his lies?

26

Emma

Tomas steps into my consulting room to have his crown fitted. Smart City suit. George Clooney eyes. He hugs me and kisses me lightly on both cheeks. Is this friendship? Or is he coming on to me? I step away from him and frown.

'What's the matter?' he asks.

'I don't think I should treat you any more.'

His mouth drops open in surprise. 'Why ever not?'

'Jade thinks you're in love with me. We need to be careful. Keep away from each other. She seems most unhinged.'

'You have to treat me. You're my dentist. I don't want to see someone else halfway through my treatment.'

I shake my head.

'I should have explained,' he continues. 'She's unwell. But it's under control, with the right meds. Believe me. Please don't worry. Please let me continue as your patient. She'll be like this whoever I go to.'

'Even if it's a man?'

'Then she'll decide I'm bisexual or gay.'

I shake my head. 'You really, really need to sort things out with her.'

'Our marriage is fine. When she is balanced we have an excellent relationship.'

An excellent relationship? I'm aghast. How can anyone have an excellent relationship with someone who is so unwell?

'It must be hard,' I say.

'Sometimes. But then she can be wonderful in between. The best wife out there.'

The best wife? Is he in denial? Fooling himself?

He takes my hands in his. 'Please, please fit my crown. I'm really busy at work. I'm here now. I don't have much time to arrange to go anywhere else.'

'OK, if you're sure. I don't want to cause any trouble between you.'

He smiles his generous smile. 'Sure, I'm sure.'

As I remove my instruments from the autoclave, as I buzz for Tania to come back from her break, I remind myself that however unsuited they seem, no one can see into someone else's relationship.

27

Jade

You are getting closer and closer to the Stereotype. Now you can't keep your hands off her from the moment you arrive. I can see you from my hiding place behind the willow tree. I see you hug her. I see you kiss her. I do what my counsellor says and count to twenty. Breathe. Breathe. I look up and you are still holding her. Now she is pushing you away. You are standing, eyes locked, fixated by what she is telling you. Infatuated. She has put a spell on you. You hold her hands, melting with love.

Memories

Shouting, so much angry shouting from my father, coming from the lounge. I ran upstairs to hide in the wardrobe in the spare room again. But no. He found me there last time. I stepped into my parents' bedroom instead. I wasn't allowed in there. He would look there last. It was cold. I shivered as I crept past Mother's empty dressing table. No jewellery. No perfume. No photographs. No mementoes.

I opened the wardrobe door. Dad's clothes on the right. Mother's clothes on the left. Colourful dresses hanging. Colourful clothes I had never seen her wear. I stepped inside, shut the door and curled up on Mother's side.

I knew the pattern by then. The screaming, the crying. I thought the screaming had almost reached a crescendo. I sat hugging my knees, breathing deeply, silently praying for it to stop. But it didn't stop. Mother was screaming like a feral animal. Today – this – was worse.

And then the bedroom door burst open. I could see through the crack where the wardrobe doors met. He was carrying her in his arms. She was sobbing now, her body limp against his. The screaming had stopped. He threw her on the bed and the screaming started again.

28

Jade

Despite the change in my drug regimen, the CBT and our session with Siobhan, it is still eating me up that you are so infatuated with the Stereotype. And I warned you, Tomas, what would happen if you betrayed me again. You have done this so many times. Your liaison with your gym instructor. The girl from accounts. The woman who lived around the corner who you used to meet when walking our elderly dog around the block at night. Men are like dogs. A dog bites once and gets the taste for blood. A man strays once and gets a taste for extramarital sex. You cannot trust him again.

I'm frisking your clothes, your possessions. Looking for evidence of your betrayal, even though I have seen you with my own eyes, holding her, touching her. Pretending you have pain in your teeth so that you can see her regularly.

I open your bedside table. I flick through your socks and underwear. Does she like your bright orange Emporio Armani boxers? Into the wardrobe, checking every pocket of your suits. Brooks Brothers. Ermenegildo Zegna. Roderick Charles.

Nothing. Only loose change. Receipts from Pret. A pair of broken cufflinks. In the last pocket of the last suit I find a receipt for a pair of women's Brora gloves, purchased yesterday. Seventy-nine pounds. Wow. Lovely. You've got me a present.

But where are they? I check the drawers in our bedroom. I can't find them anywhere. Maybe they are in your office. Maybe you will bring them home tonight.

29

Emma

The doorbell rings and I answer it. A chubby woman is standing in my porch, wearing a baggy dress, knee-high boots and an old-fashioned velvet jacket with wide lapels. Her hair needs washing. It is dry like a bird's nest.

'I'm Heather Brown, Alastair's ex-wife. I need to talk to you. Can I come in?' she asks.

I hesitate. She has caused so much trouble for Alastair. Is letting her inside my home appropriate?

'Please,' she begs, running her fingers through her bird's nest. 'It's important.'

'OK, fine. But I hope it won't take long. I need to leave for work soon.'

She steps into my hallway. 'Can we sit down?' she asks.

'Come into the drawing room,' I reply, leading the way.

She sits down and crosses her legs, glancing at the Murano glass painting on the wall. The photograph of Colin and me, in front of Cotswold yellow stone grandeur, taken on our honeymoon. Greedy eyes weighing up my possessions. I shudder inside, but I force myself to be polite.

'Would you like a drink?' I ask.

She turns towards me. 'No thanks.'

'Is everything OK?'

She swallows. 'I need to warn you about Alastair. You must believe me – or you'll end up in trouble. He's controlling. He's aggressive.' She pauses. 'Not to begin with. He gradually envelops you. I had to escape.'

'If he's so dangerous, why did you leave Stephen with him?'

She flicks her hair from her eyes. Eyes with panda bags beneath them. 'Because he threatened to hurt him if I took him.'

I shake my head slowly. 'All the more reason to take him, and report Alastair to the police.'

A wry smile. 'You're naive if you think reporting the situation to the police would protect us. People regularly break restraining orders. Believe me, I had to leave Stephen with his father, to keep the man sweet.'

'You should have stayed with him then, to protect Stephen.'

She looks as if she is about to cry. 'I could only cope with so much pain.'

'But what about your son?' I push.

'Alastair doesn't hurt children, only women. Children are safe. It's you who needs to mind your back.' She clasps and unclasps her fingers on her lap, nervously, swallowing to push back tears. 'He treated me unfairly – try to understand that.'

I take a deep breath. 'Alastair is my boyfriend, and I love him. Please go away. Leave us alone. I've heard all about you. I know you're the difficult one.'

'You'll regret this.'

30

Alastair

I've just arrived at work and am collecting my day's box of evidence for analysis. The clerk, a woman in her forties with shoulder-length black hair, hands it to me, pursing her cherry-red lips into a reluctant smile as she does every morning. Smiling and frowning at the same time.

I step away from her, into my changing area. Pulling off my outdoor clothes and hanging them up. Slipping into my scrubs. Going through the rigmarole of wrapping myself in my Tyvek suit. Grabbing my sealed box and stepping into my lab.

I yawn inside. Another day working alone for hours and hours. Changing gloves, taking swabs. Hours and hours to think. Too much time to think. About you, Emma. About my monstrous ex-wife, Heather. Trying to cause trouble. Trying to come between us, and between me and Stephen. Telling him I'm a bad man. What if you turn against me, Emma? What if people believe her?

I doze off and drift into a dream. Stephen is sitting in the middle of a roundabout, at the local playground. Heather is pulling it around. Pulling and running. Wearing a grey baggy tracksuit. Her hair is tangled. She runs and runs. Her hair becomes lighter, smoother, longer. Smooth as gossamer. Her face transforms into yours, Emma. My body jolts and I wake up.

I need you, Emma. I need stability. For myself. For Stephen. For the rest of my life.

31

Emma

Back home from work, I park the car. A few minutes later Tomas is standing on my doorstep in his smart City suit and Hugo Boss coat, brown eyes smiling into mine.

'Is everything all right?' I ask.

'Yes. But I would like to talk to you. Can I step inside?'

'Do I need to remind you about Jade's attitude to our relationship?'

He shakes his head. 'You don't need to worry about Jade. Her bark is worse than her bite.'

'Good job.'

He laughs, mouth curving into a wide smile. 'And she's at a late Pilates class, so she won't know I'm here.'

'Even better job,' I reply. 'If Jade is out, of course you can come in.'

He steps into my hallway. He rummages in his coat pocket, pulls out a gift bag and hands it to me.

'What have I done to deserve this?' I ask.

'I just wanted to say thanks for helping me with my teeth.'

I open the bag and pull out my gift. Black cashmere gloves. Softer than soft.

'They're exquisite, thanks.'

A grin. 'I just didn't want you to think I was taking you for granted.'

'I was pleased to help. I didn't think that.' I pause. 'Would you like to stay for a cup of tea, or do you need to get back?'

'I'd love a cup.'

He follows me into the kitchen. I lay the gloves on the windowsill and put the kettle on. I make a pot of tea and pour us both a cup. We sit opposite one another at my kitchen table.

'I know Jade's attitude towards you is difficult, but I need to maintain my relationships with my friends. I need to fight back.'

He leans across the table and takes my hand. Is this friendship? Or is Jade right? I do not want to get in between a warring couple. I pull my hand away.

32

Jade

I lied, telling you I would be out at a late Pilates class tonight. I parked my Porsche around the corner, outside the church hall, to confuse you about my whereabouts. Now I'm hiding in her garden, behind the rhododendron bush, warmly dressed. Puffa jacket. Beanie hat. Watching your every move. Watching my breath condense in front of me as I breathe. The rhododendron bush is in full bloom, its blood-red flowers dropping petals. Its spicy scent enveloping me.

I knew you were unreliable. I've been putting up with your infidelity for years. So many other women. But this is the end of the line; giving the Stereotype my present. Seventy-nine-pound cashmere gloves, lying on her windowsill. Seventy-nine-pound cashmere gloves from Brora that should have been for me. The present I was so excited about.

You are sitting holding hands with your loved one.

It's over between us, Tomas. I cannot put up with this any more.

Memories

It wasn't just violence. It was far more invasive than that.

I remember coming home from school on a soft spring day, not long before I sat my GCSEs. Sitting in the kitchen, filling out my application for sixth form. Mother frying chicken thighs in butter for her signature chicken casserole, the warm aroma making me feel hungry. But it would be hours before it was ready to eat. Dad, home from work early, was sitting next to me, leaning over my shoulder.

'Science A levels? Is that really what you want to do? You're punching above your weight,' he said in his sharp, shrill voice. The voice I had grown to hate.

I looked up. His eyes were hard and flat; lips pinched.

'I need science A levels, I want to be a scientist, not sure which type.'

A smile. Insincere. Mocking. 'A scientist? Science is complicated. I'm not sure that's a good idea. Wouldn't you rather be a big fish in a small bowl than try something too ambitious?'

'It's what I'm interested in, Dad. I need to try.'

A dry laugh. 'Try being the operative word, don't you think?'

'Whether try is operative or not, I'm going to go for it.'

'Good for you. Good for you.' There was a pause. 'But I'll eat my hat if you succeed.'

33

Emma

Jade is standing on my doorstep, short hair sharp and shiny, make-up-free face scrubbed and washed. She stretches her mouth into a smile.

'I wondered whether you'd like to come around again. For a drink? A girls' night?'

I'm not in the mood for difficult company. 'What date did you have in mind?' I ask, determined that whatever date the Cluster-fuck suggests I intend to be out.

'Well, Tomas is away at the moment. So any night except Wednesday. Wednesday night is book club. Apart from that I'm around all week.'

I can't be unavailable every night. She has already asked me three times. I take a deep breath. I might as well get it over with. 'What about tomorrow, then?'

'Tomorrow's good,' the Clusterfuck snaps back. 'See you at eight p.m.'

34

Alastair

I can't get you out of my mind, Emma. Your silken hair. Your taut body. Your emerald eyes. I love you. I so want to make our relationship work. I need to hold you. I need to see you. To inhale your scent. Taste your breath. I need to catch up midweek.

I call your mobile. It rings ten times, then you pick up.

'Alastair, how are you doing?'

Your voice sounds cheery and positive. Pleased to hear from me.

'Fine. Good.' I pause. 'I was just wondering whether I could pop over for a drink tonight?'

'I'm sorry, but I'm going to Jade's.'

'Tonight? I thought you didn't tend to socialise midweek? And I know you don't like Clusterfuck.'

'She coerced me. I couldn't get out of it.'

Is it poster boy Tomas who really invited you? 'Will Tomas be there?' I ask.

'No. He's travelling on business apparently. It's just me and her.'

I laugh. 'A mind-blowing party. You and Clusterfuck. I'm jealous.'

'Come and join us if you like.'

'No thanks, I'll pass.'

35

Jade

You stand on my doorstep holding a bunch of lilies in your hand. You pass them to me with a smile. 'Thanks for inviting me.'

As you step inside I silently admire your dress. Navy velvet caresses your slender figure. Your blonde hair falls in carefully blow-dried ringlets. How many hours a day do you spend manufacturing your appearance? Do you realise there is always a whiff of artificiality about you that spoils your perfect looks? We walk into my boudoir with the bar in it. My main drawing room.

'I've made you my favourite cocktail,' I say.

I give you a simpering smile as I pour it. I hand it to you. 'Thanks,' you say.

I put some music on to relax us. *Fingal's Cave* by Mendelssohn.

You take a sip of your drink. I haven't touched mine yet.

'Delicious. What's in it?'

'My secret recipe with cherry liqueur.'

Do you really think I will tell you the truth? Rohypnol. My favourite drug.

'So where's Tomas?' you ask.

Asking for Tomas already. Two-timing whore.

'Don't you know?' I ask.

You frown and shake your head. 'Why would I?' you ask.

Clever posturing, you superficial bitch. When you are sleeping with a man, you usually know where he is.

I smile a wry smile. 'He's just away overnight. He sometimes stays overnight in London when he has to entertain clients.'

Another frown. 'I thought you said he was away this week travelling.'

'I probably thought that when I said it. His plans change all the time.' I pause and hand you the peanuts. 'Do have a nibble.'

You take a handful. You continue to sip your drink. I go to the bar and produce a whole jug of Cherry Bomb. I smile at you and top you up.

'Tell me, have you had many different partners?' I ask.

Your body stiffens as if you are affronted by my question. Come on, drink up bitch. Relax.

You shake your head. 'Not really. One or two. The main ones have been my husband Colin, and now Alastair.' There is a pause. 'What about you?'

'Tomas is my only love. You know the Barry White song? The first. The last. My everything. That's him for me.'

I top up your glass again.

'How long have you owned your dental practice?' I ask.

You don't reply. Your eyes are staring and confused. Your mind is about to go. Your body slumps across the sofa, head back, arms wide. Your breathing is shallow. Chest hardly moving. I hope I haven't overdone it. But no, I can't have. I calculated the dose so carefully. I lean over you. I feel the exhalation of your breath on my cheek. Relief floods through me.

I put on the latex gloves from my pocket. With trembling hands I begin my task, fetching the wrench I bought yesterday from beneath the sink.

36

Emma

I wake up, unsure for a second where I am. I see yellow and cream curtains. In my own bedroom. Must be. A loud buzzing sound. But it isn't buzzing, it's purring. Casper is lying on top of me. My mouth tastes dry. As if a hamster has died in it. My tongue is like sandpaper. I roll over in bed and disturb the cat. He grumbles with a loud meow. As I roll, clothes pull against my skin and I realise I'm still wearing my velvet dress. I wriggle my toes. I've gone to bed in my black suede boots.

Oh my God. What has happened? Where have I been? Have I been robbed? Where is my phone? Where is my jewellery? I check my bedside table; my phone, my favourite gold jewellery, all there. Then I remember. Drinking Cherry Bomb. Not being able to think. Not being able to speak. I feel really, really guilty for having too much to drink. Not a very sensible way for a professional career woman to behave. Another reason for Jade to hate me. Thinking I have no self-restraint.

Drinking so much my memory has gone? Is there something wrong with me? I need to see my GP.

Memories

I had just returned from my A level biology field trip to Anglesey, tired after days of counting crabs and square metres of seaweed. Longing for a hot bath and an early night. Mother was sitting in the kitchen staring into the air in front of her, tears streaming down her face.

I held her against me. But she yelped and pulled away, rubbing her lower right arm.

'What is it? What's the matter?' I asked.

'Nothing,' she said. 'It's just my arm's a bit sore.'

'Let me see.'

'No, no,' she said, walking towards the sink, reaching for some kitchen roll to dry her tears. 'It's nothing to fuss about. Let me put the kettle on and get you some supper.'

She always said it was nothing when he hit her. When he did 'something', what would that look like? I laid the table and peeled the potatoes, shuddering inside. I was seventeen. I needed to take responsibility for my mother. Not just to be subservient to my father and help her peel potatoes. I needed to do something real.

37

Jade

'Shall we have a quick drink together before I set off for book group, darling?' I say with a smile.

'That would be nice.'

'I'll get us a sloe gin with ice.'

We sit in the kitchen, by the window, looking out onto the garden. It is early spring, the daffodils starting to brighten the world with their sun-ray heads. I hand you your sloe gin mixed with Rohypnol. A high enough dose. No need to take any risks.

'Cheers.' We clink glasses. 'Here's to our new life in Henley.'

We sit in silence for a while.

Then, 'It's a bit cold in here.'

'The boiler needs servicing. A guy is coming tomorrow. I switched it off.'

'Well, being cold is a lot less uncomfortable than toothache. I'm so pleased to have finished all that dental work,' you say.

I know your pain was never there. I know you made it up so that you could go to the surgery and take her in your arms. Emma, the plastic blonde with a stereotypical personality. The woman who has killed you.

'Her surgery is very nice. It has a fish tank. I like the guppy best,' you mumble as your body begins to slump. Your head lolls. Your torso leans backwards. You are out for the count.

I fetch the plastic box with all my equipment from the

cupboard beneath the kitchen sink and place it on the table. The latex gloves. The Tyvek suit. Plastic sheet. Masking tape. Sellotape. Cling film. Tape measure. Pipette. Wrench.

This is going to be difficult. I step into the Tyvek suit and put on the latex gloves. Hand trembling I pick up the wrench, taking care to make sure I'm holding the right end. I take a deep breath, pull my arm back as I have practised, and swing it at the back of your head. A gash. A small gash. I have not hit you hard enough. I pull my arm back further and, with all the strength I can muster, I swing again. This time your skull cracks. Blood pools in the wound. Your chest falls still. An almost imperceptible stiffness. And I know you have gone.

I take a photograph of the blood splatter and make notes. Measure the distances. I wipe the blood with bleach and toilet paper and flush the tissues away down the lavatory. Slowly, carefully, I lift you from the chair and place you face down on the plastic sheet. You are heavy. My back hurts. I straighten your arms and place them by your side. Heart thumping, knowing I need to act quickly, I wrap you in the plastic sheet and leave you on the cold stone kitchen floor. The heating has been off all day. Lying on the floor wrapped in plastic will keep your body cool. The low temperature will disguise your time of death. Time of death can be hard to ascertain. Real life is not like *Silent Witness*.

I take the pipette and fill it with blood from your wound. Now I need to keep the wound fresh. I cover it with cling film and Sellotape. I hide the wrench, wrapped in latex, beneath the kitchen plinth, in the corner by the bin. I will deal with it later. I place the blood-filled pipette in a plastic bag in the fridge.

Job done for now. I wrap my suit and gloves in a plastic shopping bag, stuff them in my handbag, and grab my jacket and car keys.

I drive off, looking at the time. Just right. I sigh with relief. My heart begins to slow. Everything is in order. I stop the car and dump the suit and gloves wrapped tightly in a Waitrose bag at the local roadside recycling bin. Then I continue on my way to book group. Time for my life to move on.

38

Emma

The Angel on the Bridge; my favourite pub. Warm and cosy.
Wood-panelled and characterful. Andrea arrives at the same time
as me, for our Wednesday night ritual, our early evening drink.
She is looking as good as ever, with her shiny auburn hair.
Wearing her black leather coat and signature pale-pink lipstick.

We find our table in the corner by the window, the one we
always take if we can. I go to the bar to get the drinks. Gin and
tonic for Andrea. Bombay Sapphire and Fever-Tree, of course.
Nothing but the best for my glamorous receptionist. A small
glass of white wine for me.

'I've got an assignation after this. I'm meeting someone at
eight-ish,' Andrea says, voice slightly breathless.

'An internet date?' I ask.

'Yes,' she replies. 'And if the photograph is accurate he looks
pretty fit.'

And for a second I envy her. When I'm starting a new relationship I always enjoy the swiping and tasting stage.

39

Jade

Book group is such a bore. But I need an alibi, so I have to put up with it. After tonight I won't need to come any more. The book group takes place at a different member's house each month. The person who hosts the group chooses the book and chairs the meeting. Tonight it's Josephine's turn. She is a large woman with ginger hair and freckles. A voice that is long-vowelled, overpowering. A friend of hers has self-published a book so, to support her friend, she chose it. I forced myself to read it. It wasn't very good.

Josephine opens the comments. 'I thought the book was excellent. Very well structured. The twist about the DNA evidence was brilliant, so incisive.'

I know the DNA evidence twist is incorrect, but I do not say anything. I don't need to contribute, I just need to be here. I mustn't draw attention to my forensic knowledge.

Another woman, Anna, with a big nose and curly hair that frizzes, is rabbiting on about the main character in the book; criticising her every action. I close my eyes and see your body lying there. You hurt me, Tomas. You deserve to be gone. But then my stomach knots. I see your tender face moving towards mine, the first time we kissed. When you were obsessed with me. Before my novelty wore off. We loved each other once. Memories of your love come hurtling towards me like a flood. I push them away. I want book group to end. I need to get home to finish what I have started. I pinch myself and open my eyes again. The conversation is beginning to dwindle. I look at my watch and stand up.

'It's ten thirty,' I say loudly. 'I'm afraid I must be off.'

Josephine steps out of the sitting room and accompanies me to the door.

'Thanks so much for coming. See you next month.'

I drive home. The pivotal time. I enter the house, heart palpitating. I have to act fast. No room for any mistakes. I turn the central heating on, and step into the kitchen. You are lying face down, wrapped in plastic. I feel sick at the sight of you, marble-skinned and stiff. Already bearing no resemblance to the animated man I once loved. I brace myself and swallow. I put on a fresh pair of latex gloves, and the second Tyvek suit, from my store beneath the sink.

So little time, so much to do. I mustn't panic. I mustn't forget a thing. I take a deep breath. I brace myself by bending and stretching, then I lift your body back onto the chair. Putting you into the same position, or as close as I can remember, as when I hit you. Trying not to think of this monstrous pile of stiffness as you, but as an empty shell I need to attend to. Unpeeling the cling film from your head, I'm relieved to see the blood is still wet and fresh. The back of your skull is such a mess. Hands trembling, I look at my measurements and photographs. Mind trembling, I recreate the original blood splatter as carefully as possible with the blood from the wound, using the pipette to get the right droplets. Pushing back tears, I take some blood and hair and put it in a plastic container and hide it in the freezer, just in case I need it later.

Almost finished. Pushing away love that has veered to hate. Gathering the incriminating evidence, all of it. Dirty evidence to be discarded, placed in one Waitrose bag – Tyvek suit, gloves, pipette, plastic sheet. Keeping the wrench in a separate one. Mind fragmenting, heart pulsating, I race upstairs to the loft, pull a mask over my mouth and nose, and dig into the insulation to bury the bags. I need to move them as soon as possible. But I know, from studying police reports, they won't have the patience, or the time, to look there tonight.

Finally, I dash downstairs, two steps at a time, looking at my watch to check that I have been quick enough. Hands trembling more than ever, I dial 999.

40

Emma

I'm back home, after my trip to the Angel with Andrea. Good intentions about not drinking alcohol midweek over, the small glass of wine at the pub whetting my appetite, I open a bottle of Chablis and pour myself a large slug. Still envying Andrea's excitement about finding a new relationship, I need to distract myself. I sit drinking the bottle of wine and watching *Stranger Things* on Netflix.

At eleven-ish, just as I'm about to pad upstairs and go to bed, I hear a police siren. I look out of the hall window. Blue flashing lights. A police car pulling into Tomas and Jade's drive. There must have been a burglary. I hope Jade and Tomas haven't had too much taken, I'll contact them tomorrow to check they are OK. Shuddering at the thought that an intruder might be on the loose, I check my doors are double locked, and my windows are firmly shut.

Up to bed. The usual routine. Removing my make-up. Cleaning my teeth. Dousing my face with cream. I slip into bed and Casper snuggles next to me. His tractor-engine purr increases, soothing me, singing me to sleep. Telling me that Jade and Tomas must be all right.

41

Jade

The police are here, skewing their car across my drive, alarming the area with flashing blue lights. The doorbell rings. Two police constables are on my doorstep.

'Are you Mrs Covington?' the taller one asks.

I nod my head.

'I'm PC Rosco, and this is my colleague PC Hall. May we come in?'

They step into the hallway.

'What happened?' PC Rosco asks.

I look at the ground, wracked with distress. 'I came back from book group and I . . . and I . . . I found him.' I swallow back tears. 'In the kitchen.' I pause. 'Sorry. Excuse me. I'm going to be sick.'

I rush to the downstairs cloakroom and vomit. Then I flush the loo, wash my hands and splash my face with cold water. I take a deep breath to calm myself and step out of the cloakroom to go and find the police officers. They are in the kitchen inspecting your body. I walk towards them, looking down at the floor in front of me. I cannot even bear to glance across. How could I have done this to you?

PC Rosco is on his mobile requesting a crime scene investigator urgently. PC Hall is pacing the kitchen, inspecting the windows. 'No sign of a break-in,' he announces.

No sign of a break-in. Murdered by someone who knew you.

But not me. They will never work out it was me. I feel blood suddenly rushing from the back of my head.

'I need to sit down,' I tell PC Hall. 'I'll be in the drawing room if you need me.'

'Can I get you anything? The family liaison officer is on her way.'

'Please tell her not to come. I'm so shell-shocked, I just want to be alone.'

I pad into the drawing room and sit, head in hands. After a while PC Rosco comes to sit next to me.

'Mrs Covington, I'm so sorry for your loss.' There is a pause. 'But, we need to declare the house a crime scene and request you sleep elsewhere tonight. Do you want to stay with a friend? Or in a hotel?'

I hesitate. 'I'll stay at the Red Lion.'

'OK, I'll ring and book a room. We'll try and get you back home as quickly as possible. Are you sure you don't want to see a family liaison officer tonight?'

I bite my lip and shake my head. 'I feel so awful; I just want to be left alone,' I mutter.

'Before you go to the hotel I will need to take you to the police station, where our detective sergeant will take a detailed statement, and some forensics. You need to bring something to change into this evening as the DS may want to examine the clothes you are wearing.'

Number one suspect already. Imagination so limited they always suspect the one who finds the body. Just as I expected. Breathe. Breathe.

'Now I have to watch you pack your overnight bag, is that OK?'

I nod my head.

'Do you feel up to it right now?'

'I'll manage.'

I stand up, still feeling faint. My body sways. I need to sit down again, and put my head in my hands to compose myself. On my next attempt, PC Rosco helps me up and holds my arm to support me. He guides me upstairs. He watches me fling things into my bag. Toiletries, clean underwear. Three clean outfits. My coat. My beanie hat. My phone charger. It looks random. It feels random. But my mind is still functioning, and despite the fug of mixed emotions, I have carefully put together the things I planned I would need. Heart rate calming, I zip up my bag. PC Rosco carries it downstairs, leaving me to trail behind him.

'I'm taking Mrs Covington to the station to make a statement,' he explains to his colleague. 'And then I'll come back and pick you up. The murder team will have arrived by then.'

PC Hall nods his head. We step outside, the night air brushing against my skin. I feel sick as we walk towards the police car. Sick with an overdose of nerves. There is no room for any hiccups in my statement. Everything needs to be consistent. Ducks in a row, lined up straight.

In the front of the car with PC Rosco, I look across at him. He is short and broad, with rugby-player shoulders. A neat compact look about him, a bit like Tom Hollander, with strong wavy hair.

Into the police station. A woman is walking towards me with toffee-coloured skin, and dark eyes. We meet face to face in the corridor.

'Hello. I'm DS Miranda Jupiter.'

I don't reply.

'I'm sorry to have to put you through this when you must be feeling so traumatised,' she continues. 'I need to take you to the medical room to take some DNA and also to remove your clothes.' She puts her head on one side and almost smiles. 'It's routine. Just for elimination purposes.'

I know it's routine. Most people who are murdered are murdered by someone close to them. Find a dead body. Suspect the person who finds it, especially if they are a spouse.

We go to the medical room. She watches me studiously as I remove my clothes. She bags every item individually into brown evidence bags. I dress in clean clothes. Jeans and a jumper. Trainers and socks. Then she swabs my mouth for DNA and takes my fingerprints.

'Just to help clarify the DNA we find at the crime scene.'

Just to clarify, DS Miranda Jupiter, I know why. I know more about forensics than you.

'We need to take a statement from you,' she says gently.

'That's fine.'

She leads me along a corridor into an interview room. The usual. No windows. A recording machine. Grey plastic table. Grey chairs.

'Would you like tea or coffee?' she asks as I sit down.

'I'm fine.'

'If you don't mind me saying so, you don't look fine. You look shell-shocked.'

'I am.' I bite my lip and almost manage to feign tears. But the tears that fell earlier won't come again.

There is a plastic jug full of water and some plastic cups on the table in front of her. She pours some out and hands it to me. 'Here, drink this.'

'Thanks.'

I sip the water. It is tepid. Its warmth sticks in my throat. PC Rosco enters the room and sits down next to DS Jupiter.

'However awful you're feeling we need you to try and concentrate,' DS Miranda Jupiter says. 'We need as many details as possible about the lead-up to your husband's death. We'll start the machine to record this interview in a few seconds. I need you to keep calm and really, really think.'

She nods at PC Rosco who starts the recording.

'Wednesday twenty-seventh March 2019. Interviewing Mrs Jade Covington. PC Rosco present.'

'DS Miranda Jupiter.'

The DS leans back in her chair and crosses her legs. 'When was the last time you saw your husband alive?'

I see the blood haemorrhaging from the wound at the back of your head. Feel the force of the wrench as I hit you again. I see your loving face leaning in to kiss me on the day we were married. Your golden voice resonates in my head. I look at the ground. I close my mind to the past.

'At breakfast time, before he went to work.'

'Did he seem OK?'

'Yes.'

'Was everything all right between you and Mr Covington?'

I bite my lip. 'Not really. We'd been having a few problems.' Her eyes tighten. 'He was having an affair with Emma Stockton, our neighbour. I had caught them together several times. I told him I was going to leave him.'

'When?'

'Yesterday evening.'

'How did he react?'

'As he always does. Says he's sorry. That he can't bear it if I leave. That he'll never stray again.'

'So he has been unfaithful before?'

'Yes.'

'Would you like to tell me more about your relationship?'

I push back tears. 'It's too painful to talk about right now. All I can say is I loved him so much.'

She stirs in her chair. 'Where were you this evening?'

'At Josephine Brooker's house, 76 Vale Way – at a meeting of the Henley book group.'

'All evening?'

'It started at seven thirty p.m. I left at ten thirty p.m.'

Seven thirty, the time you are always home on Wednesdays, Stereotype.

'Are you happy for me to contact your book group to verify that?'

'Of course I am, yes.'

She leans forwards. 'So you came home from work briefly, did you, before you went to book group?'

'Yes.'

'And you didn't see your husband?'

'No. I didn't see him until . . . until . . .' My voice is breaking now.

'Do you have any idea who might have wanted to hurt your husband?'

'No. Not really. Everyone always loved Tomas.' I pause and shake my head slowly. 'I suppose Emma must have been upset, if he had finished with her. He told me he was going to.'

Memories

Home from school. Walking into the kitchen to see Mother. She turned from the kitchen sink, where she was peeling potatoes, to greet me. Mother, but not Mother. A monster stood before me. Right eye swollen. Lids closed. A kaleidoscope of purple and black bruising decorating her face.

I went to the fridge, poured myself a glass of milk. I sat at the kitchen table.

'Mother, you've got to do something about this.'

'About what?' she asked.

My hand shook. I spilt the milk. It skimmed across the table like white blood. I took a cloth from the sink and wiped it up. She walked towards me, and stood in front of me.

'I opened the cupboard at the back of the garage too quickly, and the corner of the door banged into my eye.'

'Do you expect me to believe that? If you don't do something about it I will.'

She put her hand on my arm. 'I'm begging you not to, Emma. It'll only make things worse.'

42

Jade

Into my bedroom at the Red Lion. Body trembling as I throw myself across the four-poster bed. Tomas, I cannot get you out of my head. Remembering you when we first met, after hooking up on Tinder. Watching you walk into the café in Sunbury, thinking I was punching above my weight. Your golden looks. Your flat torso. Shoulders as broad as bricks. So much better-looking than me. I knew as soon as I saw you that I would never be able to keep a man like you. You smiled at me and my insides twisted.

I smiled back. You kept on walking towards me. You sat down opposite me.

'How do you do? I'm Tomas.'

'I'm Jade.'

'Jade, how should we start?'

'Tell me a few things about yourself.'

'OK then. I've never dated on Tinder before. But I've never met anyone I really, really want to be with, so I thought I'd give it a try.'

Silence fell. You looked embarrassed. You grimaced.

'Go on. Next thing,' I pushed.

You shrugged your shoulders. 'Do we have to do this?'

'Yes,' I insisted.

'Can't we just have a normal conversation?'

'No. Because I'm spiky.'

'I like spiky.'

'Actually, I'm aiming for sardonic wit but it always comes out wrong.'

You put your head back and laughed. 'I like you, Jade. I think we could have fun.'

And we did, for a while, back then. We married quickly. Our wedding was a small affair, as we were both only children with no surviving parents. It was easier that way. Just us and our witnesses, two friends from work, at the local registry office. Afterwards we ate at a trendy Italian restaurant near the river. We were so full of love for one another. So sure it would work.

I lie across the four-poster bed and sob. Loud, body-wracking sobs. Fighting for breath, too emotionally wrought to give way to the soft release of tears. I see your wound. Your blood gushing. And my sobs increase.

Then I see you in our bed with Emma. Face contorted with passion. And I know what I did was right. You betrayed me. You didn't deserve to live.

43

Alastair

First thing in the morning, I'm sitting in the scrubs area, when the buzzer sounds. A few seconds later a robotic voice announces, 'To the incident room immediately.'

Blood pulsates around my body, heightening my sensation. This part of the job is what makes it worthwhile; coming together as a team, to solve a crime. Tingling with anticipation I make my way along the corridor, into the incident room. The incident room is buzzing with curiosity and chatter.

A murder. Must be. DS Miranda Jupiter and her boss DI Hamilton are here. Miranda is looking as unruffled as ever. No frowns. No smiles. Always straight-faced. She would look pretty if she smiled. DI Hamilton is scribbling on the whiteboard. He turns to face us. Silence descends.

'We have a forty-five-year-old Caucasian man, Tomas Covington, found dead in his kitchen. The death was phoned in at ten fifty-eight p.m. by his wife when she returned from book group, or so she said. Large wound on the back of his head. No forced entry.'

My stomach tightens. Tomas Covington dead? Emma's neighbour. Should I tell them I knew him, and even had a meal in the house where he was found?

Not yet. I only met him once, after all.

'So,' DI Hamilton continues. 'We have investigated the crime scene fully, all samples from the crime scene are waiting for forensics. Sarah Dickinson, Alastair Brown and team, you're going to be very busy. We look forward to you reporting back.' He pauses.

'The autopsy is taking place as we speak, but the pathologist has already confirmed it looks like blunt instrument trauma. We haven't found a possible murder weapon yet. We're waiting for a full report on the time of death, which will be critical. Miranda, do you have anything to add?'

DS Miranda Jupiter steps forwards. 'I spoke to Mrs Covington last night, shortly after she had found the body. Evidence gathered so far supports her story. The interesting point is that Mrs Covington told us that her husband, Tomas, was having an affair with their neighbour, an Emma Stockton.'

My heart feels as if a fist is squeezing it. I can hardly breathe. Emma, having an affair with Tomas? No. I can't bear it. No. Heather has betrayed me, and now Emma? The air tightens around me. I need to tell them that I know Emma. But . . . but, they never ask who we know. If I tread carefully, they won't find out. Anyway, Emma and I haven't known each other long; we are not married, we don't live together. Air tightens in my gullet and I decide not to tell my boss, Sarah Dickinson. At least not now. I need to stay on the case. I need to know whether Emma is honest.

44

Emma

I'm between patients, having a slug of coffee, when a policewoman steps into my consulting room. Long dark hair. Cupid's mouth. Chocolate-drop eyes. Beauty laced with an acidic expression.

'Are you Emma Stockton?' she asks.

'Yes. Can I help you?'

She whips her ID card out of her wallet, then whisks it away so quickly I hardly see it. 'I'm DS Jupiter. I need to ask you a few questions.'

'Fire away,' I reply, as I have no reason to believe she isn't who she says she is.

'Do you know Tomas Covington?'

'Yes. Not very well. He lives next door to me. He and his wife, Jade, have just moved in.'

'Are you having a relationship with him?'

'What?' I splutter. 'No. Of course not.'

DS Jupiter scribbles something into her notebook.

'Ms Stockton, if you're lying to me I have to warn you that there may be serious consequences.'

'His wife's told me from time to time that he finds me attractive, but he's never made any advances to me. Or I to him. He's my patient – that's all. What's the matter? Why on earth are you asking me this?' I reply.

'Because I'm very sorry to have to tell you your *patient* is dead.'

My sharp intake of breath makes a slicing sound. 'What? How?'

'That's why I'm here, trying to find out.'

45

Alastair

Sitting in your drawing room, glass of wine in my hand, watching the sinews and shadows in your face. Sad and taut. Shaking your pretty head.

'I can't believe Tomas is dead.'

My heart stops. *Tomas.* What did he mean to you?

'Why is Jade saying I had an affair with him?' you continue. 'What's wrong with the woman?' There is a pause. 'What's *wrong* with the woman?' you repeat, louder this time. Is this genuine? Or are you over-egging it? Heather was a liar. Are you a liar too, Emma?

I take your hand in mine. 'I don't know. Her attitude worries me, Emma. She's definitely trying to push the focus onto you.'

'She was from the start. Warning me he might be attracted to me. How could she tell? You can't predict attraction, can you?'

I look at you and smile. 'Maybe. I mean you are attractive, aren't you?'

You shrug. 'You tell me.'

'You know I find you attractive.'

I kiss you. You push me away. 'But did he?' You pause. 'He never insinuated anything. All he ever did was tell me how much he loved Jade. Not exactly an extramarital seduction line. The whole situation is ridiculous. The Clusterfuck is dangerous. That's all there is to it.'

I shudder inside. 'Mad and dangerous,' I say as I pull you towards me and kiss you again.

46

Jade

Another night at the Red Lion, in my ancient beamed bedroom. And another, perhaps? Pushing the family liaison officer away during the day. I don't want her breathing down my neck. How long are they going to keep me here, now that my life and my home have become a crime scene? Are they going to tear through my house looking for evidence? Rip out the loft insulation and uncover my plot? Sitting in my hotel bedroom, I know I need to act.

I wait for dusk. Too light. I wait for darkness. Too many people walking past. Two a.m. A quiet world now. I want the receptionist to think I'm still in my room, so I slip out of my bedroom window onto the hotel portico's roof. Climbing down, balancing on the jutted wall at the front, landing heavily, almost twisting my ankle. A sharp slice of pain. There for a second and gone.

A cold, damp night. I shiver and zip up my jacket as I walk across the bridge over the river, head down, hoping no one will see me. Along the path by the Leander Club, through the car park towards my house. I stand outside. Unlit. Silent. I sigh with relief. The police have decided not to work through the night.

I pull the latex gloves and overshoes from my handbag and put them on. I carefully unpick the police tape across the doorway. So carefully that I can replace it. Turning the key. Stepping inside.

Darkness and silence pressing against me but I do not switch on the lights. Using the torch on my iPhone, I move through the hallway into the kitchen.

Moonlight floods through the large picture window, illuminating the shadow of your memory. For your body is gone, Tomas. And only your ghost is left, stepping towards me, telling me that you are sorry. That you will never cheat on me again. And for a second I wish I could hold you, touch you, pull your warm body towards me again. But I shake my head. It is too late now. Our last goodbye has been said.

Heart pounding, I move upstairs to the loft to find out whether the police have found the evidence they need to prosecute me. I put on a dust mask from the pile you kept at the entrance. Fingers trembling, I grasp at the insulation in the corner of the loft and scrape it back. Breathe. Breathe. The tremor in my fingers decreases. The bags are still here. I pull them out. I push the loft insulation back and step away.

Breathe. Breathe. I need to pay attention to detail. One mistake, however slight, could incriminate me. Into the bathroom. Washing the blood from the wrench down the sink. Wrapping the wrench in clean plastic. After my dirty work, I put on a fresh pair of gloves. All the debris from my deed is in my 'dirty' Waitrose bag. The wrench is carefully stored in a new clean one.

Almost there. Time to leave. Step by step, guided by light from my iPhone. Step by step downstairs. Opening and then re-locking the front door. Slowly, carefully, replacing the police tape. At last, with a sigh of relief, moving back into the safety of the night. The headlights of a car pierce through the darkness towards me. I duck down behind my crinodendron bush as they move past.

Slowly, slowly, creeping through the side gate into your garden, Emma. Towards your shed. Opening the door. New latex gloves. Taking the wrench out of its bag. Removing the plastic off the wrench. Placing it in your tool box.

Off and away, feeling elated. My planning is really paying off. Along the footpath by the river, whipping off the latex gloves and overshoes, adding them to my debris bag. It's a silent night, apart from the occasional hiss of a passing car and the plaintive cry of a lonely river bird.

Through the silent streets of town, avoiding the CCTV cameras. I know where they are. But the clothes I managed to remove from my bedroom when I was being watched by PC Rosco happen to be black. A black phantom, even if captured by a camera, is difficult to see. A black phantom, wild and invincible. Along to the roadside plastics recycling bin, where I deposit my debris bag.

Back to the Red Lion Hotel. I stand looking up at the portico. My mind freezes. Climbing back up looks difficult. Harder than climbing down. I can't reach high enough to stand on the small row of bricks that juts out. I must climb up the plastic drainpipe. Will it be strong enough?

I've come this far. There is no going back. I will have to take the risk. I grab on to the drainpipe and pull myself up like a monkey. It holds my weight. I heave my legs across onto the flat roof of the portico and collapse into a relieved heap, sliding in a pool of stale rainwater. So stale it smells like sewage.

Bedroom window left open, I drag my exhausted body inside.

Memories

Sitting in a room at the police station in front of a female officer.
DS Simpson. Short blonde wavy hair. Wide Marilyn Monroe
lips. Telling her everything that has happened to you, Mother.
She listened intently. Then she leant forwards.

'It all sounds very serious, but your mother needs to report
this herself. Can you try and persuade her to do that?'

I shook my head. 'She won't. I've tried so many times, but
she always says it'll make things worse. She's so afraid of him.'
I paused. 'Isn't there anything you can do to help?'

'Call us next time something happens and we'll come round,
ring the doorbell and ask your parents if everything is all right.
But your mother needs to make a complaint about your father.
She needs to tell us. And a doctor needs to be shown any injuries.
If he hurts her a doctor needs to verify it.'

'So you just have to wait until my mother is hurt?'

DS Simpson looked sadder than sad. 'To arrest and charge your
father, yes. But if she would only come and talk to us, we could
advise her. There are charities that help women like your mother.'

'Can I contact them?'

'No. She needs to do it herself. They won't be able to help her
without her permission, otherwise it's an invasion of her privacy.'
Frustration welled in my stomach. 'But I can give you a leaflet
for her,' DS Simpson continued.

She handed me the leaflet and I accepted it.

'Thank you,' I said limply, crushed with disappointment. As if a leaflet was going to protect her.

'What about you?' DS Simpson asked.

I frowned. 'Me?'

'Yes.' She paused. 'Has he hurt you?'

'Not physically.'

'Never?'

'Never. He shouts. He frightens me. He minimises me. Tells me I'll never succeed.'

DS Simpson leant across the table of the interview room and put her hand on my arm. 'If he ever hurts you, you must come and see us immediately.'

'I've told you, it's not me he hurts, it's my mother.'

47

Jade

Home at last, after my incarceration in the Red Lion. But the DS with the sultry face is here again. She comes every day. Watching me like a hawk.

'Can I get you a cup of tea?' I ask, stretching my cheeks into a forced smile.

'Yes, please.'

Her eyes dart around my kitchen, resting too long on the wall calendar. What is she looking for?

'Do you mind if I pop to the loo?' she asks.

Oh. The usual trick. Go to the loo and snoop around the bathroom. Or if the toilet is upstairs, snoop around the bedroom too. Hard luck, Miranda Jupiter. Our downstairs cloakroom is compact and minimalistic. No evidence there.

'Step into the hallway. It's the second door on the right.' Another stretched smile.

'Thanks.'

She is gone a while. I make the tea and lay a few biscuits on a plate. When she returns her eyes are more doleful than ever.

I hand her the tea and we sit opposite one another at the kitchen table.

'Have you remembered anything more about the day of the murder?' she asks as she takes a sip of tea and helps herself to a custard cream.

'No. I keep running it back – how awful it was finding my

husband so . . . so . . . dead, his body so badly damaged. I can't get the sight of it out of my head.' I pause. I wipe my eyes. 'It was terrible when I came home when he wasn't expecting me and I caught him with Emma Stockton, having sex in *our* bed.' I shake my head. 'That was bad enough at the time. But nothing to the pain of losing him.'

DS Miranda Jupiter sits drinking her tea. 'Have you changed the bedsheets since you saw Emma here?' she asks.

I frown. 'No. I haven't been finding it easy to do normal chores like washing. You know . . . what with everything.' I pause. 'I haven't even been sleeping in our bedroom, since Tomas died. I can't bear being in it without him.'

'I'm sure it must have all been very difficult.' There is a pause. 'I'm sending a police constable around with evidence bags to collect the bedding later today. We need to take a look at it.'

I smile inside. I so wanted her to organise that.

48

Emma

I drive to the police station, nose streaming from a cold I've caught from one of my patients. I'm not feeling well. Why on earth do they want to see me, and at short notice?

I check in at the reception counter, and am asked to sit and wait by a young PC with a stern face. After what seems a long time, DS Miranda Jupiter puts her head around the door.

'Thanks for coming in, Ms Stockton.' There is a pause. 'Do come here and follow me to the interview room.'

I pad across the waiting area, following DS Jupiter along a thin winding corridor until we reach the interview room. We sit down opposite one another.

'I asked you in today because we would like to take a swab of your DNA, if you don't mind.'

My stomach knots. 'I've nothing to hide. Why would I mind?' I force myself to smile. Anything to disguise the tumult inside.

'Good. Good.'

She produces a paper package from a cupboard behind her and unwraps it, withdrawing a thin test-tube with a cotton bud in it. She unscrews the top and pulls it out. 'Open wide,' she instructs.

Slowly, gently, she uses it to scrape the inside of my cheek. She puts the swab back in the tube and closes the lid.

'Why are you taking this?' I sniff. I blow my nose. 'Am I a suspect?'

'Everyone is a suspect in a case like this.'

'But I hardly knew him.'

'Well, you've got nothing to worry about then.'

49

Alastair

It's the murder team's morning briefing. There's the usual interested buzz, tinged with excitement. Revelling in death as if it
is a mere puzzle to solve. DS Jupiter standing at the front, back
arched, like a cat about to preen herself. DI Hamilton is on
secondment today and she is in charge.

'Good morning, team.' She smiles and nods her head. An
ice-queen bowing to her subjects. 'Yesterday Jade Covington told
me she came home unexpectedly and caught Tomas and Emma
in the Covingtons' marital bed, together.'

My stomach flips. My heart races. Emma. Tomas. Emma, how
could you betray me? I'm bleeding inside. I cannot keep a woman
faithful to me.

'The sheets may not have been changed since then, so we
have removed them and put them into evidence bags.' DS
Jupiter looks across at me. 'Alastair, will you analyse them as
soon as possible?'

And then I will know who to believe; whether I have been
betrayed again.

Seething inside. 'Of course. As soon as the briefing is over,' I
say with a tight smile.

'We now have swabs of DNA from Jade and Emma, so that
will help clarify anything we find,' DS Jupiter continues.

DNA.

Emma is a suspect. I need to tell the team I know her. I should have told them as soon as it happened. My mind rotates. Will another twenty-four hours make any difference? If I hang on a bit longer I can find out if she is honest. I will not speak out yet. I want to know the truth first hand. Sometimes doing the right thing is not the most important priority.

Feeling low, feeling confused, contorted, I change into my scrubs and pad to the evidence store to collect the sheets. Heart pulsating, I step into the sterile area and put on my forensic suit. Then I enter my lab and start work. Jade's sheets are king-sized and pale gold. The same colour as Emma's. They look like Emma's, but then a lot of people have pale-gold sheets. I busy myself putting swab after swab into the machine. DNA. Fragments of tissue. Strong white hairs. They look like Casper's. I pick one up and look at it through a magnifying glass. It's obviously not human hair.

My heart stops. Has Jade got hold of your sheets to set you up? We need to see if these hairs are Casper's, because Casper never leaves your house. He always sleeps by your pillow. Exactly where I have found this nest of hair. I turn my mind in on itself and concentrate. The more I think, the more I figure that there is no other possible explanation. Jade must have swapped the sheets. You are faithful to me, my darling, my love.

My mind fragments. But if she swapped the sheets, wouldn't my DNA be on it, too? That would stop her little plan from working. I push and push. Not if she changed them midweek. Emma always changes the bedding on Monday. She has a thing about airing bedding to dry it, hanging it out on the line. Emma and Jade's houses are so close, Jade would know that.

I step outside the lab, and pick one of Casper's hairs off my jacket. I return and place it on a slide next to one from the bedsheet. I put them under the microscope. Magnified, they look as if they are the same type of hair. They are the same. They must be. My body is electric with happiness because you are not dishonest. Jade has set you up. My beautiful Emma. My true love. The Clusterfuck has set you up. My heart trembles with love. My body trembles with anger.

I come out of the lab and peel off my sterilised clothing. I walk to my boss Sarah Dickinson's office. She is sitting at her desk, staring at her computer screen.

'Please can I have a word?'

She looks up. 'Of course. What is it?'

Trying to keep my voice calm, I say, 'I've found what look like cat hairs on the bedsheets. I'm puzzled as I wasn't sure whether Jade and Tomas had a cat? I want authorisation to send them for analysis.'

'Look Alastair, you know the difficulty with pet hair analysis. We have to send samples abroad and that's expensive. Even then they are not that accurate. But go and talk to Miranda. If she thinks it's a good idea we might get the budget for it.'

I leave the forensic area and walk across to Miranda's desk, still dressed in my scrubs. She is reading through a thick file. 'I need to talk to you,' I say.

She looks up. 'Fire away.'

I try to explain, but I'm not sure she is listening properly. Her eyes keep straying from my face back to the file she was reading.

She shakes her head. 'What's the point? I can check whether Jade has a cat. Even if she doesn't a stray might get in. Why is it significant?'

'This isn't a small amount of hair from a random visit. And Jade's a potential suspect. She might be setting Emma up.'

Miranda leans towards me. 'Why would she?'

I shrug my shoulders. 'To cover up her crime.'

'What makes you think she committed this crime?'

'She has motive. Envy. Jealousy. She said Tomas was a serial womaniser who always loved her, but she could easily have resented his infidelity far more than she has admitted.' I shrug my shoulders. 'I think that's more likely than the angle you are pushing.' I pause. 'What makes you think she didn't do it?'

Miranda Jupiter's body stiffens. Her mouth turns down further than usual.

'I'm the detective working on this, so you can leave this to me.' She pauses. 'I'll talk to Jade and let you know if we need any more tests.'

I ache to say more. To tell her about your precious cat who is never allowed to leave the house. The cat that lives in your bedroom. If I tell her the cat shares your bed with me, I will be off the case. Now I fear you are being set up, I need to stay to protect you. For now, until I can distance myself, Miranda will have to work out the cat situation herself.

Memories

Fingers trembling as I dialled the police. The sound of my mother's cries echoing in my head. Lying in bed, head beneath the covers, trying to block the sound in my ears. The repetitive sound of kicking and thumping that I heard when I went downstairs.

The doorbell rang. I crept onto the landing and held my breath, craning my neck to watch my mother hobbling across the hallway to answer it. Two officers on our doorstep. One male, one female.

'Is everything OK?' the female officer asked.

'Yes.'

'We had a call. A neighbour heard noises. Shouting, as if there was a fight,' the female officer said, eyes darting into the hallway.

'Everything is good here. We were watching a film. Maybe we had it on too loud.'

'Are you sure? We can come inside if you want.'

'No, honestly officer — I'm fine.'

50

Jade

DS Miranda Jupiter is standing on my doorstep. DS Miranda Jupiter is crossing my threshold, chestnut eyes searing through my hallway. Staring at my paintings, at my orchids. Frowning as she glances at my cowhide rugs.

'Can I get you anything?' I ask.

'No thanks, I just came to ask you a few questions.'

What more does she need to know? She's already taken a swab.

'I just want to check that you didn't see your husband when you came back from work on the evening he died. One of his colleagues thought he left work late afternoon. Which means, given the distance you had to travel, you should have had half an hour together – unless he was late, or delayed.'

'He used to get back from work any time between six thirty and eight p.m. Maybe he caught a later train. Sometimes he went shopping before he came home.'

She purses her lips. 'We're checking the CCTV at Paddington Station. So we should be able to get to the bottom of this.'

Breathe. Breathe. CCTV can be unclear. One man in a City suit looks much like another. And half the time the cameras don't work, or the cop on duty falls asleep watching the CCTV tapes as they are so very boring. Sifting for CCTV evidence is tedious in the extreme. Breathe. Breathe.

I confused time of death adequately. I'm sure I did.

51

Emma

DS Miranda Jupiter is sitting on my sofa. She leans back and crosses her slender legs.

'I've got a few questions about your relationship with Tomas.'

'What relationship?' I snap.

'He was your patient.'

'Yes. As I have already told you, I had a patient–dentist relationship with him.'

'Jade Covington says she found a receipt for some black ladies' cashmere gloves, which he never gave to her.' She pauses. 'She thinks he may have given them to you.'

'He did.'

'Isn't that a bit of an odd thing for a patient to do?' There is a pause. 'Give his dentist an expensive pair of gloves?'

'Yes. It was a bit over-the-top. I treated him at the house out of hours when he had an infection in his wisdom teeth. I didn't charge him. Then he had to come and see me at the surgery, later. We fitted him in at short notice, and he gave me the gloves to thank me. I was rather taken aback.'

'Thank you for explaining,' she says, mouth turning downwards. 'And now I need to inform you, I have a search warrant for your house and garden. A team of officers are about to arrive.'

The doorbell rings almost immediately, before the news has sunk in. I must be a suspect. I can't believe this. The police are here, wearing latex gloves, armed with piles of brown paper evidence bags. Three of them. Two men, one woman. Marching across my property as if they own it. Opening drawers and cupboards. Flicking through the contents. Rifling through my kitchen cupboards, my bin, my fridge. Ransacking my bathroom cabinet, my bedroom. Tromping across the garden. Rummaging through the tools in my shed. I don't know what they'll find in there. I haven't been in it for months.

52

Alastair

It's a full meeting today. Everyone assembled. DI Hamilton is standing shoulders wide, neck stretched. Miranda Jupiter's lips are almost curved into a smile, faced tuned into DI Hamilton's, as if she can't wait for the meeting to start.

Silence descends. DI Hamilton steps forwards.

'We've found the murder weapon in Emma Stockton's shed. Pathology tells us that the wrench matches the trauma wound in Tomas Covington's head,' he says.

No. Not you Emma. My darling. My love. You wouldn't do this. You couldn't. You're not even strong enough.

I dwell on the cat hairs. I know you are innocent, I know that Jade is setting you up. What did she do on that night you can't remember? The night you went to hers for a drink. She is a conniving, heartless bitch. I need to stay on the case. I need to help you fight back. We need to box clever. We need to sort this. Even though you are now the main suspect we must keep our relationship quiet. I've had an idea. I can do something to help.

'Alastair, please could you examine the wrench this morning; and send anything you find off for analysis?' DI Hamilton asks.

I nod my head. 'Yes sir, of course.'

Memories

'No honestly, I'm fine.'

The words she said to the police, after I rang them, in the middle of one of my parents' rows and they finally came. No honestly, I'm fine, twists and turns in my head. Twists and turns into my memory of what happened next. After school the next day, visiting her in hospital. Leg in plaster. Two fractured vertebrae and a broken leg.

Her hand clasping mine. 'I told you if you tried to do something about it, it would make things worse. Remember. Remember. I fell downstairs.'

53

Alastair

Another day, another meeting. All the usual. DI Hamilton standing up straight at the front of the room, looking smug. DS Jupiter, petulant and depressed. My boss Sarah Dickinson smiling and equivocal – I'm glad I report to her, not Miranda Jupiter.

DI Hamilton begins, 'Congratulations team, we're moving forwards well on this case.' He looks across at Miranda. 'Please update us on the time of death.'

She steps forwards, pursing her lips. 'The pathologist has come back to us and says it was sometime between seven thirty and nine thirty. He can't be more precise than that. Jade Covington has a strong alibi, she was at a meeting of the Henley book club. Ten people can vouch for her. Emma Stockton, however, was home alone watching Netflix. She had been out for a drink earlier but would have been back in time to kill Tomas.'

My heart sinks. Emma is definitely the lead suspect. All the evidence points to her. So definitely. So precisely. Too precisely. When will the police realise it's a set-up? Murder investigations don't normally progress as smoothly as this.

'What about the wrench, Alastair?' DI Hamilton asks.

I step forwards. 'As well as a bit of Tomas' blood and hair, it has female DNA on it. DNA not on the database yet. So we're waiting to receive the results of the swabs from Jade and Emma – to see if either match.'

'And the bedding?'

'Same thing. We need to wait for the swab results.'

'Taking their time, aren't they? Phone the lab. Tell them to hurry up.'

Miranda Jupiter raises her hand. 'We've checked the CCTV from Paddington Station and we can't find any evidence that Tomas came home earlier than Jade said.'

I am sure your DNA will be on the sheets and on the wrench, Emma. I think Jade has concealed the time of death and set you up. She knows the drill. I bet she kept the house cool and wrapped Tomas' body in plastic. Anyone with mine and Jade's forensic experience knows you can do that. Why are the police so blinkered? They need to check her background. I will find the right moment to remind them.

Memories

Clutching my A level results in my hand. Jumping in the air. UCAS had just confirmed my place. Soon I would be on a train to Dundee University. The best university in Europe to study dentistry. Soon I would be living on the banks of the River Tay.

Hugging my friends. Wanting to dance on the ceiling. To sing and sing, and never stop.

I ran home at full pelt to share this with my mother. A mobile phone conversation just wouldn't hack it. I burst into the kitchen. My heart sank: Father was there too. Sitting at the pine table with her, doing the crossword. Mother was engrossed in one of the romantic novels she was always reading. They looked up.

'I'm going to Dundee. I got into my first choice.'

She stood up and walked towards me, pulled me close and hugged me. 'Emma, I'm so very proud of you.'

I was inhaling her love, her warmth. But my father was prising us apart with his hands, physically separating us.

'I don't know why you're so excited. The top Scottish universities are for Oxbridge rejects. Second choice for people like you who like to think they're clever.'

My body stiffened. My stomach coagulated. 'I wasn't an Oxbridge candidate. Oxford and Cambridge don't have dental schools.'

He stood in front of me and folded his arms. 'Congratulations, Little Miss Self-Important. So proud of yourself, aren't you?'

'Yes Dad, I am. And you should be proud of me too.'

54

Alastair

I open the email. The DNA results from Jade and Emma's swabs have come through. I take a deep breath and read the words on the screen in front of me. Emma's DNA is on Jade and Tomas' bedsheets. Emma's DNA is on the spanner. I knew the Clusterfuck was dangerous as soon as I met her. I'm not informing the police about this until tomorrow. I am off to see Emma tonight.

'What are you doing here in the week?' you ask as you open the door to me, red-nosed and sniffing with your cold.

'That's a warm reception.'

'Don't snap. Of course I'm pleased to see you. I just hope everything's OK.' You step away from me and blow your nose. Your heavy cold is dragging on, pulling you down. 'I won't kiss you, I don't want you to catch this.'

'I'll take the risk.'

Our lips meet. The usual desire when we touch pulses through me. But I pull away. I know I need to act quickly.

'I need to check something.'

I dash upstairs, two steps at a time. Into your bedroom. I inspect the sheets. Pale gold. The same colour as ever. I slip a pillowcase off and look more closely. Debenhams label, not John Lewis. You always joke you live in a John Lewis house, with the exception of what you buy at Waitrose. I need to use your credit card bill to prove where you bought your sheets. All in due course.

Back downstairs, I find you in the kitchen. I pull you towards me and hold you, panic simmering inside me. I need to help you, quickly.

'Jade is setting you up, we need to talk about this,' I say.

You pull away from me. 'What do you mean?' you ask.

'It's complicated. Let's talk.'

We sit down opposite one another at your pine table. I lean across and take your hands in mine. 'She's double-crossed you. Taken your DNA and put it on the wrench. That night. That night you can't remember. She must have done it then, when you were out for the count. The DNA swab results came back. It's your DNA on the murder weapon. And on the sheets.'

You are wide-eyed with panic.

'I have to tell my colleagues at the meeting tomorrow, then you'll be arrested,' I continue. 'We haven't got much time to sort this out.'

You take a sharp intake of breath. You look as if you are about to faint.

'But . . . but . . . how can we?' you stutter.

I put my hand on your arm. 'I can change the evidence. Just listen. First things first. She needs to catch your cold. Trust me. I'll tell you what to do. Two can play at this game. She has no more forensic knowledge than me.' I pause. 'I'm not letting anything happen to you, Emma. Believe me. I'm in control of this.'

55

Emma

On Friday morning, I phone Andrea and tell her to cancel my appointments, trying to suppress the panic that is rising inside me. I need to keep calm and follow Alastair's instructions immediately. Fortunately for our plan, my cold is becoming worse. My nose is red raw with all the blowing. My eyes are watering. My throat feels as if I have swallowed sandpaper. Jade's car is in the drive. This is my opportunity.

I pull on an old tracksuit and force myself to walk up her garden path, past all the new conifers her gardener has planted. Past rose bushes and catmint. Past rhododendrons, crinodendrons and choisya. I ring the bell. She answers, still in her slippers and dressing gown.

'I've finally got a morning off work so I've popped over to tell you in person how sorry I am about Tomas. I know I sent you a card, but it isn't the same as speaking to you.' I pause. 'Can I come in for a quick coffee?'

We stand looking at each other.

'It's a bit early. I'm not even dressed yet.'

'I know. I'm sorry. It's just I've got to go to work later and I thought we could have a chat.'

'OK, OK. As long as you don't mind me looking like this.'

She steps back from the door, I walk into her weird hallway of mirrors.

'Let's go into the kitchen,' she suggests.

I blow my nose as I progress towards the kitchen, following her, then I wipe my hankie on the door handle when she's not looking. As she fills the kettle at the sink I wipe it across her kitchen surfaces. She sits down at the kitchen table. I sit opposite her.

'How are you coping?' I ask.

'I'm missing Tomas so much. It hurts so much without him.'

Lying Clusterfuck. When she pops to the toilet I wipe my handkerchief on the strap of her handbag, on the cruet, on the teacup she was drinking from. You want DNA evidence, you'll get it.

Memories

Entering Caird Hall as graduands, dressed in black flowing robes, lined with ruby silk and trimmed with white fur. Waiting in a hall, heady with a mixture of boredom, pride and anticipation, to receive our degrees. Giggling. Chatting. Staring at the pantomime characters dressed in bright colours and lumpy hats on the stage in front of us.

Silence fell. The chancellor, decked in canary yellow and paint-pot blue, spoke words of pride in our fine university, words of praise and encouragement. I sat listening and a strong sense of my life opening out in front of me overwhelmed me. I took my turn and walked across the stage to receive my degree.

Leaving the hall, we stood in front of fine stone pillars to have our photographs taken. Throwing our mortar boards and laughing. Freeze frame.

I stepped away from the group and my parents walked towards me. Mother was dabbing her face with a tissue, Father was frowning.

'What now?' he asked.

'I booked a table for lunch at Collinson's.'

'Your mother mentioned that.' He paused. 'Do you think that I'm made of money? Cancel the booking. We're going to the café over the road.'

56

Emma

I'm still dumbfounded after being arrested, when I'm pushed into a cell at the police station. A compact cell, containing only a bed, a bench and a toilet, cold and unwelcoming with a concrete floor and concrete walls. I sit on the bench, arms tightly cuffed behind my back. The constable uncuffs me.

'I need to see my solicitor,' I say, voice trembling.

'Give me the name and I'll get in touch.'

'Benjamin Watts. From Barnham and Watts. His number is in my mobile.'

The constable nods his head and leaves. I feel hot. Cold. Empty inside. I will not speak to them until my solicitor is here. My stomach spasms. I feel sick. Why is Jade doing this to me?

Time stops. And I am back remembering the first time I met her. The weird way she invited me into the kitchen to tell me Tomas had a wandering eye. Her spiky personality. Her face moves towards me, neat-featured and masculine. Broad, strong cheekbones. Dark eyes pushing into mine, as she handed me the Cherry Bomb cocktail. What did she do to me that night? The night I can't remember. I must tell the police about it. I must tell Benjamin. Her masculine face becomes my father's, becomes Colin's. A pealing, haunting laugh.

A click of the lock. Benjamin is here. Stepping into my cell, let in by the constable who immediately disappears. Benjamin Watts. Tall with brown, almost red, hair. His beard and moustache are straggly. He kisses me on both cheeks and his facial hair scratches my skin. I cling on to him for a second too long, imagining he is someone I know, a soulmate. Then I step back, embarrassed. He sits on the plank–like bed, I sit on the bench.

He leans forwards. 'Tell me what happened, Emma.'

The kindness in his voice makes me feel like bursting into tears. 'I think I've been stitched up,' I reply with a sniff.

'Stitched up is a very tricky defence. We need to run very carefully through your movements that evening.'

'I went for a drink with my receptionist, Andrea. I was home by seven thirty, watching Netflix.'

'Home, alone?'

'Yes.'

Tears well as I remember the way Miranda Jupiter spoke to me.

No alibi around the time of death, she snarled with her lips and her eyes.

57

Jade

DS Miranda Jupiter is here, sitting in my living room, by my shiny arrangement of black orchids. She leans forwards.

'I have come to tell you we have arrested Emma Stockton for your husband's murder.'

I have rehearsed this in front of the mirror, so many times. Hours and hours in front of the bathroom mirror. A sharp intake of breath. An almost imperceptible widening of my fingers and nostrils. I shake my head. I compose myself.

'Thank goodness,' I say slowly. 'Thank goodness she's been caught.'

I put my head in my hands and cry tears that are dry. Tomas, I have cried for you so often for so long. Now the person who caused your death has been arrested, try as I might, more tears won't come.

58

Alastair

A briefing meeting called at short notice. DI Hamilton and DS Jupiter are standing by the whiteboard. Smug. Preening. Gloating. Like a pair of pedigree cats. DI Harrison steps forward, beaming from cheek to cheek.

'Well done, team. Emma Stockton has been charged now. Over to the CPS.' He raises his arms in the air. 'Drinks on me at the Cock and Bull tonight.'

The team are smiling, chatting, laughing, joking.

'And I've bought some doughnuts,' DS Jupiter adds, waving a cake box in the air.

She places the box on the table by the window. I walk across and take one. I bite into it. The jam is so sweet, it makes me feel sick.

Memories

Living in a converted warehouse in Rotherhithe, working at a local dental practice. Looking for love in all the wrong places. And swiping left too many times on Tinder. Until I saw Colin. An older guy. A silver fox. Streaks of silver in fine black hair. Craggy features; Liam Neeson style.

I swiped right. So did he. A few days later we went for a date. By date I mean I went to meet him at his workplace. And that was how our relationship began.

59

Alastair

I'm missing you, Emma. I miss the feel of your arms around me. The way we used to laugh. The way we used to smile.

But however much I want to, I cannot come and see you. The police might realise we are involved with one another and knock me off the case. So I have sent you a note, with the request that when you have read it, you destroy it. A note to reassure you, Emma, that Jade will not get away with this. You will soon be free. I will make her pay. For what she did to Tomas. For what she has done to you. No one will get away with harming you, my darling. Jade and Heather pervade my mind. Enemy fire trying to destroy our relationship. Enemy fire which has failed.

60

Emma

I'm being transferred from the police station to prison in what looks like a cattle truck, in a compartment with a high window. I can see sky if I crane my neck. No horizon; no buildings, no trees. Travel sickness engulfing me.

61

Alastair

Jade should have caught your cold by now. I dial her number to find out. She picks up.

'Ted Leicester here, from UK Polling. Would you mind answering a few questions?' I say.

'Yeb, I do minb,' she replies through a blocked nose.

And I know that she has a very, very bad cold. The sound of sniffling down the phone makes me smile inside.

62

Jade

Despite the inconvenience of the cold I am suffering from, meaning I have to blow my nose every few minutes, I'm drinking a bottle of Champagne to celebrate the fact that you are in prison. You deserve to be there, you superficial bint. For flirting with my beautiful Tomas. Touching him. Hugging him by your surgery window for all to see. You had every opportunity to stop. I even gave you a heads-up. You are the one who has taken him away from me.

Have you any idea how ridiculous you looked out for the count on my sofa? Mouth lax and open. Saliva dribbling. As I rubbed your inert fingers on the wrench. So many skin cells, ripe for plucking.

Out for the count, such tedious company. And I was waiting until it was late at night, no one in sight, so it was safe to take you home without being spotted. To while away the time, I decided to do what I always do when Tomas is busy. Watch a romcom on Netflix.

I love them, but they are always the same. Two people, who hate each other, meet and argue. Then they fall in love. Three quarters of the way through, a major impediment makes them split up. The conflict is resolved in the last few minutes.

I flicked one on, and sat engrossed. It starred Josh Duhamel. The more I watched, the more I fell in love with him. So much better-looking than Tomas. So much better-looking than any man I've ever seen. In the film, his love interest dumped him, found a new dishy man nowhere near as sexy, and missed him. He came back to visit the town she lived in, told her he loved her, always had. And they got back together. I cried with happiness as I watched them kiss at the end. I so wanted a man to love me like that. To love me beyond all. To make me the centre of his universe.

I've finished the Champagne. I'm going to have a whisky and a Lemsip, and watch that film again.

63

Alastair

Wearing my latex gloves, I pick up the spare keys from beneath the watering can. Emma, you knew they were there because you saw Jade and Tomas use them from time to time.

I unlock the door, open it and step inside. I have been following Jade's movements. She has gone to Pilates; I know I have an hour and a half to raid her house. A voice coming from the kitchen makes me jump out of my skin. I stand still and listen. The dulcet tones of Radio 4. No other sound. No one pottering about. A radio on a timer to deter thieves. It won't deter me.

I dash upstairs to her bedroom. She has changed the look. No longer into soft golden sheets? The double-crossing fuck. Black silk. Black satin pillows. Black orchids on the dressing table, now. Looking like a shiny funeral parlour. I open the door to the en-suite. Black marble, gold taps, white suite. I open the bin. It's empty. Bugger. The cleaner must have been and taken my DNA proof away. I try not to panic and rush back into the bedroom. I look under the pillows. Three large hankies, bruised with snot and crinkled. I exhale in relief. These will do.

Downstairs. Into the kitchen. Tidy and clean, no debris. Into the sitting room, everything minimalistic. No photographs. No ornaments. I check by the side of the leather armchair. Bingo. A Champagne glass with a tissue inside it. Slowly, carefully, I put it in an evidence bag.

This is enough.

I hear a car on the drive. I dash to the side of the window and look. It's you, Jade, home early. I have no choice but to hide behind the sitting room door.

The key turns in the lock. The front door opens. Footsteps go upstairs.

I creep to the front door, hardly breathing. Softly, slowly, I open it, and walk away, heart thumping, body pressed to the wall of the house. Creeping through the shrubbery. Climbing over the side wall. Jumping down. Trying to look as if I am casually meandering towards the Leander Club and the river.

64

Emma

In a prison cell. The air is thin and stale. So thin that breathing is unsatisfying. First the cell is too hot, then it is too cold. At least for now I'm on my own. One of the guards told me that in this prison sharing a cell comes later, when you are settled in. I have a bed. A shower. A basin and a toilet. And a window that looks out onto a red–brick wall.

I lie on a bed so hard it feels like concrete. Six thirty p.m: lockdown. Alone until tomorrow morning. Nothing to do but read or watch the small TV with its limited selection of channels. I didn't have time to grab a book. I'm not in the mood for TV. TV will tell tales of the outside world and that is too painful right now. I close my eyes and think of Jade, and what she has done to me. My fists clench as I imagine what I could do to her. Bury her alive and listen to her suffer. And then my mind turns to you, Alastair. How you warned me about her behaviour. Do you really love me enough to save me?

65

Alastair

Wearing my scrubs, I cross the outer office to speak to my line manager, Sarah Dickinson. I knock on the door and step inside. She looks up from her paperwork.

'Alastair, how's it going?' she asks.

I sit in the chair in front of her desk and cross my legs.

'I need to ask permission to give the murder weapon in the Emma Stockton case a second sweep.'

A frown ripples across her forehead. 'The wrench? Why's that?'

I lean forwards. 'Because we need to be really careful. There's been a false positives scam in America recently and some criticism of the techniques we're using. There's no harm in double-checking. A new technique has just become available.' I pause. 'I can handle the swabs today.'

Sarah puts her head on one side. 'But it's expensive to carry out more tests.'

I expected her to say yes without thinking. I take a deep breath. 'What would you prefer? A scandal because we've got an incorrect result, or spending a bit more money?' I push.

She gives me her crooked smile. 'I suppose you're right. Go ahead.'

Sighing with relief, I walk back to reception to collect the wrench, and carry it, in its paper bag, back to the laboratory area. I put on my sterilisation clothes, my Tyvek body suit, my gloves, my hairnets, my glasses, my mask, my overshoes.

I'm doing this for you, my love, everything for you, I tell myself as I step into my lab and smear a tiny fragment of Jade's DNA from one of her snotty hankies onto the wrench. The tiniest amount, consistent with a slight mistake made by someone with forensic knowledge – wearing latex gloves and wiping their face by mistake then touching the wrench. I swab the wrench, and send the samples off to the central laboratory for analysis.

66

Alastair

Two days after I carried out the second sweep of the wrench, I'm sitting in the lab, thinking of you again. Always thinking of you. This time I'm remembering the first time you invited me to your house. We sat in the kitchen together drinking red wine; a Spanish Rioja, soft and spicy. Resonant on the tongue. We were laughing. I frown as I try to remember what was so funny. You laughed so much it made your mascara run. After a while you went to the bathroom. When you returned you had cleaned up your face.

'I've never laughed so much with anyone that they made my face look like a panda's, before,' you said. 'I'm so glad I found you on Tinder.'

'And I'm so glad I found you too.'

I leant across and kissed you. I can still taste the tenderness of that kiss. Emma, I love you. You will never know how much.

My computer pings. An email. The results are in. Jade's DNA as well as yours has been detected on the murder weapon now. A result that will liven up tomorrow's progress meeting. Well on the way to getting you off the hook, my darling, my love.

67

Jade

I relive the moment your body finally succumbed, Tomas. The moment I smashed the wrench so hard you didn't have a chance. Your head lolled forward and I knew you were dead. I wish I could have let you live. That you still loved me. That you always had. That you had never been unfaithful.

I run it back in my mind, again and again. I tell myself your death was painless, as you were comatose from Rohypnol when I crushed your skull. I try and rationalise it by saying even if you had felt the wrench, it wouldn't compare to the pain you have given me. Why did you do it? Why did you fool me into loving you, and then play the field? Why were you serially unfaithful?

But you are still giving me pain. I miss you so much it hurts. I force myself to think back and remember why I did it. To remember the time I caught you out at a neighbour's Christmas party, snogging a woman I had never seen before, beneath the mistletoe in the porch. I sidled past you to go home. You were so busy enjoying her, you didn't even see me.

You rolled home hours later and snapped on the bedroom light. I sat bolt upright and blinked.

'What do you think you were doing, kissing that woman?' I asked.

'What woman? What are you talking about?'

You bastard, pretending you didn't know.

'You tell me!' I shouted.

'I don't know what you're talking about. You must have been hallucinating,' you said as you fell, fully dressed, into bed.

That snog was just the tip of the iceberg. Usually your behaviour was far more serious. Every time I caught you, you denied it and begged me not to leave you. I didn't want to leave you. I have made sure you have left me instead.

When I'm not crying over your loss, I just sit here and feel pleased that your latest squeeze, the Stereotype, is incarcerated.

Dealing with her wasn't easy. Calculating the dose of Rohypnol, waiting for the right moment when she was so out of it that she would never know. Rubbing her hands vigorously on my brand-new wrench, to get as many of her skin cells on it as possible.

Watching a romcom on Netflix, waiting for darkness to fall, so that I could carry her home without anyone seeing me.

She was still comatose. Breathing shallowly. She wouldn't wake up for hours; and when she did she would remember nothing. I put on a fresh pair of gloves. Gathered her coat, her handbag, and the new sheets I bought for her bed from Debenhams last week, and put them in my rucksack. I rummaged in her handbag to find her keys and put them in my pocket. Rucksack on, keys easily accessible. Time to lift her up. I know she's only a lightweight, but it's a good job I sometimes work out. I struggled as I pulled her up from the sofa. As I put her arms over my shoulder, and held her tightly against me, by her buttocks. Far heavier than she looks. My back hurt. I clenched my jaw and braced myself. This wouldn't take long.

But I began to panic. I hadn't been thinking clearly enough. What if she had put a burglar alarm on? I dropped her back on the sofa. She stirred a little. Was she coming round? No. She settled. My heart was in overdrive. I needed the password. A pet, usually, wasn't it? I knew she had a cat. I'd seen it sitting on the windowsill. It was white with brown stripes, like a weird fluffy baby tiger. But I didn't know its name. No. No. That's computer passwords. Burglar alarms are numbers. Birthdays, etc. My panic increased. What if she came round and was still in my house? My plan would have failed.

My panic was stifling me. I couldn't think clearly. I breathed deeply, in, out, to try and calm down. If she came round and was still in my house I would just tell her that she drank too much. She would have no way of knowing otherwise. But I would need a new plan.

In. Out. Breathe. Breathe. I rummaged in her bag. She had a diary. I flicked through it. Notes at the back. BA 12 12 2012. That must be it. BA is burglar alarm. I decided to take the risk, and determined to carry her back. My hands trembled as I returned her diary to her bag.

I put her handbag into my rucksack, and pulled it onto my back. I gritted my teeth and lifted her again. She was breathing more deeply by now, but was still way out of it. Slowly, slowly, I carried her across the sitting room, through the dining room, into the hallway. No one could see in. The blinds and curtains fall automatically at dusk. I pressed a button by the front door to switch the outside lights off.

Across my driveway. Along the pavement. Hoping no one was out late, hovering, watching this. Glad I had insisted Tomas stayed over in London that night. I reached her drive and stumbled. I fell. I dropped her. The back of her head hit tarmac. She lay splayed on the floor, motionless. I bumped my knee and struggled to pull myself up. I took a deep breath, put my arms around her and strained my back to pick her up. So slim, but so heavy. It isn't fat. It must be muscle.

I hobbled up the drive with her across my shoulders, jumping as security lights, bright as stage lights, snapped on, illuminating us. I looked around nervously. No one watching.

Car headlights. I ducked down behind a bush at the edge of her drive and almost dropped her again.

After the car had passed, I scuttled up to her front door, rummaging for her key in my pocket. It was double locked but I managed to turn it without dropping her again. In the hallway, the burglar alarm box was humming on the landing to the right of the staircase – a yellow light on a screen in the middle of it flashing. I laid her down in the hallway. The cat was brushing against her and meowing, trying to wake her up. A stupid cat. Not able to sense she was out for the count. Hands shaking, I put in the code from her diary, and the flashing light on the box went off. The humming stopped. Relief flooded through me.

So far, so good.

I walked upstairs and into her bedroom, heart pounding. Her bedroom; yellow, cream and frilly. Frilly curtains. Frilly duvet. Sickly and sweet. It suddenly made me think of lemon bonbons, my favourite confectionery when I was a child. I changed her sheets, replacing them with my new ones, and thrust hers into a plastic bag in my rucksack, ready to carry home. I carefully put her handbag by her dressing table, with her house keys on top.

Walking across the landing, I looked at the framed photographs on the wall of her with an older man. Dishy. Faded rock-star looks. I dashed back downstairs to fetch her.

She was still breathing deeply, fast asleep. The cat was lying on top of her. I pushed it off and lifted her. The stairs were going to be difficult. Maybe I should have just left her on the sofa. No. No. If she got home herself, she would have been able to get herself into bed.

My back was seizing up. The muscles in my arms tightening. She was so heavy, I was finding it hard to breathe. But I gritted my teeth, and managed. Step by step I managed. To the top of the stairs. Across the landing. At last, I entered her bedroom and slipped her body between new sheets.

'Goodnight, darling. Sweet dreams.'

Memories

Colin, it turned out, was a professor at Guy's Dental School. So we had dentistry in common. He invited me to attend one of his lectures, and go for a meal afterwards.

I arrived early and sat at the front, waiting for the talk to start. A plastic environment. Artificial light. No windows. A wall-to-wall whiteboard. Professor Colin Stockton, recognising me from my Tinder profile, walking towards me smiling. Stopping in front of my bench. 'Thanks for coming.'

My stomach tumbled. Even nicer-looking than in his photograph.

He walked away to stand in front of the whiteboard by the projector. The lecture began. I listened, entranced. But I didn't understand the benefits of the new type of filling material he was waxing lyrical about. He stopped talking.

'Any questions?' he beamed confidently.

My hand went up. Among a sea of hands, he chose mine.

'Please could you expand on the benefits of the Devon amalgam?' I asked.

'Well, it's complicated,' he said and began to explain.

I watched him, transfixed. Rugged good looks, the sort that turn me on. Deep, resonant voice. He could have been an actor in another life. I lost track of his exact words, just enjoyed his intonation until I heard him ask,

'Does that answer your question?'

He was looking straight at me. I nodded my head. 'Yes, thank you.'

'Next question,' he said, scanning the room.

A forest of hands shot up. I was still not listening. In a daydream, wondering why he was on Tinder. Surely he would have almost every student after him? Surely he didn't need a dating app? The lecture ended and people filed out. Chatting, laughing.

He walked towards me. 'I could explain a bit more about all the amalgams that are available now, over a spot of lunch as we agreed.' He raised his eyebrows questioningly. 'I know a good fish restaurant nearby, it's called Fish! Not a very innovative name, but great food actually.'

'That would be nice,' I replied. 'But I'd like to talk about more than amalgams.'

68

Alastair

The team is gathering for the morning meeting, with a hum of background chatter. DI Hamilton and DS Miranda Jupiter are standing at the front of the room by the whiteboard, hands behind their backs, feet slightly apart. An expectant silence falls. My heart beats so loudly I fear someone will hear it. Its pulse thumps against my eardrums.

DI Hamilton steps forwards. 'Emma Stockton has been denied bail. Her case should come to trial in six weeks. Before we move on, are there any remaining comments on this one?'

'Yes please, sir,' I say.

'Carry on, Brown,' he instructs in his gruff monotone.

'I ran a second sweep on the murder weapon. This time we found Jude Covington's DNA, as well as Emma Stockton's.'

A murmur spreads across the room.

'Where does that leave us?' DI Hamilton asks, turning to my boss.

Sarah looks across at me. 'I think Alastair should lead on this. He has been concentrating on the Stockton case, not me.'

'Go ahead then,' DI Hamilton barks.

I take a deep breath. 'I found just a tiny fragment of Jade's DNA on the murder weapon. An amount so small that it could have been left by mistake by someone who was trying to avoid leaving it. Someone with forensic knowledge. It raises the possibility that Jade Covington has set up Emma Stockton. I've been concerned for a while, because of the suspected cat hairs on the bedsheets when Jade does not own a cat. My first suggestion is that we send these hairs to be analysed, to find out whether they do indeed belong to a cat, and if it is possible they could belong to Emma Stockton's cat. In which case, we should ask the question why it would be in Jade and Tomas' house.'

'If she was having an affair with Tomas, do you think she might have brought the cat with her, when she visited Tomas?' a young PC suggests.

The team titter.

'Cats are territorial – not the sort of animal you'd take to someone else's house like a lap dog,' DI Hamilton snaps.

'May I suggest we send the hairs for analysis,' I continue. 'And we need to check Jade's background – does she have forensic knowledge? We need to put our minds to whether she could have disguised the time of death to give her her alibi.'

'Good God man, are you taking over the investigation?' DI Hamilton asks with a wry smile. 'Action all this, team. Good work, Brown,' he barks.

69

Jade

Today is the day, a warm day at the beginning of May, Tomas. The day I must say goodbye to you. I'm laughing silently inside because your lover is in prison, unable to attend, even if you wanted her to. I'm keeping it simple. A private ceremony. We were both loners when it comes to family. But you were far more 'sociable' than me. So we had to move home every time you were indiscreet. And after so much angst, it has all just boiled down to you, me and the minister. A twenty-minute service.

And then your body will burn in the clinging fires of hell. You will be cremated sometime in the next twenty-four hours. I have to be satisfied with that. I always thought bodies were incinerated immediately, descending into the furnace as soon as those curtains had crept to a close.

But no. Your body will be stored and placed individually in a furnace later. Let me explain what will happen. The cremating chamber will be sealed. A column of flames will aim at your torso. First your soft tissue will tighten and burn. It will vaporise. Then your skin will become waxy, discolour and split. Your muscles will char and elongate, moving your legs and arms so that for a second you will look like the living dead; a zombie.

And last your bones will begin to crumble. Bone will be the hardest of all your body parts to destroy. Larger fragments of bone may need to be pulverised later. Ashes to ashes. Dust to dust.

Ashes weigh a similar amount to birth weight. You were big, weren't you? Ten pounds, you told me. Ten pounds of detritus to be sprinkled in the rose garden at the crematorium. I paid for someone there to scatter your remains for me, and plant a bush. I couldn't bear to touch your ashes. I will miss you in spite of everything. When your body has been cremated no one will ever find out what I have done. When your body has been cremated my life will move on.

70

Alastair

'The hairs are from a cat, and eighty per cent likely to be from a Siberian Forest Cat,' I announce as I step into Sarah Dickinson's office. She looks up and frowns. 'Same breed as Emma Stockton's pedigree,' I remind her. 'The results just came back. They can't specify the exact cat's DNA – or be more precise about its breed.'

'So where does that leave us?' she asks.

I shrug my shoulders.

'Still in a quandary.' I pause. 'Jade Covington said there were pet hairs on the bedsheets because Emma's cat often came into her house. Emma Stockton says Casper is an expensive pedigree who's not allowed out due to kidnap risk. As far as she knows, Casper has never escaped.'

Sarah pushed her wavy chestnut hair back from her face. 'So what should we do next?'

I sit down on the chair in front of her. 'Two things. One – contact the vet Emma uses. Vets keep a record of this sort of detail about the pets they treat. They'll know whether the cat is allowed out. Clients always discuss issues like this. It affects the pet's health and diet.'

She shrugs her shoulders, leans back in her chair and crosses her legs. 'That would be good to know, but it's indicative, not proof. This bloody cat may have broken the house rules.'

'Then we need to carry out tests on the cat. I've contacted

the Royal College of Veterinary Surgeons. They've recommended a specialist who can look at the cat's claws and paws to determine its habits.' I pause. 'As I said before, the amount of cat fur on those sheets can't have been from a one-off visit.'

Memories

We walked through Borough Market, which was bustling with young people and tourists, the aroma of spicy food floating in the air, making me feel hungry. Healthy food. Food from all around the world. Vegetarian. Vegan. Brightly coloured. Full of vegetables and lentils. Street sellers calling. A busker as good as anyone I had heard at the O2 serenading our walk.

Into the more sedate ambience of Fish! Suits and solemnity in there. After checking in at reception we were shown to a table by a svelte young waitress with shiny hair, wearing a black mini-skirt and pumps. We settled by the window. A table rammed so close to the next one, you had to keep your elbows in to stop them from touching its occupants.

My silver fox from Tinder leant back in his chair.

'You said you'd like to talk about more than amalgams. What did you have in mind?' he asked.

'I don't know you well enough to tell you what I have in mind. Not yet.' My skin felt hot and I knew I was blushing. 'What's an attractive guy like you doing on your own at your age?' I continued.

He grinned at me. 'It's complicated.'

'Like the film?'

He laughed at me and shook his head. 'Oh no. I'm not shagging my ex.'

'Who are you shagging then?'

'I don't believe in shagging. I believe in love.'

I raised my eyebrows. 'Which brings me back to my question.'

He shrugged. 'I guess I've just not met the right person yet.'

'So you've had to resort to Tinder?'

His eyes held mine. 'It's not such a bad place to resort to. It turned you up.'

'I might be a bunny boiler,' I point out.

'I might be a psychotic murderer with a dark message from God.'

'Shall we take the risk and find out?'

He leant across and took my hands in his. 'I would like to do that.'

71

Alastair

After a long day in the lab I clump up the stairs to my flat. As soon as I walk through the door Stephen is running towards me in his Batman pyjamas. He clings on to my legs, so tightly, as if he will never let go. I bend down and hug him. He smells of his favourite lemon bubble bath – the bubble bath that he says is like kryptonite and gives him superpowers – and of the coconut shampoo my mother always washes his hair with. Sweet as a nut. Sweet enough to eat.

'Why aren't you in bed?'

'I couldn't sleep. I was waiting for you to come home.'

'Where's Gran?' I ask.

'Resting in her room.'

He grins a devilish grin, displaying the gap at the front of his mouth where his front milk tooth has fallen out. Why do kids with gappy teeth always look so cute?

'She thinks I'm in bed. I pretended to be asleep when she checked.'

My poor mother. She must be exhausted if she doesn't realise he is up, waiting for me.

I take Stephen's hand in mind. 'Come on Stephen. I'll settle you back to bed.'

He shakes his sweet coconut head. 'But I don't want to go to bed. I can't sleep.'

'Just resting does your body almost as much good as sleeping.'

'But it's boring. Lying in bed when I can't sleep makes me feel too hot. I feel as if I have something twisting in my arms and legs, and in my stomach, so that I can't get comfy.'

'Boring or not, twisting or not, you are going to bed, young man.'

I hold his hand tightly and lead him through the living area of our flat, into his bedroom. His small room that I have painstakingly decorated with Farrow & Ball paint and a super-heroes border. He slips under the duvet. I smooth it over him and kiss him.

'Mummy popped in to see me this evening,' he said.

'That's not like her. She doesn't usually come midweek.'

'She said your girlfriend Emma is in prison. You must be a bad man, Daddy, if you have a bad girlfriend.'

I sit on the bed staring at my son, trying to keep calm. To breathe deep. I didn't want him to know about this.

I kiss his forehead and go downstairs. I sit at the kitchen table, head in my hands, and picture you, Emma, incarcerated. Bored. Lonely. Pushing my mind to work out how to rumble the Clusterfuck. I need to prove she disguised the time of Tomas' death. Jade Covington needs to be totally fucked.

151

72

Emma

Miranda Jupiter nods her head at me as I am escorted into the interview room.

'Hello again Emma,' she says, almost smiling. I don't smile back.

'To what do I owe this pleasure?' I ask.

'We want to know which vet you use for Casper.'

My stomach twists. 'What's happened?'

She shakes her head. 'Nothing. He's fine. Please don't worry. We want to ask the vet to verify a few points about his habits.'

I sigh inside, with relief. 'Henley Vets, Reading Road.'

She leans forwards. 'And where is he now, if we want to examine him?'

'At my receptionist Andrea Smith's house, 2 Water Lane. She's looking after him for me.'

And my heart sings, Alastair, because I know you are fighting for me.

Memories

Lying in bed with Colin. The first morning. After our first night together in his stylish flat near Borough Market. Full of modern art and classic books.

'You haven't talked about your parents, yet,' he said.

'My time with them was difficult. I'm trying to push it away.'

He pulled me towards him and kissed me so gently. A soft, silken kiss.

'I don't want anything to be difficult for you ever again.'

I smiled and shook my head. 'No one can make someone's life perfect. Life isn't perfect. Not for anyone.'

'I'll try though. I promise I'll do my best.'

'You sound like a boy scout.'

He laughed. 'I'll be an Emma scout. What about that?'

73

Alastair

The rain this early summer morning is so ferocious it beats against the police station windows horizontally. People are arriving soaked to the skin, water dripping off hair and noses. It takes longer than usual for us to assemble in the meeting room. Coats being hung up carefully to dry. Queuing at the drinks machine – morning coffee will take our minds off the dampness in our bones. The dampness that pervades the thoughts in our heads.

'Get a move on,' DI Hamilton bellows.

Team assembled at last, DI Hamilton widens his shoulders and starts, 'I need to ask if there have been any developments on Operation Titanic Case 301 – Tomas Covington?'

I step forward to reply. 'The Harrier Vets, recommended by the Royal College of Veterinary Surgeons, have inspected Casper, Emma Stockton's Siberian Forest Cat, and are willing to testify that, from the condition of his claws and paws, he doesn't go outside. This corroborates with Casper's own vet, who believes he is an indoor cat.'

Miranda Jupiter raises her arm to speak. DI Hamilton nods to encourage her.

'We have been covertly observing Andrea Smith's house, where the cat is now living. We have also questioned her neighbours. During the period of our investigation the cat has not been seen outside at all. By us, or anyone else in the area to the best of our knowledge.' She takes a deep breath and pauses. 'There is now reason to believe that Jade Covington was lying.'

A murmur pulsates around the meeting room.

'OK,' DI Hamilton says, 'let's investigate the make and time of purchase of the gold bedding found in both houses.' He looks across to Miranda. 'As soon as possible, DS Jupiter.' There is a pause. 'Anything else?' he asks.

The youngest member of the team, PC Johnson, steps forward.

'Jade Covington was head of forensics at the University of West London, resigning two years ago. She used her maiden name Fischer at work.'

'As I suspected,' I say, smiling inside. 'In keeping with the trace amounts of DNA on the wrench. I think we need to check the smart meter of her central heating. The heating will have been switched off around the time of the murder and the body wrapped in plastic if she did kill Tomas and wanted to disguise the time. Her strong alibi was very convenient. Too convenient. I expect she doesn't bother to attend book group now.'

'I'll go and check the smart meter with an expert,' Miranda Jupiter says with a shake of her silken hair. 'And I'm going to get the team to trawl the CCTV cameras at Paddington again. Tomas' colleague says he left work early that day, and so even though Jade denies it there is a possibility he was at home with her before she left for book group.' She pauses. 'Good idea, Alastair. I'll contact them to see if she still goes.'

I take a deep breath. Nearly there. So nearly there.

Memories

We went to the Donmar Warehouse theatre together. Standing in the bar before the play began, necking large glasses of Chardonnay.

'I love coming here,' he said. 'The theatre is as small as a school stage, so you get an exceptionally good view of the actors.' He paused. He shook his head slowly. 'And they get such talent here, it's breath-taking.'

He held my hand as we swept into the auditorium, nursing the remains of our wine in plastic cups. Small indeed. Sitting in the front row, toes almost touching the stage, knees close to my face.

Lights down. The sudden hiss of silence from the audience. Mournful music with an overdose of trumpet. The play began. A couple were drinking and arguing. The argument became heated. Ten minutes in the man was verbally abusing the woman. Fifteen minutes in he was hitting her.

I began to tremble. I began to sweat. I could hardly breathe.

'I'm ill. I need to leave,' I whispered to Colin.

'Sorry, sorry,' he muttered as we stood up and disturbed our row.

Through the auditorium door, blinking in the bright light of the corridor. A young female usher was hovering there anxiously. 'Are you all right?' she asked.

'I don't feel well. I need to go home.'

Onto Earlham Street in the pouring rain. Colin standing holding my hands in his.

'What's the matter, Emma?'

Still having difficulty breathing, I gasped for air. Tears streaming down my face. 'The play was a trigger. It brought it all back.'

He held me against his chest and stroked my hair.

'Calm down, Emma. You're with me now.'

74

Alastair

I bump into Sarah Dickinson at the coffee machine.

'Good morning Alastair,' she says as she presses the buttons for her habitual 9 a.m. cappuccino.

'Good morning,' I reply.

She turns around, coffee in hand, eyes sparkling. 'I met Miranda last night just as I was leaving and . . .' she pauses.

'And?' I push.

'You were right about the bedding. Bedding the same make and style as Emma's was purchased recently by Jade, at Debenhams. We checked with the store and they found the credit card transaction. The bedding on Jade's bed was Emma's, we think, as Emma remembered buying it about a year ago, and again that checked out with a John Lewis card transaction.'

I smile. 'Good stuff.'

'Not only that, but as you suspected the central heating had been turned off on the morning of the murder – atypically. It was usually on from six a.m. to nine a.m., and six p.m. until eleven p.m. in March. It was switched off all day and turned back on at ten forty-five p.m., programmed to stay on until midnight that night.'

I want to dance on the ceiling. To jump in the air and shout *yes*. But I take a deep breath, try not to smile too broadly.

'What happens next?' I ask.

'Miranda Jupiter says there are a few last things to tie up, and then DI Hamilton will call a meeting. They're still trawling through CCTV from Paddington Station, and a young PC is looking into Jade's background.'

Hallelujah, my heart sings. The evil Clusterfuck will soon have to pay.

75

Emma

Cuffed and escorted to a prison interview room by an overweight guard, thighs so heavy they roll past one another as he walks.

'Why are we going to an interview room?' I ask.

'You'll find out when we get there.'

We arrive. He jerks his head.

'In here,' he barks, as he holds the door.

I step inside. The room opens out in front of me; grey upon grey. Grey plastic table. Grey plastic chairs. And two people: DS Miranda Jupiter, and my solicitor, Benjamin Watts, sitting either side of the table, ignoring one another. Benjamin Watts is studying the floor. Miranda Jupiter analysing the wall. They look up at me as I enter.

'Ms Stockton, do sit down,' DS Miranda Jupiter commands, gesturing to the seat next to Benjamin's.

He turns his kind face towards me, trying to reassure me that it will be all right. I sit next to him. His presence, and the tangle of stale cigarette smoke and peppermint he exhales, comfort me.

'I need to ask you a few questions about the statement you gave to the police the night you were arrested,' Miranda Jupiter says, voice harsh.

'Why are you going over old ground?' Benjamin asks.

She turns her face towards him, slow and imperious, eyebrows arching. 'I do not need to disclose a reason at this point.'

'What do you need to know?' I ask, limbs and heart trembling.

Miranda presses a button to switch the tape recorder on. Frowning, she announces the names of those present.

'So you said in your initial interview that you went to Jade Covington's house for a drink, a few weeks before Tomas died.' She pauses. 'Can you run me through what happened when you got there?'

'That's the thing, I can't remember.' I hesitate. 'Except . . . except . . .'

'Except what?' Miranda Jupiter asks.

'Jade gave me a drink she called Cherry Bomb, and I woke up the next morning, fully dressed, in bed.'

Miranda leant forwards, pushing her head towards me across the grey plastic table. 'Your own bed?'

'Yes.'

Large brown eyes widen. 'Are you sure?'

'Yes. Sure. Sure. Sure. Fully dressed. I even had my suede boots on. My cat was asleep, purring on top of me.'

She grimaces and shakes her head. 'And you have no memory of walking home, or opening the front door?'

'None at all. That's why I went to see my GP, because I was worried about what was happening to me.'

'And what did your GP say?'

'He said that I may have drunk too much but I was showing the same symptoms as someone whose drink had been spiked with a date-rape drug.' I pause for breath. 'He didn't think I would have any permanent damage. He told me to watch my alcohol intake and come back to see him if I had any further problems.'

Miranda Jupiter flicks her hair from her eyes. 'Please can I have your permission to talk to him?'

'Of course.'

She snaps the tape machine off. 'Thank you. That's all.'

She stands up to go, mouth in a line. Slowly, elegantly, she leaves.

'I request some privacy with my client,' Benjamin says, turning towards the guard.

'OK Guvnor,' the guard replies, dragging his heavy body through the doorway.

The lock clicks behind him.

'Checking past evidence. That's good news, Emma. I know we told them about this but they didn't seem very interested. I don't want to get your hopes up too much – but revisiting statements sometimes happens when they've charged the wrong person.'

My heart misses a beat. Alastair, we can't meet. We can't speak. But I would like to take you in my arms and thank you. Run my fingers through your dark hair. Run my hands down your muscled back. Hold your body against mine. Tell you that I love you and that I will be grateful to you forever.

76

Alastair

DI Hamilton is standing at the front of the meeting room, shoulders wide, feet apart, with a smug look on his face.

'Quiet please,' he barks. 'I have to make an important announcement.' Silence falls. 'There's been a development in the Tomas Covington case.' He takes a deep breath. 'We now have reason to believe that Emma Stockton was telling the truth. It seems that Jade Covington committed the murder and set her up. We have proof the bedsheets on Jade's bed were Emma's; purchased by Emma and covered in cat fur. Sheets purchased by Jade were recovered from Emma's bed.'

Another pause. Murmuring and tittering float across the room. When it has subsided he continues.

'We now believe Jade drugged Emma and placed her DNA on the wrench. We have firm evidence that she lied and swapped Emma's bedsheets. We believe she disguised the time of death by switching off the central heating. And we have an image of a man who looks very like Tomas coming through Paddington at five p.m. on the evening of the murder. She has forensic knowledge. It all hangs together and so we are releasing Emma Stockton, and arresting Jade Covington. DS Jupiter and PC Browning are on their way to the Covington property now.'

My body sings with relief.

'Well done, team. This is a complicated case. We have worked together well and cracked it. Drinks are on me at the Black Bear tonight,' DI Hamilton announces.

Memories

A pod to ourselves at the top of the London Eye. Colin's arm around me as we looked out at the view. An orange glow over parks and buildings. A silhouette of my favourite city.

'The most beautiful city in the world,' I muttered beneath my breath, because to speak out loud would have intruded on that perfect moment of suspense between dusk and daylight.

'And I'm with the most beautiful girl in the world.' There was a pause. 'Will you marry me, Emma?'

My heart sang. 'Yes please.'

He pulled a small box from his pocket, opened it and thrust it towards me. A ring with two almond-shaped diamonds glimmered inside it. He took the ring out of the box and slipped it onto my finger. It fitted perfectly.

'It's wonderful, thank you,' I said as my lips melted into his. On top of the Eye. On top of the world.

77

Jade

I open the door. DS Miranda Jupiter is standing in front of me, almost smiling. She looks like the *Mona Lisa*. A younger officer is beside her. A man in his twenties I have not seen before. He has cut himself shaving. He has a spot on his cheek.

'Do you mind if we come in?' she asks.

'Of course not.' I try to stretch my lips into a smile, but my skin feels tight.

I step back from the door and my visitors enter. They push past me a little roughly. I shut the door and turn to face them.

'You are under arrest on suspicion of murdering your husband Tomas. You do not have to say anything, but it may harm your defence if you do not mention when questioned something which you later rely on in court. Anything you do say may be given in evidence,' DS Miranda Jupiter spouts.

I stand watching her, mouth open in shock. I panic inside. What has happened? It was all sewn up.

'But what are you talking about? You know I didn't do this.'

'New evidence has come to light, so we are arresting you and taking you to the police station.'

'What new evidence?'

'I'll explain at the station.'

'I can't come to the station without my meds.'

Her body stiffens. 'What meds?'

'Diazepam, aripiprazole and paroxetine. I can't manage without them.'

'OK. Tell me where they are and PC Browning will get them.'

'In the bathroom cabinet, where do you think?'

PC Browning, the boy with the spot, disappears upstairs.

'We'll take you to the station and get an appropriate adult to help you,' Miranda Jupiter continues. 'A doctor will assess you.'

The young policeman bundles me into the waiting police car. He scrapes my leg on the car door as he pushes me in. Miranda Jupiter is driving. She presses a button on her central control to lock the car doors. She turns the ignition and we set off. She even drives haughtily, with her proud head held high. I am trembling and scared.

'What's happening?' I ask.

'We've arrested you, Jade, and we're taking you to the police station to make a statement. If we have enough evidence we will charge you.'

'You won't manage that.'

'Our case against you is pretty solid,' she says as we wait at the lights.

I wriggle away from Spot and kick the back of her seat. She presses her talons on the steering wheel and the siren wails. We jump the lights. The car skids into the police station car park, like a scene in a TV car chase.

Frogmarched between them, I am rushed into the police station and thrown into a cell. The door locks behind me. I am in a cell with a barred window. A holding cell, just a bench to sit on, no other facilities. The grid in the door opens and Miranda's voice floats towards me.

'We'll send a psychiatrist to assess you and an appropriate adult to assist you. Do you have a family member who could act as an appropriate adult?'

'No.'

'Would you like us to find someone?'

I don't reply. I sit on the bench, put my head back and scream.

The cell door opens. Two women enter. A tall, thin, elderly woman with grey hair and a short, dumpy blonde with a neat face. The door locks behind them.

'Hello Jade,' the tall thin one with grey hair says.

They stand in front of me.

'I'm the psychiatrist here to assess you. To make sure you get the medicine you need. My name is Penny.'

'And I'm Constance, your appropriate adult,' the dumpy one says.

They stand in front of me like holograms, not people I can relate to. The short dumpy one stares at me wide-eyed, until her eyelids droop and she blinks. 'I'm here to represent you, to make sure you are treated fairly.'

'Well, if I was being treated fairly I wouldn't be here.'

'Not necessarily. That depends on what you've done.'

I shake my head. 'I don't understand why I need you.'

'DS Jupiter infers from the medicine you are on that you must have mental health issues – so you need help to make sure you get all the treatment and understanding that you require.'

Pushing back tears. 'I just need to go home,' I whimper. 'I always feel all right at home.'

'We need to talk to you Jade,' Penny starts up in the syco-phantic, syrupy tone that some therapists use. Hands held together in front of her stomach, lips simmering into a 'look at me, I'm kind' smile. 'We want to ring the guards and get you taken to an interview room where you will be more comfortable.' Voice silky smooth. 'Is that OK?' she continues.

'It's not OK. Nothing is OK.'

'So you'd rather talk here?'

I know the routine. Give two bad choices, second one worse,

so the difficult child acquiesces to the first. 'That is not what I said.'

They exchange glances.

Penny pulls a pad and pen out of her pocket. 'I've checked your medical records.'

'You're breaching my legal confidentiality,' I shout. 'I never signed anything to allow you to look at my medical history.'

Calm. Kind. Smarmy. Body relaxed, head slightly tilted. 'That's not correct. I'm a doctor assigned to treat you. Unless you specifically signed a form denying use of your data I'm allowed to look at it. And I need to, to help you.'

'I do not want your help,' I yell, as I stand up, heart pumping fast, blood pounding against my eardrums.

Constance presses a button on a cord around her neck. The cell door opens. Two guards run in and hold me back.

I feel flattened. As if all my energy has been punched out of me. There's a knock on the door. It opens slowly. Miranda Jupiter and her sidekick. Walking towards me in tandem; feet in unison. She puts her head on one side. Mouth in a line. Time passes. And somewhere in the distance of my mind her words contort.

'I am charging you with murdering your husband, Tomas Covington, and with attempting to pervert the course of justice by creating false evidence.'

Charged with murdering you. Don't these people understand it was your behaviour that was killing me? Not me that was killing you. Don't they understand I love you? I had to kill you for your own good, and mine.

Memories

On top of the world. Rotating in the London Eye. Admiring the broad sweep of the tree-lined river. The motherly dome of St Paul's dominated now by a plethora of modern buildings. The Shard, the Gherkin, the Leadenhall. The sleek modernity of Canary Wharf. Cleopatra's Needle. Alexandra Palace and its radio mast. Down we moved, almost imperceptibly. Seeing the fragile beauty of the Houses of Parliament, and Big Ben. The wedding-cake magnificence of the old M16 building. Nelson's Column. Buckingham Palace. The Post Office Tower. Park after park of green.

We emerged at the bottom, looked at the photograph taken and laughed as we decided not to buy it. We walked hand in hand to Skylon and ordered a bottle of Krug to celebrate our engagement.

'Come on,' I said, a little tipsy as we finished the bottle. 'Let's go to my parents' house and tell them.'

Colin's dark eyes turned to flint. 'I don't want to. Let's keep this evening special. Let's keep it to ourselves.'

'Let's get it over with. Colin, please.'

An hour later, having stopped at the off-licence to buy another bottle of Champagne, we arrived at 17 Downton Road, East Finchley.

Mother answered the door in her denim apron, looking paler than ever. Her face lit up as soon as she saw me. She pulled her body against mine and held me.

170

'Come in,' she almost squeaked. 'It's so fantastic to see you, isn't it, Terry?'

My father appeared in the hallway, hovering behind her. Wearing green corduroy trousers, a checked shirt and a frown.

'Always a pleasure to see my favourite daughter,' he said, voice gruff.

'Your only daughter,' I replied with a hollow laugh.

We followed my parents into the small living room of their 1930s semi which seemed to shrink every time I visited.

'What can we get you to drink?' Mother asked.

'We've come to tell you we've just got engaged so I think Champagne is in order,' Colin announced, handing my father the chilled bottle of bubbles.

I stretched my left hand out to show off my pretty almond-shaped diamonds.

'Congratulations,' Mother said, with her mouth, but not her eyes.

'We didn't know. You didn't ask my permission.'

'I thought that was a little dated, old chap,' Colin said, patting my father on his back.

My father stiffened and pulled away from Colin. He handed the Krug to my mother. 'Come on Sally. Get this opened. Find the glasses.'

'Emma, come with me,' Mother said. 'I need a little help with the Champers.'

I followed her into her tidy kitchen. Neatly lined plants on the windowsill. A cookbook open ready on a stand on the shiny counter top. She placed the bottle on the table and stretched up to a cupboard above the sink to pull out four Champagne flutes. Flutes in hand, she stood staring at me.

'It's all a bit quick. Are you sure about this?'

'Yes. Of course I'm sure.'

'Colin's a Leo, isn't he?'

I nodded.

171

'Do be careful. Leos can be so controlling.'

And my stomach tightened. How could she be critical of Colin when she tolerated my father? Could she see something I couldn't? Or was she just scared of men?

78

Emma

Two guards are approaching: a man and a woman. The woman is thin and pointy. Sharp nose. Skinny arms. Darts for elbows. Long blonde hair tied back in a ponytail. The man, who has a much softer face, is going grey around his temples. They stand in front of the plastic dining table. The man places his arms on the table in front of me and leans towards me.

'Guvnor wants to see you,' he announces.

'Now?' I ask.

'Yes, if you can tear yourself away from your food.'

'Of course.'

'Come with us,' the sharp, pointy one instructs, with a toss of her ponytail.

I abandon my egg and chips, and follow them across the canteen. Eyeballs slide towards us as we leave.. Into the corridor that looks like a giant metal pipe, decorated with white paint spread like butter over rust. White paint flaking like dandruff. Flaking dandruff and rust. We push through gate after gate. Opened with their keys, automatically locking behind us. The corridor twists and turns into a section of the prison I have never seen before. It looks like school offices. It has an open area with low chairs and big windows, blue carpets and homely child-like artwork. The female guard knocks on the prison governor's office door.

'Come in.'

She opens the door and puts her head around it. 'Emma Stockton for you.'

'Fine, fine, send her in.'

The guard opens the door and gesticulates for me to enter. Heart in my mouth, I step towards the prison governor, Fiona Perry-Jones, who is sitting behind her desk, looking at me over the top of half-moon glasses. Her iron-grey hair is cut into a statuesque bob. Something about her tailored black trouser suit and white polo-neck jumper make her look like a female version of James Bond. Elegance and simplicity.

'Do sit down,' she says.

I accept her invitation and sit in the armchair in front of her desk.

'Good news. You're being released.'

I jump up from the chair, excitement pulsing through me like electricity, smiling from cheek to cheek. It is all I can do to stop myself being inappropriate and hugging her.

'Fantastic. That's amazing news. Thanks. What changed things?'

'New DNA analysis.'

Alastair came good at last.

Released. A whirlwind of activity. I am escorted back to my cell and allowed to hurriedly collect my belongings, putting them in a clear plastic bag with a hole in the corner. Not that I had much. A few clothes. A pad. A pen. A few toiletries. Back along the rusty corridor to the holding area. The area I passed through when I came in. Forms to fill in. The possessions they took off me when I came in to prison are here for me to collect. My jewellery. My phone and charger. My handbag. My credit cards. I sit on a sofa and one of the volunteer inmates brings me a cup of tea. My hand shakes as I drink. What if this is a dream? What if I wake up in a few minutes in my cell and it isn't real?

But it is real. They let me out through the front gate to wait for my taxi. Wind caresses my face. I breathe deeply and drink the air. It tastes sweet. It tastes of trees and flowers and rain.

My taxi arrives. A young man, with a shaved head and a tattoo of a snake on his neck, is driving.

'Wotcha,' he says.

'Wotcha,' I reply.

'What's a nice girl like you doing coming out of a place like that?'

I smile at him. 'What makes you think I'm nice?'

I get into the back of his Prius. Smooth FM is playing. He drives. The world moves around me. Colourful. Explosive. I want to dance. I want to sing. I want to hold you, Alastair, and thank you. Is it safe? Can I text you? No. I must just wait for you to arrive at my house under cover of darkness. My stomach knots in anticipation. I can't wait to get home.

79

Jade

The psychiatrist, Penny, is back with two prison guards. Slowly, slowly she walks towards me, flanked by her entourage.

'I am sectioning you, under the Mental Health Act 1983, as I and one other doctor have certified that we consider you to be a danger to yourself,' Penny says. 'You'll be transferred to the psychiatric unit at the local hospital,' she continues.

Hospital? Prison? The hospital seems like a prison to me.

Magistrates' Court. Waiting in a cell with a seat. No bed. No windows. Into a court. People talking. People listening. No one listening to me.

Crown Court. Somebody talking. Making up lies about me. Saying I killed you Tomas, when you killed me first. When I loved you. And I miss you. When really they know that Emma did it.

Closed doors and windows. No way out. The nurse is here, making sure I take my tablets, handing them to me with a cup of water and watching me swallow. Satisfied, she bustles to puff up my pillow and pads away, closing the door behind her.

80

Emma

Twilight glows orange over the river as I cross the bridge in a taxi. I see the familiar shapes of the houses along the bank of the river, the willow trees, the boathouses.

'Nice area, love,' the driver mutters.

'It's good to be back.'

'How long were you in for?'

'Three months.'

'Not too long then.'

'It felt like an eternity.'

Left at the pub, past Jade's house, into my drive. I pay him and stagger out of the back of the car, grabbing my handbag and my plastic bag. His Prius glides silently away.

I fumble for my keys and turn the lock. Into the hallway. Hearing the background throb of the burglar alarm. Pressing the code to switch it off.

And Casper is here, pushing his head against my feet, purring like a lawn tractor. Andrea brought him back home to welcome me. Not her; just the cat. After so long incarcerated I need peace and privacy. I lift him up and hold his warm body against me. I press his fur against my face. A living, breathing cuddly toy, soft and pliable in my hands. Nothing aloof about him; totally unlike any moggy I have had. Not just a cat. I expect he became vital evidence. The reason Jade couldn't shaft me. I'm longing to hear all about it from you, Alastair.

I carry Casper into my living kitchen and put him down gently. The luxury of my shiny kitchen unfolds in front of me. Soft oak. Glittering granite. Cream sofas. A fifty-inch TV. Floor-to-ceiling windows so that I look out into the garden with a view so clear, I feel as if I could reach out and touch my plants and bushes. I have loved gardening ever since my unhappy days with Colin. I never have much time for it now that I have my own practice.

I reach for the letter on the table that Andrea has left for me. I sit and read it. It makes me smile. Updates on the surgery. The locum. How she has managed. Good girl. She will get a big pay rise.

So long since I drank alcohol, I pull a bottle of Fleurie from the cupboard. Casper tangles his body around my ankles, as I open the wine and pour myself the largest of glasses.

I snap on the sound system. 'Take Five' by Dave Brubeck slices into the room, every instrument so clear it sounds as if the musicians are playing live. I kick off my shoes, sink into the sofa, Casper on top of me. The music pierces me. I drink as twilight bleeds into darkness. When I'm surrounded by the solidity of the night I press a button to close the blinds. Waiting for you to arrive, Alastair.

81

Alastair

I take you in my arms and hold you, so tight. I want to engulf you. I could stay like this forever, feeling your heat, drinking the aroma of your body. But you pull away.

'Come to the sitting room. I've opened some wine.'

I follow you, watching the willowy grace of your figure as you walk. A bottle of Fleurie on the coffee table, a half-full glass and an empty one waiting for me. You pour me a glass. 'You knew I was coming?'

'I hoped.'

We sink together onto the sofa.

'Are you pleased to be home?' I ask.

Your eyes shine. Your face creases into a smile. 'You bet.' You lean across, pull me into your arms, and kiss me. You taste of heat and wine. Desire spills through me. 'Thank you for my freedom,' you whisper. 'No words can explain how grateful I am.'

Memories

I leant on my father's arm. The organ trumpeted me up the aisle to Toccata *in* Fugue, *followed by two cousins I hardly knew, swathed in pink and garlands of rosebuds. Davina and Nicole. Mother had insisted they were my bridesmaids. Past a sea of smiling, turning heads. Friends from Dundee University. Friends from the practice. Towards Colin, and his best man, Tony, a colleague from work who I hardly knew, beaming at me from the front of the church. Colin's smile making my heart flutter. Towards my mother wreathed in worry. A frown coiling around her from tip to toe.*

Colin was so much older than me, his parents had already died. He had squeezed a tear the night before, talking about how much they would have loved to see him meet the woman of his dreams, and marry her. I secretly wasn't sorry not to be saddled with a mother-in-law. Trying to be nice to my own father was bad enough. Trying not to be angry about my mother's subservience. From what I had heard from girlfriends, the mother-in-law/daughter-in-law relationship tended to be a nightmare.

Standing at the altar in front of the vicar, a bull of a man, my bouquet of roses and lilies trembling in my fingers, looking into the dark eyes of my fiancé.

Repeating the iconic words: to have and to hold. For better, for worse. For richer, for poorer. In sickness and in health. To love and to cherish, until death do us part.

The wedding ring was slipped on my finger, and I slipped a ring onto his. My heart was seared with happiness. Wrapping a cloth around our ringed hands, the vicar said,

'Those who God has joined together, let no man put asunder.'

My heart trembled at the power of those words. I was so happy, I wanted nothing more than to press a button and stop my life right there.

But the day moved on. Dripping with Champagne, confetti and photographs. A rich wedding breakfast. Compliments and kisses. Admiration and advice. Sycophantic, insincere speeches, even from my father. But I preferred that to honesty. I glided through the day, a beautiful princess in my silk meringue of a dress. The most beautiful girl in the world.

Something old: my dead grandmother's necklace. Something new: my wedding dress. Something borrowed: my mother's pinprick diamond earrings. Something blue: a blue silk garter from Harrods.

We drove away in Colin's BMW, dragging cans tied together with string, and pans and pan lids. Someone must have put a kipper in the boot. The car stank of smoked fish.

82

Alastair

I have put Stephen to bed and insisted that Mum relax in her bedroom watching *EastEnders*. Heather is here, sitting on the sofa next to me. She has put on even more weight. Her stomach now looks as if she is six months pregnant. She's trying to disguise it by wearing a baggy dress, but nothing can camouflage a figure like that. Tangled hair, blotchy skin. Teeth like a donkey's. How did I ever find her attractive?

'To what do I owe the pleasure of this visit?' I ask, voice fermenting to vinegar.

She frowns. Her already small eyes narrow. 'I want some money. Otherwise I'm going to tell people what you did to me.'

My body stills. I thought that whole business was behind us. Heather had made it all up, of course, but that didn't make facing the investigation any easier.

'But . . . but . . .' I stutter, hoping to head her off, 'we've already been through this. The CPS dropped the case, several years ago. They're not going to believe any more of your lies.'

'I'm not talking about the CPS. I'm just saying I'll make it known around here.' She shrugs. 'In the pubs where Shelly and I drink. I'll tell Stephen. I'll tell the staff at his school. Your mother. Your girlfriend.' She pauses. 'Actually, I've already tried to warn Emma about you. But she wouldn't listen. Maybe I should tell her the whole truth, just to make sure she really, really understands what you are.'

Pressure rises, pulsating against my skull, pressing against my eardrums. The room fragments into red dots around me. The dots coagulate into a sheet of red. Flames are licking, rising from a furnace beneath. Hotter and hotter. The sheet is white hot. White heat storming through me. It is going to explode if I cannot contain it. I close my eyes. I turn my mind in on itself, and lower my head.

'Please, Heather, go away. Just get out of here.'

83

Emma

I'm back at the surgery, smiling inside.

Smile and the world smiles with you. Cry and you cry alone.

My mother's mantra to help her cope with her difficulties. Did that help her tolerate my father for so long? But I am not tolerating anybody or anything. High on freedom and comfort, I'm smiling inside and out, with a genuine smile from deep inside me. Standing outside my surgery, admiring the tumbling willow tree, the brightly coloured border of roses, clematis, hydrangeas and daisies, beyond. I pull my eyes away from this beloved garden, perfectly maintained during my absence, and step inside.

The surgery smells of lavender. Mozart's horn concertos play quietly from the sound system. Andrea stands up and walks from behind the counter to greet me. Dog's-tooth culottes and mustard silk blouse today. We hug. We kiss each other's cheeks.

'Welcome back.'

I hand her the flowers I have chosen for her. The largest pink and white lilies I could find. And a bottle of vintage Champagne. 'I will never be able to thank you enough.'

Tania steps from my consulting room, flashing her precise porcelain smile. I walk across and hug her. Her cheap saccharine perfume engulfs me. I hand her a bottle bag containing pink Champagne, her favourite.

'Thank you so much Tania, for holding it together with all the different locums.'

'What else would I do?' she asks.

I smile. 'Some people would have run a mile with their boss in prison.'

I walk across to the fish tank, and stand watching fish glide around each other like dancers.

'Wow. You've added an angel fish, and . . . what's the turquoise one with stripes?'

'Symphysodon,' Andrea says.

'Beautiful,' I mutter, watching its fins tremble as it swims.

I look across at Tania and Andrea, standing in the middle of the waiting room, staring at me as if they can't believe I'm actually here.

'The fish are a present to welcome you back,' Tania says, head on one side, biting her lip.

And I know from the glint in her eye and the turn of her head that this was her idea.

'Thank you.' I swallow to push back tears. I take a deep breath. 'OK, OK. Back to business. What time is our first patient?'

'Nine thirty. Botox this morning. Quite a long list,' Andrea says.

Good, good, I think. Injecting Botox on my first morning back will be far easier than filling teeth.

84

Jade

The air is lighter. Easier to breathe. According to my appropriate adult, Constance, I'm in a secure psychiatric unit, awaiting trial, as I'm a danger to myself and others. I know that, really, but Constance keeps reminding me. And she keeps reminding me that bail was denied on two court applications. First to the Magistrates', and then to the Crown. Do I remember either of them? If I really push, I do, a little.

I lie on a bed, my room blurring around me, looking across to try and see through the window. A collage of green rotates and dances in front of me. The lock of the door to my room clicks open. I look up; someone is here, walking towards my bed.

'Hey Jade,' a female voice asks, 'how are you feeling today? Are you still crying for Tomas?'

I bite my lip. 'I will always cry for Tomas. He was my passion. My love.'

'Do you think he is here now?' the voice asks softly.

I open my eyes. I shake my head.

'That's good. One minute you're talking to him, crying for him. The next you're shouting at him and telling him he's unfaithful.'

The person pulls up a chair and sits next to my bed. It is a woman wearing a grey tweed suit today. Grey upon grey. Grey hair. Grey clothes. Grey eyes. My psychiatrist, Penny. 'Are you going to get out of bed and get dressed today?'

I frown. 'Maybe later.'

'Has Constance been in?'

Constance. The dumpy one. Appropriate adult. I laugh inside. What a stupid name for the job. Has she been in? So many questions.

'Not yet,' I snap. I hear my voice sharp in the air. I know I need to tone it down. If I make too much noise they give me more medication.

Penny pulls a pad and pen from her briefcase. 'OK. I just want to ask you a few questions.'

More questions. Too many questions. I pull myself up, to sit up in bed. Puffing up my pillows. 'Fire away,' I say, trying not to sound aggressive. Aggressive always seems to get me in trouble in the end.

She leans forward, pen in hand. 'Are you sure he cheated?'

I feel hot. I feel sick. 'Of course. All my partners have let me down. Tomas was the worst.'

Penny smiles, a soft kind smile. Head on one side. 'Can you prove he cheated on you? Real proof? Not just clues you manufactured.'

I clench my fist and bang it on the bed. 'I saw him.'

Her grey eyes lighten. 'Jade, tell me everything. What did you see?'

I shake my head, teeth clenched. 'I saw him, hugging her, in the surgery. I watched through the window.' I pause. 'Hugging the willowy blonde dentist. The one I knew would get him as soon as I saw her. The one that was so attractive I knew he wouldn't be able to keep his hands off her.'

The memory screams in my head and my nausea increases. Penny makes notes, scratching and scribbling in her pad. She looks up.

'Were they just hugging to say goodbye at the end of the consultation?'

I begin to cry inside. I want to shout. I want to scream. 'No.

No. He wanted to put his tongue down her throat. He wanted to fuck her. All day and all night.'

Penny inhales deeply. 'But did you see them snog?' There is a pause. 'Or was it a peck?'

I feel tears running down my face. I try, but I can't stop them. 'I'm not sure. I can't remember.'

She leans forwards. 'Did he ever admit to being unfaithful?'

I wipe my tears with a tissue. 'No.'

'Did he ever tell you he wanted to leave you?'

'No.' I close my eyes, and see him coming back from dog walks, eyes shining with exhilaration. 'He kept meeting the last one, Sylvia, when he was walking our old dog. I know because I followed him.'

Sylvia. She was the most unfathomable. So hard to understand what he saw in her. She was old like our dog. Old and ugly. Such an insult that he could run to her from me. At least the dentist is good-looking.

I open my eyes. Penny is looking at me with her still grey eyes, almost silver in the sunlight pooling through the window. 'What was he doing with Sylvia?' she asks.

I wince at the memory. 'Chatting by the lamppost.'

She frowns. 'Chatting? Only chatting?'

Anger pulsates through the core of my body. 'They were arranging to meet up. The bastards.'

'Did you hear that specifically?'

The word 'specifically' punches into me and annoys me. Clever fucking Penny trying to trip me up.

'Specifically,' I mimic. 'Fucking specifically. Yes they were fucking muttering. Keeping their voices down. But I knew. They couldn't fool me, I knew,' I shout.

Penny puts her hand on my arm. 'I'm going to up your prescription of aripiprazole.' There is a pause. 'I really think it will help.'

I grab her arm and thrust it away. 'I don't know why you

need to give me more aripiprazole. I'm telling the truth. I'm not delusional.'

'You do need to take your drugs, Jade. If you take your drugs you will start to feel better. The reason you've been so confused is because you stopped taking them.'

'No. No. There's nothing wrong. I don't need them any more.'

'You do need them. That's why you're here. In the psychiatric unit.'

Memories

In a bedroom at the Lygon Arms Hotel, in the Cotswolds, surrounded by stone arches and antiques. Trying to remove the smell of smoked fish from my nostrils by spraying perfume into the air. Unpacking my suitcase containing all my carefully chosen honeymoon finery, I experienced a sudden adrenalin trough. Flopping backwards onto the silken bed, exhausted after so much excitement and euphoria. All I wanted to do was pull the Egyptian cotton sheets around me and sleep. Colin looked at his watch.

'Come on, it's seven p.m. Dinner's booked for seven thirty. You need to crack on and get changed.'

'Can't we push it back a bit?' I asked, bloated after too much Champagne and a late afternoon wedding breakfast.

His face stiffened. 'Emma, we're eating at seven thirty. It's what I've arranged.'

'OK, OK. Great.'

I pulled myself from the bed and forced myself to shower and change. The heat of the shower tumbling against my tired skin imbued me with enhanced energy. I stepped from the bathroom wearing the new dress I chose at L.K.Bennett, feeling like a princess again. Loose-fitting and comfortable, black with lace edging and sleeves. A dress for a pyjama party.

Colin looked across at me and shook his head. 'You can't wear that.'

'Why not?'

'It's baggy.'

'No, it's tasteful. It was expensive.'

He raised his left hand in the air, and shook his head more vehemently. 'I don't care what it cost. I've bought you something else. Something more snazzy.'

He reached into the wardrobe and pulled out a large gift bag – gold with a red heart on the side. He handed it to me, pulled me towards him and kissed me. 'For my beautiful wife.' There was a pause. 'You can put these on now.'

I opened the bag. A red silk dress with large gold buttons. Very 'look at me'. Handbag and shoes to match.

'Thank you,' I gasped.

He looked at his watch. 'Hurry up Emma, we can't be late for our special meal tonight.'

I changed into his gift as quickly as possible, and even managed to find a lipstick in my handbag with a similar tone. Red upon red. Little Red Riding Hood.

I looked at myself in the full-length mirror in the corner of the room. So bright, so garish, it made me look pale as a ghost. Colin stood behind me, wrapping his arms around my body. He put his head on my shoulder to look at my reflection.

'Lady in red, you look so beautiful,' he said, kissing my ear. He fumbled in his pocket and produced a jewel box. He handed it to me. 'I wanted to give you this as a reminder of today.'

I opened the box. Ruby earrings. Stones as big as rocks. He took them one at a time and put them in my ears. So large I thought they were going to tear my earlobe as I looked at myself in the mirror. I have never thought red suited me. My colouring is too pale. Garish jewellery has never been my thing. But for Colin I will do this. I will be his Lady in Red tonight. That insipid song blasted into my mind.

'Thank you,' I repeated, turning to kiss him on the lips. His lips clung to mine. I pulled away.

He patted my bottom. 'Let's go and eat.'

The restaurant was empty. We were the only diners.

A flurry of waiters greeted us, leading us to our table by the window.

'Where is everyone?' I asked.

'I paid the hotel the amount they would have made if they had been open to the public tonight, to keep it just for us.'

'It must have cost a fortune.'

Colin smiled. 'It did and I'm not telling you how much.'

Waiters dressed in black tie pulled out our chairs, placed cushions behind our backs, and tucked us in to the table. They bowed as they receded, fawning and obsequious. Another stood over us, a bottle in each hand.

'Still or sparkling?' he chirruped.

'Sparkling for both of us,' Colin replied.

'What do you fancy to eat?' I asked him.

He leant across the table and took my hand in his. 'I've already ordered. We're having sweetbreads for starters. Sea bass with coriander, lime and ginger, followed by bread and butter pudding.' There was a pause. 'Does it suit you?'

I don't like fish, or offal. I rarely eat pudding and, if I do, I would rather just have fruit. I would rather have eaten in a vibrant restaurant with a choice. But, flattered by his over-whelming attention, I replied, 'Yes, lovely, thanks.'

We ate slowly, washing down the meal with expensive wine; heavy, with an aftertaste. We finished our meal.

He wiped his mouth with his linen napkin and smiled across at me. 'That was good. But the best part of the evening is yet to come.'

In the bedroom, he undressed me, slowly. Red silk slinking into a pile on the floor. He stepped back to admire my body.

'I have another present for you.'

Another flamboyant parcel appeared from the wardrobe. I sat on the bed to open it. A red and white box containing a nurse's outfit. Not a real one. It looked like a child's dressing-up outfit. Short blue dress. White apron with a red cross on. A plastic stethoscope as well.

'Come and make Daddy better,' he said with a grin.

My heart raced. My stomach tightened.

'I'm a woman, not a doll,' I told him.

85

Alastair

Sitting in my lab, wearing my full sterilisation suit, starting the forensics for a new case. Operation Titular – Max Jones – T3178. Taking swabs from a bottle. I sigh inside as I pull off my gloves and fling them in the bin. I reach for a new pair and stretch them carefully over my fingers. I smile inside, as I remember pulling you towards me, and you whispering in my ear:

'No words can explain how grateful I am.'

I'm riding high on love, excited about the future of our relationship. A relationship I can rely on at last.

Memories

We returned from our honeymoon to live in the house Colin had chosen in a gated community in Esher. A surprise for me. A property I had never seen. Colin had been having it built anyway. Before he even met me. But the timing of completion was a dream. Ready when we returned from our mini-moon in the Cotswolds.

A code to get into the private road. Black iron gates creaking slowly open. Six houses standing back from the road, surrounded by manicured lawns and carefully tended bushes, guarded by more turrets of shiny ironwork.

Colin leant out of the car window and pressed a code into the entry point. The gates parted and we entered the drive of a modern red-brick mansion with stone-framed windows. Colin parked the car, and we stepped out and stood in the doorway, ready to meet the next level of security.

Facial recognition. Colin pressed buttons, cameras whirred. Our photographs were taken and noted. The front door opened.

'Welcome family,' a female voice spouted through a speaker.

We stepped inside. I couldn't believe my eyes. The house had internal glass walls. I had never seen anything like it. Not even on Grand Designs. *You could see straight through the house, from the hallway to the dining room on the left, to the sitting room, and drawing room on the right. To the gardens, swimming pool, tennis court and acres beyond.*

I took a sharp intake of breath. So surprised. So shocked. And turned around. Behind me a staircase of stone swept upstairs. A staircase grand enough for a palace.

'Welcome to your new home,' Colin said.

I kissed him. 'The most beautiful home a woman could ever have.'

Later on, tired after unpacking all day — my belongings had been delivered and left in the garage while we were away — I stepped into the less formal sitting room, and flopped into the chair closest to the TV. Closest to the fireplace. Colin walked in and tapped me on the shoulder.

'That's my chair. Get out of it please.'

'We're married now. What's yours is mine and vice versa.'

I smiled. He didn't smile back.

'Except in the case of that chair. That's my chair.'

He walked towards me, grabbed my wrists and pulled me up. He pushed me down onto the sofa. He flicked the remote at the TV screen and an action film began. No women. No dialogue. Screeching car wheels. Punches and grunts.

Why do I remember the little things, when the big things hurt so much?

86

Emma

Driving home from work, my mobile rings, flashing your name across my navigation system. I press a button on my steering wheel and your voice fills the car, as I wait at the lights.

'I've won a trip for us both to a fancy hotel in the Lake District, next weekend. The Lodore Falls Hotel & Spa on Derwentwater. Three nights dinner, bed and breakfast. Bar bill paid as well.'

Every syllable you utter bubbles with enthusiasm.

A stone sinks in my stomach. 'Alastair, I'm sorry, I just can't.' Your disappointment simmers down the phone line. 'I've got a special fillers clinic all day Saturday,' I explain.

'Come after that. I just need to get away from everything with Heather.'

'And arrive in the small hours of Sunday morning? Impossible. I've got to remove four wisdom teeth on Monday. That's a big operation. I need to rest on Sunday, not travel to the other end of the country.'

The lights change.

'OK,' you say, voice cold and sharp.

OK but not OK.

'Let's talk later.'

I end the call to push away the coldness in your voice.

Memories

Difficult news comes from nowhere. Out of the blue. That is why people say there is no point in worrying. The things we worry about never happen. The things we don't even consider do.

Sitting in my study in my house of glass, reading a text book on paediatric dentistry, an area where I wanted to improve, sipping an espresso to perk me up. Colin was in his study preparing for a lecture.

My mobile rang. I picked up. It was Mother, weeping down the phone line.

'What is it? What's the matter?' I asked.

'It's your father. He's got terminal colon cancer. It's already spread to his liver and lungs.' There was a pause. More sobbing. 'They think he's got about two weeks.'

I went to tell Colin. He pulled me towards him and held me, head against his chest. 'I'm sorry Emma. So sorry.'

I drove over to East Finchley, not really believing what I had been told. My father was such a strong character I had always thought he would live forever. Dominating us. Menacing us. I think I expected to arrive at my family home and find it was a very bad joke.

Mum answered the door, face red and puffy, tears streaming down her face.

'He's in the sitting room,' she managed between sobs.

'Did you tell him I was coming to see him?'

'Yes.'

I stood by the door and took a deep breath. If I was religious I would have prayed for strength. All I could do was breathe deeply and brace myself. Inhale. Exhale.

I entered the sitting room. A room that hadn't been decorated for twenty years. Stuck in the past. A photograph on the mantelpiece of Mother holding me when I first came home from the hospital. My graduation photograph.

Father was sitting in his black leather armchair, staring at the air in front of him, looking the same as ever. Whatever was happening internally wasn't changing his appearance yet. Until he turned to look at me. Face towards mine, I could see he looked thinner. Frail. Brittle. But still strong. Still my dad.

'Have you come to feel sorry for me?' he asked. 'I do not want any sycophantic gloating. I asked your mother not to tell anyone.'

'Don't be ridiculous, Dad. You can't not tell me, I'm your daughter.' I walked towards him. 'And I haven't come to gloat, I just wanted to see you.' I sat down next to him and took his hand. 'Why would I gloat?'

He squeezed my hand. 'I have never been very demonstrative with you, Emma, but I want you to know, I have always loved you in my own way.'

'And Dad, I love you too,' I said.

It wasn't true. I didn't understand him. I didn't know him well enough to love him. It was a knee-jerk response to what he had said.

I paused. I swallowed. 'What treatment are they giving you?' I asked.

'The treatment's only palliative so I've decided not to have it. Why should I punish my body with chemo that isn't going to do anything but reduce the pain a bit? I might as well move straight on to morphine when I need it.'

'Sometimes—' I started, about to give him a lecture on prognoses *being wrong, new immunological wonder drugs, and people's bodies responding unexpectedly to chemo.*

But he interrupted me. 'I'm going to die soon. Period. That's it.'

And he did. In less than a week. The first night he asked for morphine. Mother got out of bed at four in the morning when he asked her to get him a tablet to relieve his pain. She brought him a morphine tablet and a glass of water to help him swallow it. He took the tablet and without saying anything, not even thank you, he rolled over and died. At five past four. He didn't live long enough to suffer.

Mother was so upset. Far more than I thought she would be, after how much he had put her through. I thought she would have recovered quickly, and enjoyed some peace. I felt empty and bereft. I had always hoped one day I would be able to forgive him for his aggression and have a relationship with him. That opportunity was gone forever, and so, hope fragmented, Mother and I grieved together. And his declaration of loving me in his own way — whatever that meant — stayed with me and haunted me.

87

Emma

You are here. Ringing my doorbell. I open the door. You step into my hallway, and stand looking down at me, pushing your dark hair from your eyes. You put your arms around me and kiss me gently. I kiss you back. You taste of mint and beer. You smell of lemon and sandalwood. My kisses are urgent. Insistent. Lips entwined we move upstairs, towards my bedroom. I fall backwards onto my bed and pull you on top of me.

'Let's take our time; make it last,' you say.

'How are we going to do that, Alastair?' I ask, as I reach for your penis.

'Not sure,' you murmur as you enter me.

We melt together. We move together. We climax in unison.

I roll away from you and lie on my back, arms above my head. Stretched. Relaxed. I close my eyes, about to drop off to sleep.

You move towards me. And lie on top of me. Your body is crushing me. I feel your erection, throbbing on my stomach.

'Hey; get off, you're hurting me.' You lift your right knee to push my legs open. 'Alastair, stop. We've just finished. Let's relax.'

You enter me again. Pumping, thrusting, pushing, so hard it hurts.

'Stop,' I cry. 'Stop.'

Eyes closed. Face tight. You can't see. You can't hear. Your breath quickens. All you can do is climax. You grunt, gently at first, then like a wild animal dying. It is over. Your body softens and collapses on mine. Silence solidifies around us, interrupted by the ticking of the clock on the mantlepiece.

Pain rises inside me. A burning pain as intense as fire. I roll away from you and rush to the bathroom. To wipe away the pain. To wipe away the fire. You didn't mean to hurt me, did you? You just got carried away.

Your ex-wife Heather's eyes move towards me, as they did when she tried to tell me about you. But you didn't mean to hurt me, did you? I tell myself again.

88

Alastair

I climax inside you, but this time I do not feel your muscles tightly clamped around me, encouraging me like they used to.

89

Emma

It's Thursday evening and I'm sitting at the kitchen table. A background hum of Casper purring as he sits at my feet, and the wall clock ticking. Checking through some paperwork from the surgery. Sipping coffee, enjoying being alone after a day with patients. Peace. Pure peace.

The doorbell rings. I look at my watch. Nine p.m. I frown. Not expecting anyone, I pad across the hallway to the door and look through my spy hole. Alastair. You are holding a genetically modified bunch of flowers, so large they cover your chest. Staring at the door, tapping your foot, as if willing it to open.

My body tenses. We still have our arrangement not to see one another midweek. We both have work. You have Stephen. Sighing inside, I open the door. Eyes shining, you step towards me and hand me the bouquet. An army of tumbling flowers; lilies, campanula, carnations, chrysanthemums, germini.

'Thank you so much Alastair. They're beautiful.'

Your face softens into an expression I have not seen before. An overdose of love. You take the bouquet from my hands and place it gently on the dresser. You wrap your arms around me and hold me so tight it hurts.

'I need you to love me, Emma. I want to be the centre of your universe.'

And I tremble inside. Surely this is too much? Surely there has to be balance?

90

Alastair

I put my arms around you and hold you tight. You pull away from me, holding the flowers I bought you, and pad into the kitchen. I follow you.

'Thank you so much Alastair, they're beautiful,' you repeat.

You busy yourself at the sink, cutting their stems, pulling off their lower leaves. I stand watching you. Admiring your slim, toned frame. Painted-on jeans, clinging to your every contour. Tasteful pink cashmere jumper, fluffy and youthful. Tumbling blonde hair caressing your shoulders. As you arrange the flowers into a large crystal vase, desire rises inside me.

'Mum's happy to get up early with Stephen so that I can stay over tonight.'

You turn and face me. Green eyes pale as ice.

'No, Alastair.' You gesticulate towards the pile of papers on the kitchen table. 'It's lovely to see you but I need to get on.'

'But . . . but . . . I can just watch a bit of TV while you finish off.'

'This isn't fair. We agreed to stick to weekends.'

I step towards you, put my arms around you and hold your body against mine. 'We have a relationship – not a business contract.'

Your body stiffens. You put your hands on my chest and push me away. 'But I'm running a business. I'm a dentist with my own practice. It's a big responsibility. What don't you understand about that?'

You stand in front of me, so cool, so beautiful, so superior, letting me know with your words and the twist of your head that you are out of my league.

'Are you saying I don't have responsibilities?' I ask.

You frown and shake your head. 'I didn't say that.'

A band is tightening in my head.

'I risked my job, my life for you. You won't come away with me and you still don't want to see me midweek?'

Memories

Mother. Bereft at my father's funeral. We sat in the back of the funeral car together, holding hands. Her hand trembled so much it felt as if her nervous system had been pushed into overdrive.

In the church with its fine stone arches, still holding her jerking hand, I watched her sitting, eyes glazed and disinterested. The day seemed to move around her and she seemed to step through it mentally comatose.

The vicar said all the usual clap-trap. About celebrating a life rather than mourning a person who had died. What is natural about that? Unless a person is so old and ill it is a relief they have died, how can anyone empathetic expect people to be pleased? Most people die too soon, when their families love them and need them. The vicar continued to be hypocritical by eulogising the difficult man who was my father. Terry was kind. A family man. Good husband. Good father. A stalwart of the church. At least that last part was true. He even helped clean the church's silverware. If the vicar was to be believed, my father would be riding into heaven through gates of gold and pearl, on the back of a white stallion, serenaded by trumpets, and angels. But . . . but, I remind myself, he did once say he loved me in his own way.

The worst part was the burial. Intense. Elemental. Depressing and terminal. Watching his coffin lowered into the ground. Closing my eyes, thinking about decomposition too much. Opening them again and watching my mother throw a red rose on top, looking as if she was auditioning for RADA.

And then, just to jolly things along, the party. Tea and sandwiches in the draughty church hall. Making small talk with an army of elderly women I didn't know. Women dressed in hats, who seemed to think my father was Superman just because he had been a church warden.

Funeral over, I waited for my mother to thrive. I truly believed that the special flower inside her, the one my father had deprived of water, would drink and survive. Flourish, even.

But no. She stayed at home, sitting in his armchair, looking out of the window. Looking at old photographs. Every time I visited all she did was talk about the past, showing me black and white prints.

'Here he is on the beach when he was two.'

Sitting in a rock pool. Sweet and cheeky. No premonition of the adult he would become.

'Here he is at a Butlin's holiday camp with his parents.'

Sitting on his mother's knee at a table eating. So small the cutlery looks heavy in his young arms.

A colour photograph now; 'This is what he looked like when we met.'

A dreamboat in his army uniform. Was it his strong, balanced face that attracted her? Did she just fall in love with his looks? I looked across at her doting face as she sat mesmerised by his photograph. I took a deep breath.

'When did his temper start?' I asked.

She looked up and frowned. 'Temper? He didn't have a temper.'

'He was always shouting. Always lashing out at you.'

She shook her head and smiled. 'You had a very different impression of him to me,' she said, turning back to stare at his picture again.

I was so angry about how she could be in such denial, when he had put us through such hell. But then later I began to realise denial was the way she coped. The pivot she rotated around. She had an image of what her marriage should have been, and she wanted to put a veneer over it and pretend it was real.

She couldn't live without him. No individual spirit. No back-bone. Three months to the day of his funeral, she died in her sleep. The post mortem showed she'd had a stroke. I think she just didn't want to live.

So over a period of twelve weeks I became an orphan. And after both my parents died, instead of experiencing the heavy grief people describe in novels and poetry, that people talk about at self-help groups and on radio phone-ins, I felt free. Almost. Apart from Colin of course. Free to concentrate on the challenge of my marriage. Marriage can be such a burden at times.

91

Jade

Joy upon joy. My medicines are balanced and they are moving me from the secure psychological unit to the prison. In a van with high windows, no view of the horizon, being buffeted about like cheap cargo, feeling sick. The van draws to a halt. My stomach aches. I sit bent double until the guards open my horse box to let me out. I stagger out clutching my possessions.

Fresh air. Inhale. Exhale. Sweet and clean. Fresh air sweeter than Champagne. Two guards escort me across the car park. A large man, so fat his body makes his head look small, and a wiry young woman. I walk as slowly as possible, drinking in as much fresh air as I can.

Through rotating doors into an open area with sofas and a reception desk. Pretending to be a cheap hotel, not a prison; fooling us before they incarcerate us. And Constance is here, walking towards me.

So much paperwork; rules, regulations, agreements. Papers to sign. So many instructions, my head is spinning. How will I ever remember it all?

Constance holds on to my arm, 'Jade, don't worry, it will be all right,' she whispers.

The guards are taking me away from her. New guards. Guards I have not met before. One male, one female. Slim and young. I do not look at them. I walk down the corridor, balancing my belongings and paperwork, trying not to drop them. The guards stop at a cell door. I stop with them.

'This is your new home,' the female guard says, gesticulating for me to step inside.

I do as she asks. But someone is in my cell. How dare they? A big woman with hands like a man's.

I put my head back and scream, 'Constance, come back, I need you.'

92

Emma

I wake up and open my eyes. Saturday morning. You are here, lying next to me in bed; arms tangled around me. Pushing me too far over to my side. Why are you taking up so much space, Alastair? You are poky and bony. All elbows and knees. I extricate myself from your arms and pad to the bathroom.

I pull off my black lace nightie and step into the shower. I turn the temperature up, so hot it scalds me. I like it like that. Hot water is cathartic. I savour the pressure of the shower as it pummels my back, my chest. I soap myself, and rinse the suds off, slowly, carefully. Until every crevice in my body is clean enough to lick.

You pad into the bathroom wearing your white towelling dressing gown.

'Good morning. I need a shower too,' you announce.

I push my wet hair back from my face. 'I'm just getting out,' I say.

You step into the shower cubicle, closing the door behind you. 'Please stay.'

Inside the shower cubicle, pulling me towards you. Erect and groping. Rubbing soap on me, into my vagina.

'I've just washed myself,' I snap.

You press your body onto mine, pinning me against the glass. 'I'm just washing you again.'

My insides tighten. I wanted to get on with my day. Why are you so demanding at the moment?

93

Alastair

A perfect weekend.

We make love in the warmth of your bed. Softly. Gently. Six out of ten. We make love in the shower. Your muscles tighten around me like they used to, telling me that you love me. I give you the best climax yet, pressed against the glass cubicle, face contorted with pleasure. Ten out of ten.

Making love in the kitchen while we wait for the Chinese takeaway. Ten out of ten again. The takeaway arrives. All my favourites. Singapore noodles. Chicken with cashew nuts. Crispy duck with pancakes. Beef in black bean sauce. We sit at the kitchen table and laugh as we try to use the cheap wooden chopsticks it came with. I top up your wine glass.

'Do you mind if I bring Stephen over to meet you next weekend?' I ask. 'Mum's going away.'

94

Emma

Do you mind if I bring Stephen over to meet you next weekend? Your words echo in my head.

'Alastair, I told you when we met, I don't do children.'

Your eyes narrow. 'Remind me why not?'

'It's because of all the kids I have to deal with at work; I just don't want the hassle at home.' I pause. 'I'm just not maternal. I've never wanted children of my own, never mind having to cope with other people's.'

'But I thought you'd like to meet Stephen. Most women are maternal.'

'Women are not clones.'

You catch my eyes in yours. 'I just thought now that we're so close it might be nice for the three of us to get together.'

You look so upset. Shoulders down, eyes deflated. Your recent words, *I risked my job, my life for you. You won't come away with me and you still don't want to see me midweek?* push into my mind.

'OK then,' I say and force a smile. 'Please bring him. I'll try and make sure my mothering skills improve.'

95

Jade

A meeting room in prison. Everything white and grey. Grey plastic table. Grey plastic chairs. White ceiling. White chairs. White walls. Constance wearing a floral jumpsuit that clings to her generous thighs, sitting next to me holding my hand. The door opens. A guard enters accompanied by a thin woman, wearing a black suit, carrying a briefcase. Short brown hair. Pale face.

The guard and the woman sit down opposite Constance and me. The woman smiles at me and leans across the table to shake my hand. It feels cold in mine.

'Agatha Basildon, your defence barrister.' She nods her head in greeting.

'Hello,' I reply.

'Hello,' Constance parrots.

Agatha Basildon opens her briefcase, pulls out a pile of papers and begins to flick through them. She brandishes one sheet in the air then places it at the top. She taps the sheets together to neaten the pile, and lays them on the table in front of her.

She stares at me, neck stretched forwards. 'We're moving towards a trial in eight weeks' time. I advise we plead guilty to manslaughter with diminished responsibility. Are you happy with that?'

'Saying I'm happy is an exaggeration.'

Agatha places her elbows on the table and leans forwards. 'OK. But is it acceptable?' she pushes.

I shake my head. 'No. I want to tell the court that I'm innocent.'

She frowns. 'Do you think that's wise when there's so much evidence against you?'

I shrug my shoulders. 'I've been set up. Why should I plead guilty?'

'Let me explain,' She pauses to cross her legs. 'If you plead not guilty to murder and are found guilty you will receive a much longer sentence than if you plead guilty to manslaughter with diminished responsibility.' She leans back in her chair. 'You've been very seriously ill. Please remember that you had to be sectioned to get your meds under control. It's as simple as this. If you plead guilty you'll get a substantially reduced sentence.'

Memories

Sitting at the kitchen table opposite Colin, eating a takeaway from our local Indian restaurant. Colin loved curry. A prawn dhansak, gobi saag aloo, chicken jalfrezi and pilau rice. I remember because I spent ages on the phone ordering it.

'I'm going out with my friends from work tomorrow evening,' I told him.

His eyes darkened. 'What friends?' he asked.

'The other locum dentists working in my area. We're getting together for a drink to swap notes.'

Face hard. Jaw stiff. 'What do you need to swap notes about?'

I shrugged. 'Everything really. How we're all finding working in this area. Problem patients. Surgeries with awkward managing partners. That sort of thing.'

His eyes seared into mine. 'We've discussed this before. You're a very attractive woman. You belong to me. I don't want you going out in mixed company.'

'What do you mean?'

A twist of the lips. 'I would have thought it was quite clear what I mean.'

'Don't you trust me?' I asked.

He leant across the table and grabbed my wrist. He tightened his fingers. 'It's not about trust. It's about obedience, Emma.'

96

Alastair

Hand in hand, Stephen and I follow you into your shiny kitchen. You look at my son and your eyes soften.

'We could order takeaway pizza and watch a movie,' you suggest.

'That would be lovely,' Stephen says. 'Thank you so much, Emma.'

I knew I was right. There is no such thing as a non-maternal woman.

97

Emma

The takeaway pizza arrives. You open the box, choking my kitchen with the stench of hot cheese and processed meat. Stephen's eyes light up as he reaches across to grab a piece. Stuffing it in his mouth. As he chews, grease dribbles down his chin.

I look across at you, Alastair, tucking into pizza with a base like fried bread, swimming in melted chorizo fat, and silently ask you, aren't you going to tell your son to wipe his face with his napkin? You seem oblivious to your son's bad table manners. Behaviour that is making me feel sick. What about the noise? The chomping? The difficulty he has closing his mouth?

I stand up and walk to the fridge. I help myself to the remains of the tabbouleh salad I made for supper last night.

'Don't you like pizza?' Stephen asks.

I smile. 'Yes, it's delicious. I just have to watch my weight.'

'My mummy doesn't watch her weight.'

'So I hear.' I take a forkful of salad, and raise it to my mouth. 'What film would you like to watch tonight?'

'My favourite. *The Incredibles*.'

'The first one or the second one?' you ask knowledgeably.

Stephen reaches for another slice of pizza. 'Both please. Please, Dad, please.'

'What's it about?' I ask.

You smile enthusiastically. 'Cartoon superheroes.'

I can't stand superhero movies. I can't stand cartoons. A headache begins to throb at my temples. I need to take an early night.

Sunday morning. You make eggy bread. Fried bread saturated in fried eggs. Are you trying to clog your son's arteries by the time he is twelve? Why not just serve him a bowlful of saturated fats?

'Would you like some?'

'No thanks.'

Breakfast done and dusted, it is time to play cricket. I bowl first. I feel as if I have dislocated my shoulder. You massage it and it feels worse. You bowl. Stephen hits a six. You disappear off to the toilet.

'What does God look like?' Stephen asks.

I shrug my shoulders. 'I don't know. Maybe we can feel him rather than see him.'

'Is he a man?' he asks, swinging his bat, revving up for his next shot.

'Maybe he's neither a man or a woman.'

'Transgender?'

'Maybe. As long as he's all-powerful what does his sex matter?'

I bowl a soft shot. He whacks it into the flower bed. He puts his head back and laughs, delighted with himself. 'Six again.'

'I suppose we'll find out more about God when we die,' I say as I tiptoe through my flower bed, trying not to damage my roses and clematis, looking for the ball.

Stephen leans on his bat. 'Why do we die?'

So many questions. Does this child ever shut up? 'Our bodies are just machines. They won't last forever.' My voice is strained. Clipped.

'What happens to our bodies when we do?'

Dwelling on decomposition and maggots, unsuitable for his ears, I do not answer. I bowl at him again, shoulder killing me.

He misses, runs after the ball, picks it up and throws it back to me.

'Where do we go when we die?'

Shut up. Shut up and stop asking questions, a voice screams in my head. 'Heaven,' I reply.

'What's heaven?'

'The place where God lives; a place of perfection.'

Alastair, where are you? Why are you taking so long on the toilet? Has that greasy pizza made you ill?

'Can we go and visit heaven before we die? Let God know whether we want to go there or not?'

I look around. Where have you gone, Alastair? How long do I have to play with your son, alone?

I bowl again. He hits the ball straight back to me. I catch it.

'Your turn to bat,' he instructs.

I hand him the ball. He passes the bat to me and we swap places. I stand in front of the wickets.

He is about to bowl. He stops and holds the ball by his side.

'One last question,' he says. I sigh inside with relief. 'Why does Daddy hurt my mummy sometimes?'

Panic rises inside me.

98

Alastair

I step back into your garden, where you are playing cricket with Stephen. You stand, ball in hand, watching me as I walk towards you, fear in your eyes. What is the matter, Emma? Things were going so well. What happened while I was reading the newspaper on the loo?

99

Emma

I'm standing in the supermarket by the toiletries when I see an elderly woman hobbling towards me. Clasping a basket, head down, intent on the ground beneath her. She arrives and encroaches on my body space, lifting her head to inspect the shower gels. She turns and sets her eyes on me.

She is short, about five two. Wavy grey hair. Intense dark eyes. Face, heavily furrowed. Wearing sensible shoes and a mac. Moving closer, staring harder.

I look down at her. 'Are you all right? Can I help you?'

'I'm Mary. Alastair's mother and Stephen's grandmother.'

'Oh. I'm Emma. Nice to meet you.'

'I know who you are.' Unfriendly. Menacing. Staring. 'From the photos Alastair showed me on his iPhone,' she continues. 'He told me you use the same supermarket as me, so I've been looking out for you.'

'Well, here I am,' I say, beginning to wilt beneath the heat of Mary's gaze.

'So I see,' she replies, voice taut. 'I'm pleased I've bumped into you. I need to talk to you.'

'Would you like to go to the café? We could have a chat and a drink there.'

She shakes her head. 'We can talk here.' There is a pause. 'I want to know why you're being so selfish.'

Her words stab into me. 'What do you mean?' I ask.

'Stephen enjoyed his weekend with you.'

'Well I'm glad he did.'

She frowns; her chin moves back and her eyes narrow as she does so. 'But given your relationship with my son, I think Stephen should also come to you both, every weekend he's not at Heather's.' There is a pause, 'So that I can have a rest.'

Every other weekend. If that happened I would shoot myself in the head, or throw myself in the river. 'I'm having a relationship with Alastair. Not you or Stephen.'

She purses her lips and shakes her head. 'It doesn't work like that. Try separating us. We are symbiotic; like trees and ivy.'

'Alastair is divorced. His child is not my responsibility.'

Her eyes spit towards mine. 'If you want to be with him, everything about his life is also yours. Including his responsibilities.' She pauses. 'I think you're a spoilt, rich bitch, trying to split up our family – what's left of it.'

Spoilt rich bitch. That hurts.

'How can you accuse me of that? I can assure you I've worked hard, really hard for everything I have.'

Her lined lips snarl. 'If you're not going to stick around to help bring Stephen up, you're not doing my son any good. I want you to back off. Leave him alone.'

'You're a heartless interfering bitch,' I whisper.

'Are you talking about yourself?' she asks calmly, placing a bright-blue shower gel in her basket.

100

Alastair

I'm walking towards your house, along the river. The sun is high in the sky, fragmenting across the water like moissanite. The river meanders today, wide and slow. Emma, how could you call someone as kind and concerned as my mother a heartless, interfering bitch? Someone who looks after my son twenty-four-seven. The only other woman in the world who cares for me as much as you do.

Across the bridge. Cutting through the Leander Club land, onto the public footpath. I arrive at your house and you stand in front of me, eyes wide, face taut. Blonde hair framing your sculptured face like an aura. Into the kitchen. Shoulders wide, head high.

'Why did you speak to my mother like that?' I ask.

You turn your head towards me, imperiously. 'She spoke to me like that first — did she tell you what she said?'

'She recorded it actually, on her iPhone. I heard every word.'

Surprised, you raise your eyebrows. You laugh. 'Wily old bird, trying to catch me out and record it for posterity.' There is a pause. 'I'll try and be more flamboyant with my language next time.'

So provocative. So irritating.

I push down my desire to laugh back. To take you in my arms and hold you.

'Are you going to apologise?' I demand.

'Only if she apologises first.'

I give in. I smile. The smile that shows my dimple. The smile I know women like. 'Why don't we go to bed? That might help take your mind off things. Off your temper.'

Your face doesn't move. 'I don't want my mind taking off my temper. I don't feel the need to dilute myself. When I'm cross I want to experience it. Really, really feel it.' You pause. 'Anyway, I'm not in the mood to play around right now.'

My body tightens. Anger incubates inside me. Hot white anger. I have taken such a risk for you. You have insulted my mother and I have forgiven you. Why can't you reward me? I push the anger down. Breathe. Breathe. It will be fine by morning, I tell myself. By morning your body and mind will have relaxed.

'Let's just go to bed and sleep.'

Lips thin. Eyes flatten. 'Alastair, please understand, I want to be on my own tonight.'

My body stiffens.

'You don't mind, do you? This argument with your mother has upset me. I'll be fine next weekend. I just need a bit of time out.'

Time out.

Your words reverberate in my head. I stand up to leave. I walk to the door. You do not follow me. What has happened to you, Emma? Were you just using me so that you didn't get convicted?

I walk back along the river. Back towards Stephen. Back towards my mother. Back towards my small little life.

Memories

The Bear in the centre of Esher; on the corner by the feeder road to the A3. Sitting in a group around the fire, on a brown leather sofa, watching flames dance and play. Sally, Joe, Frieda, Tim, Ian and me. I ate scampi and chips. Everyone had something and chips. I drank three gin and tonics – Bombay Sapphire and Fever-Tree – and finished off with a large glass of white Burgundy. We laughed. We bitched about our bosses. Their ears must have been burning. I don't suppose they realised they were so thoughtless, so controlling. We bad-mouthed awkward receptionists, clumsy dental assistants. Told tales of difficult patients.

'I had a woman who wouldn't let me do her fillings unless she had her dog on her lap,' Sally giggled. 'Every time I leant across him, he growled. In the end, one day when I was doing her crown, he jumped up and bit me.'

'I had a child who I had to sing nursery rhymes to, otherwise he couldn't relax in the chair. His mother said he had ADHD,' Tim said as he sipped his ale. 'I found it hard to sing and drill at the same time. His favourite was "Humpty Dumpty". I even gave him a stuffed Humpty Dumpty toy last Christmas.'

'You're a soft touch, mate,' Joe added.

'An old man pooped in my chair,' Ian said.

'That's not funny, it's sad,' I said. And we all laughed anyway, because we'd had too much to drink.

'What did you do about it?' Frieda wanted to know.

'We've just eaten. Don't ask.'

I left the pub feeling happier than I had in a long time. Was it the company? Or was it the alcohol? Not caring which, I ambled home arm in arm with Joe and Frieda. Joe, a big seventeen-stone hunk, a broken-nosed cauliflower-eared rugby player. Frieda, a quietly spoken intellectual who campaigned for Amnesty International in her free time.

The world moved blurrily around me. I remember saying goodbye to them, and opening the gate to our road with the code. Wobbling home, past grand modern houses, until I came to ours, three doors down on the right. I stood in front of our gate, by the camera that now recognised my face. It opened slowly. I stepped inside and padded across the drive to our front door.

The security light snapped on, making me blink. The front door opened. Colin was standing in front of me, eyes like a furnace, face spitting in anger. A stone solidified in my stomach. I had hoped he would move past this.

'Come in,' he said.

I stepped inside. He closed the door.

'You disobeyed me.'

101

Jade

Constance is here. Sitting by my bed. Pretty little Constance. Sweet despite her dumpiness. Silky blonde hair, shiny like an animal's pelt. Neat little nose. Button-mushroom mouth.

A frown ripples across her forehead. 'You do understand that it is now the beginning of October and that your trial is coming up, in less than six weeks?'

I raise my hands in the air. 'What trial?' I ask.

Her frown deepens. She leans forwards. 'I will start at the beginning . . .'

'Only joking,' I interrupt.

She laughs but the laughter doesn't move around her face. Her nose and mouth remain still.

'You do know I'm innocent, don't you? I didn't kill Tomas. I loved him.'

She doesn't reply. She looks out of the window, and stares at the view of a weed-covered path and a wall. A path that nobody uses. After a while she turns back to me.

'It's not for me to comment on your guilt or innocence. You might have killed him and not realised you had.'

I lean across and put my hand on her arm, wanting to shake her. 'How can you help me if you don't know the truth? I didn't do anything to my husband, Constance, you have to believe me.'

102

Alastair

I ring your mobile. You pick up.

'Let's go out for the day. Staying at home all the time is becoming claustrophobic.' I pause. 'I think we need to go out, do a few things together like normal couples. Life is getting in our way.'

Silence reverberates down the phone line. I picture you contemplating my words, standing by the kitchen window, phone to your ear.

'But we don't want to be seen together, not yet,' you reply.

I sigh inside. 'Come on, Emma, use your imagination.' I pause, take a deep breath. 'We'll drive away from Henley. Somewhere no one knows us. Let's go to Oxford. You can wear a hat to cover your hair. No one's interested in us. Who will see us?'

I picture you shaking your head. 'The police. One of my patients. One of your colleagues.' Your voice sounds impatient. Breathless.

'Well, even better, what about lying down on the back seat of my car, with a blanket over you, as they do in films?'

You giggle. Silence, then, 'OK. It sounds good.'

I smile inside. 'I'll pick you up next Saturday at ten a.m.'

We drive to Oxford on a soft, autumn day. You have relented. We do not use the blanket. You are wearing a long beige raincoat to cover your usual fashionable clothing, and a brown cowboy hat to disguise your face and hair. Music blasts from the sound system as I drive. You are choosing tracks from your playlist, tapping your feet to the music and waxing lyrical about each one: Savage Garden, Nirvana, Michael Bolton, Bryan Adams, Seal, Usher, Mariah Carey. This is more like it, Emma. This is a normal couple having fun.

We arrive in the City of Dreaming Spires and park outside St John's College, opposite the Randolph. A quick coffee in the Morse Bar, surrounded by wood panelling and TV memorabilia.

'What do you want to do? Colleges, museums, shops, tea-rooms?' I ask.

'It's such a lovely day – I'd like to go for a walk in Christ Church Meadow.'

Hand in hand in Christ Church Meadow, cowboy hat discarded in your bag. Blonde hair cascading onto your shoulders, serenading your perfect face. As I look at you your image fades and Heather's crumpled features sear across my mind. I blink and you are with me again, looking like a model in a TV advert. What have I done to deserve a woman like you?

Leaves beginning to fall, carpeting the ground in russet and gold. I inhale deeply, humming with happiness as a soft breeze caresses my face.

We cross the meadow and arrive at the riverbank, by the line of college boathouses. A flurry of activity. Teams lifting their boats after Saturday morning training. Lithe, muscular bodies, wrapped in bright body-hugging Lycra. Bustling importantly as if they are enjoying the tourists' voyeuristic curiosity. Shouting instructions to one another confidently. Teams so used to one another they function like well-oiled machines.

You look at me and smile. We turn right and walk along the Thames, past Folly Bridge. Admiring the river birds; mallards, swans, moorhens, grey heron, kingfishers, geese, coots, grebes. Listening to their cries.

All the way to The Perch, for lunch. We sit at a table by the wood burner, holding each other's eyes. I choose fish and chips. You pick at spiced pumpkin, goat's cheese and beetroot salad. On the way back to the car, you squeeze my hand.

'You were right, Alastair. This is what we need, isn't it? A bit more fun. A bit more time out.'

103

Emma

Monday morning. Walking past Andrea as I enter my surgery. Andrea, bright and breezy today; dressed top to toe in yellow. Mustard-yellow skirt and cardigan. Banana-yellow blouse with a bow at the neckline. Banana-yellow glittery nails. A bit too bright and breezy for me.

Smiling, nodding, 'Nice weekend?' she asks.

'Yes, thanks.'

I don't tell her that Alastair and I had a dreamy day on Saturday walking hand in hand through Christ Church Meadow. We are still quiet, even with her, about our relationship.

'I've sent today's patient list to you on email.'

'Thanks.'

I step through the waiting room to check on my fish tank. I pop some food in for them and watch my ornate fish glide towards the dropping food, open-mouthed, flapping their fins. So beautiful. So delicate. Illuminating the waiting room with their electric colours. Almost bright enough to compete with Andrea.

I pull myself away and enter my consulting room where I find Tania removing instruments from the autoclave. Before I can even greet her, the internal phone rings. I pick up.

'You have an unexpected visitor. Heather Brown. She says she's a friend and she needs to see you urgently,' Andrea informs me in a voice that sounds flustered.

Heather seems to make everyone feel flustered. Her special talent.

'Wait for Tania to step out, and then send her in.'

At the mention of her name, Tania raises her painted-on eyebrows. I put the phone down. 'Do I need to take an early coffee break?' she asks.

'Yes please. A blast from the past I need to deal with.'

She flashes her teeth, with her special smile. 'Let me know if you need a hand. I'll step back in and help.'

Tania leaves, heels clicking across the floor. Heather storms in, slamming the door behind her. Not looking at her best today. Her jeans cling to her pear-shaped thighs too precisely, and it is not a pretty sight. She looks as if she has stopped bothering to wash. Dirty hair like a bird's nest. Tendrils so thick and dry they look like twigs. A ruddy face. Has she got high blood pressure? Someone needs to tell her to go for an urgent medical check-up.

She stands in front of me, feet apart, hands on hips. Stale, malty breath washes over me. I step back. Alcohol. That explains the ruddy cheeks.

'You haven't listened to me, have you?' she asks, moving closer.

I step back further. 'I did listen but I don't believe you.' Back against the counter. Pinned there, inhaling stale malty breath.

Heather's lips snarl. She is so unattractive. The fact that he was ever with her lowers Alastair in my estimation. How could a man as handsome as him ever have been attracted to a woman like this?

'You're a fool not believing me. I know from his mother, Mary, that you're still liaising with him.' There is a pause. She smiles a rancid smile. 'Liaising – a good word for screwing, isn't it?'

Anger pulses inside me. 'Liaising. Screwing. So what? It's none of your business.'

She puts her head on one side. 'So uppity. Posh totty. Is that what you think you are?'

234

I clench my teeth. I clench my fists. Breathe. Breathe.

'I'm only trying to help,' she continues. 'I'm only trying to help you before he really hurts you.'

My mind steps back to the weekend, hand in hand with you on Christ Church Meadow, dappled sun on my face, kissing beneath the willow tree. Alastair, I do not want to believe this scruffy, self-indulgent woman. I will not let her get between us.

I force a smile. 'Thank you for your concern and advice, Heather. But I can assure you that everything between me and Alastair is absolutely fine.'

She gives me a withering look. It takes me all my energy to grit my teeth and stop myself from pulling my arm back and slapping her.

'Thanks for coming, but my first patient is due and I really need to get on with my day.'

Memories

That Saturday morning, I opened my eyes, mouth dry, head pulsating. The last thing I remembered was drinking Sambuca with my colleagues at The Bear in Esher. I turned my mind in on itself to concentrate. How did I get home last night? I felt too ill to panic about it, but memory black-out from alcohol was worrying. I pushed harder. OK. I was in the pub. I went there with the usual crowd. Sally, Joe, Frieda, Tim and Ian. I must have come home, at least to the end of the road with Joe and Frieda. They were the ones who live near me. I pushed and pushed to remember, until I saw Colin, stepping towards me. Closing the door.

'You disobeyed me.'

Frustrated, I ran my fingers through my hair. Something hurt. I winced. I pressed my index finger and middle finger down where I felt the pain, and winced again. I pulled them away from my head and looked at them. They were wet with blood.

Out of bed, ripping every muscle to move. Hobbling to the bathroom, naked. Looking at myself in the long mirror. Fresh bruises. Too many to have been from a fall.

Colin.

A flashback of Colin. Kicking my head. My sternum. My ribs. Kicking and kicking.

I pressed my fingers hard onto my head and jerked in pain. Did I need to go to hospital? I thought about what had happened to Natasha Richardson and trembled inside. But I took a deep breath, and decided to take the risk. I was not going to hospital. Ninety-nine point nine per cent recurring chance I would be all right. I wanted to sort out my problems with Colin myself. Authorities confused difficult situations. They did not help. My stomach tightened. Was I behaving like my mother? No. No. The difference was I would sort this out myself. Why did I marry him so quickly when I hardly knew him? Why did I marry anyone after what happened to my mother?

Into the shower. Water pulsing against my bruises, making me feel worse. Out of the shower. Wrapping myself in a towel, knocking down some paracetamol and ibuprofen, and rubbing on some pain-relief gel; so much our bedroom smelt like an old people's home.

I pulled on my jeans and a cashmere jumper, fancying a walk, or rather, given the condition I was in, a hobble, in the local woods, to clear my head. Sun was streaming through the window.

But the door wouldn't open. The lock wouldn't turn. I panicked. My hand tightened. I forced it. But however hard I tried, it just wouldn't move. Colin had locked me in. I banged on the door shouting his name until my fists were too sore to cope any more. I grabbed my phone and rang him. No reply. I yelled and yelled, banging my fists on the door again and again.

104

Alastair

Saturday evening at dusk I walk over the bridge in the middle of Henley, wind whipping across my face. The sun is going down, sending shards of pink across the skyline. River birds honk in the distance.

People are walking past with a sense of purpose. Everyone is on the way to somewhere. Singletons rushing towards dates. Groups of youths gathering on the bridge. Couples arm in arm meander towards the pubs and restaurants.

I arrive at your house with my carefully packed oversized rucksack. It weighs a ton. My back aches after carrying it from home. But that doesn't matter. Nothing matters except the fact that I'm spoiling you tonight. Even the overdraft that I have acquired doing this doesn't matter. This is it. This is special. My time with you is now.

You open the door and move towards me in your blue silk dress. Silk, as fine as gossamer, brushing across your slender body. You kiss me, wrapping me in your scent of musk and vanilla. I hold you so tight. I want you so much. I have to breathe deeply and slowly not to try and take you right here and now. I extricate my legs and arms from the heat of your body.

'Come on,' I say. 'Let's get the cooking started.'

I follow you, through the hallway, past your rogues' gallery of photographs. A collage of you with Colin. Soon it will be me in every collage, not Colin. You don't like to talk about him, but I would like to erase him from your home completely.

Into your kitchen. You stand watching me as I begin to unpack my rucksack. As I snap on the sound system to play my carefully selected mood music. *The Planets* suite by Gustav Holst. Wine. Always a priority. As I place vintage Bollinger and Chassagne-Montrachet in the fridge. As I open Gevrey Chambertin 1er Cru Les Champeaux, to breathe.

You sit down and place your elbows on the table, head cupped in your hands, still watching me. Tapered blue nails to match your dress tapping together as you watch. You have curled the ends of your hair and it looks prettier than ever this evening.

I unpack the food from my rucksack. Canapés, sea bass ready to bake basted in Pernod and almonds. A baked cheesecake. All prepared by me. Coming home early every evening for the last few days, I have been busy in the small kitchen in my flat. Mum and Stephen watched, fascinated. Stephen even helped me with the cheesecake. 'Are you planning on going on *MasterChef*, Dad?' he'd quipped.

I look across at you, emerald eyes almost blue tonight, taking the shade of your dress.

'How was your week?' I ask.

You tilt your head to one side and sigh. 'Relaxing. Some weeks I find going to work more restful than weekends.'

I place the canapés I made last night into the oven and stand in the middle of your kitchen looking across at you again. I smile. 'I suppose we're both lucky we enjoy our jobs so much.'

I lay the table. Arranging a bunch of red roses. Lighting a vanilla-scented candle as a centrepiece. Vanilla, your signature scent. I pour the Champagne into your crystal flutes and sit down opposite you.

'Tell me why you find work relaxing?' I push.

You sip your Champagne. You shake your head. 'I don't know

exactly.' There is a pause. 'It's where I am fully in control. It makes me feel good. It concentrates my mind. Stops me dwelling on stuff.'

'Stuff. What stuff?'

I watch your emerald eyes darken in the candlelight. 'The past. My relationship with Colin.'

I top up your Champagne. 'It's time to move forward now.'

The oven buzzes. I whip out the canapés, finish making them up, and place them on the table; chicken skewers with satay dip, teriyaki beef and lettuce cups, prawn spring roll wraps. You reach across and help yourself to some teriyaki beef. You pop it into your mouth in one, close your eyes to savour it, and chew slowly. 'Mmm . . . delicious,' you purr.

You open your eyes and they meet mine. This is it. This is my moment. 'Emma, I think we need a fresh start. Together.'

Your eyes tighten. Your brow furrows. 'What, now?' you ask.

'Yes.' I lean across and take your hands in mine. 'If you sell this place and I sell my flat, we could move to Marlow and live together. I could change jobs within the Thames Valley Police. It's only a twenty-minute drive from there to your surgery. No one would piece us together.'

'But what about Stephen? What about your mother?'

'They could come with us.'

I pull the leather box from my pocket, open it and place it on the table in front of you. Sapphire and diamonds sparkle. The flower-shaped ring I have taken out a loan to buy for you. I take your right hand in mine. 'Will you marry me, Emma?'

I look across at you. You sit staring at me like a wild animal startled by car headlights. You shake your head. You are saying no. Refusing me. My body tightens. My fist clenches.

'Alastair, this is too rushed,' you continue. 'I married Colin very quickly, and we had . . . difficulties.' You pause. 'I love you, but we need to take time to get to know each other first.'

Your face rotates in front of me. Your green eyes scream no.

Your delicate cheekbones. Peach skin. Julia Roberts smile. *Too rushed.* You don't love me. Heather didn't love me. My blood coagulates and steams up through my body, pushing and throbbing. *Too rushed.* I'm feeling hotter and hotter. I cannot contain my hurt, Emma. How can you treat me like this?

105

Emma

You are sitting in my kitchen spoiling me, and I am enjoying it. Canapés that melt in my mouth. Vintage Champagne so fine my taste buds explode. Smiling at me, over red roses and candlelight.

And now you are asking me to marry you. Offering me a ring; sapphire and diamonds, exquisitely pretty. Asking me to move to Marlow. With Stephen. My heart contracts. With your mother.

'Alastair, this is too rushed.'

Your face becomes red, then purple. Your eyes bulge. The veins in your neck protrude. You grab my wrists from across the table and you squeeze them tighter and tighter as if they were plywood or cardboard. But they are muscle, bone, veins, arteries, and the pain you are causing is unbearable. Searing through my whole body. My body is no longer a body, but a pain conduit.

'Stop it,' I scream, 'you're hurting me.'

You continue to squeeze. Black spots dance before my eyes and even though I'm sitting down I fear I'm going to faint. You let go and I exhale in relief. But now you stand up and throw your chair to the ground behind you. It clatters on the stone floor and cracks. No longer a chair, just splintered wood, suitable to build a fire with. I tremble inside, as you rush towards me.

I stand up, take a deep breath and turn, preparing to run. But you are behind me, grabbing me, pulling my body round, thrusting me against the wall. Pressing against me.

'You don't love me,' you hiss. '*Too rushed*, is all you can say after all I have done for you.'

'I didn't say that I don't love you,' I pant.

'Your reaction did. Your instinct.'

You press your face closer to mine. You spit in my face. Your spittle runs down my cheek. I try to move my arm to wipe my face, but you are holding my wrists again.

You pull back your arm, your fist. You smash it into my face and I feel another explosion of pain. When I can open my eyes again, I see your dark eyes contort into Colin's. Colin is hitting my face with his fist. Colin is slapping my cheek. Harder and harder. Again and again. But it isn't Colin. It's you, Alastair. As I start to collapse, I feel your fist crash into my face, again. Again. Again. I feel blood, sticky against my face. I smell it, heady and heavy; like the stench of a butcher's shop. I try to bend my face away from you, tears streaming.

'*Get out*. Go away, Alastair, leave me alone,' I scream. I scream and scream. And my world turns black.

I wake up on the kitchen floor, Casper lying on top of me. My head is in something sticky; it smells sour and heavy. I rub my fingers in it and sniff them. Blood. Oh my God. I am stretched out in a pool of blood. I pull myself to a sitting position, pain throbbing at my temples. I rub my temples, for a second oblivious to what has happened, then I remember.

You asking me to marry you.

Pain searing across my body. Your fist pulverising my cheek. Your spittle in my face. The world turning black. I look across the kitchen. The candle is still burning, almost to its base now. I pull myself to standing. Woozy and weak, about to faint. I hang on to the table and breathe deeply. The dizziness passes.

I drag my aching body to the light switch and turn the light on. As the room becomes illuminated I see the devastation I'm surrounded by. The debris of the meal that has been thrown from the table. Stinking uncooked fish. Fragmented canapés. Splattered cheesecake. Cracked plates and glasses. A cracked Champagne bottle. The smashed chair. Roses strewn across the floor, sliding through my blood. So weak I can hardly move, I force myself to reach the table, muscles aching. Mind and fingers trembling, I blow the candle out. The whole house could have burnt down. Casper and I could so easily both be dead. I collapse into a chair, and sit with my hands in my head. Why have I been so stupid?

Heather's face moves towards me, her sad eyes warning me. She was right; you *are* dangerous. How many times did she try and warn me and I didn't believe her? How could I have ignored the plaintive voice of Stephen, asking *why does Daddy hurt Mummy sometimes?* How could I have misjudged you so, Alastair? After all I experienced with my father? With Colin?

Memories

'Colin, you bastard. How dare you lock me in.'

Shouting, screaming, banging with both fists on the door. Turning and forcing the door handle. Shouting and screaming again.

I rang his mobile. No reply. My husband was not getting away with this. An image of his face flashed in front of me and I hated him so much. I opened the bedroom window and looked out. Too high to jump.

No way out.

I tightened my fists. There is always a way out. I wrapped my handbag across my chest and pulled off the bedsheets. I tied them together. Attaching one end to the headboard I hung my rope out of the window. I climbed onto the windowsill. Don't look down, I told myself. I slid off the sill and clung on to the sheets with my hands and my knees, like a monkey.

I slipped and gripped all the way down, like we used to do on the ropes at school. My body aching after what Colin had done to me. When my feet touched the ground I felt weak with relief for a few seconds. But I soon realised I was stuck in my back garden, with its tennis court and swimming pool. With its many acres and Fort Knox security. What was I going to do now?

I hid behind a large oak tree at the back of our land, to take a bit of time out and think. The back garden was bordered on each side of the house with high railings. Unless you had a key to the side gate it had to be entered from the house. My key was in the house. The gardener was the only person who ever used it. Our land was separated from our neighbours by a six-foot-high cedarwood fence.

Definitely no way out.

There had to be a way out.

I climbed the oak tree I was hiding behind. Carefully, slowly. Limbs bruised and aching. Balancing along a thin extended branch and jumping down, into the woods behind our house. Running, pain slicing through me, wind in my hair. Running until I fell in a heap, exhausted, and slept beneath a tree.

I woke up shivering, hungry, aching all over. I reached for my iPhone. Twenty missed calls. Colin. I switched it off. I didn't want him to find me. I wasn't too worried, though. It wasn't like on TV dramas. He wasn't a whizz with technology. Only with teeth. I heard the hiss of cars sweeping past. I followed the sound, limping my way to the main road. Walking along the side of the road into a café in town.

I sat drinking coffee and tucking into scrambled eggs on toast, dwelling on my situation. Should I call the police? Should I leave him? Should I go home and confront him, make sure he never locked me in again? I paid my bill and, without being conscious of having made a clear decision, my feet began to carry me home.

106

Alastair

I ring your mobile. You pick up.

'I'm sorry,' I say, as I sit in my living room, staring at the off-white wall that needs a lick of paint. Tapping my fingers nervously on the arm of my sofa. 'So sorry. We need to talk.'

I hear you swallow. 'No we don't. There is nothing to talk about. I don't want to see you, Alastair.'

Silence festers down the phone line.

I take a deep breath. 'I'm begging you to . . .' I pause. 'I need to explain properly.'

Silence, louder than sound.

'Alastair, after what happened how do you ever expect me to want to see you again?'

I take a deep breath. 'I know what to do, if that's how you want to play it. You *have* to see me. I have a very interesting tale to tell the police about how I doctored the evidence because I was in love with you. But that I think you're guilty. You're the murderer, not Jade.'

You laugh. A false half-hearted laugh. 'Don't be ridiculous, Alastair. You know I didn't do it.'

'Try proving it.'

You open the door to me, as I knew you would. I step into your hallway, towards your bruised, unsmiling face. Your swollen nose. Your swollen lips. A kaleidoscope of colour dancing around your cheeks. A hundred shades of purple. A hundred shades of green.

You deserve it, for the way you treated me. And I thought you were so much better than Heather.

But I also know that I love you. I want to keep you forever. I just couldn't help it. You hurt me. You had to learn a lesson.

You turn. I follow you into your drawing room, decorated in delicate shades of gold and cream, laden with elegant antiques. Georgian sofa and chairs with walnut frames, engraved with leaves and flowers. A Regency crested mirror adorning the fireplace. The crystal chandelier centrepiece. Your life that drips with money. Money oozing out of every pore.

We sit in chairs on either side of the marble fireplace. You put your head in your hands and begin to weep. 'I cannot believe you brutalised me,' you manage between sobs. You lift your face. 'Look at what you did to me.'

Closer to, your face looks even worse. Pulverised flesh, red as raw meat, beneath the purple and green bruises. I lean towards you. 'I'm so sorry. So very sorry. I just love you so much. I couldn't bear it that you rejected me. I know that I was wrong.'

You pull your face away. 'You assured me you were never violent and that Heather was lying.' There is a pause. 'Then you beat me to a pulp. When I came round, the candle was burning down – the house could have been set on fire. Alastair, I'm lucky not to have died. You nearly killed me.'

I try to take your hand but you snap your hands behind your back. 'I just lost it, Emma. I don't normally behave like that and I will never do it again.'

'*Normally* isn't good enough, Alastair. It should be never.'

Tears pour down your face. You fumble up your sleeve to find a hankie, blow your nose and wipe your tears away. You sit staring at me, lips tight, jaw stiff and strained. Another shake of the head. 'You shouldn't hurt your girlfriend. It's unforgivable.' You stretch your legs in front of you and sigh from the bottom of your lungs. 'Before this happened I thought I loved you but . . .' You pause. 'You were rushing me. I didn't want to live with you and your child. Not yet. That's how I felt.' You shrug your shoulders and raise your hands. 'It's not unreasonable to take your time in a relationship.'

But your eyes and body language tell me that 'Not yet' means 'Never'.

'And now this.' You point to your face. 'How did you think this would help? What possessed you to do something like that?'

I do not answer that question.

'We've known each other for a year now,' I tell you instead, anger building inside me like a rising tide. 'Long enough to fall in love. You've had enough time.' I pause. 'I find your reluctance intolerable after all I've done for you. I could have gone to prison for tampering with police evidence; perverting the course of justice is serious.'

Your body shrugs. Your eyes and shoulders widen. 'But I'm innocent. So how could you be perverting the course of justice? Don't you dare threaten me.'

Anger is bubbling in my skull, beneath my fingers, itching to clasp together and punch you again. 'I'm not threatening you. But I did break the law for you. Risking a prison sentence in order to protect you. I hope you fully understand that.' I pause. 'I love you, Emma. I want to make this right. And I want to move in with you.'

'I can't do it.' There is a pause. 'Not now, after what you've done.'

A river of anger bursts its banks. My fists clench.

'You must,' I shout.

You stand up, walk towards me and lean down to push your bruised face into mine. 'What are you talking about? You can't make me. You don't control me.'

I stand up and push you back. 'Oh yes I can,' I shout. 'If you don't honour your commitment to me, as I said on the phone,

I'll tell the police what I've done. Tell them the truth. I was overwhelmed, bamboozled by my love for you.' I pause. 'You'll go to jail. Yes, I'll be investigated. I may lose my job, but actually, when I really think about it, I won't be prosecuted. I can turn Queen's evidence. I will be the main prosecution witness. And you'll lose your freedom. You'll lose everything.' I take a deep breath to try and calm myself. I mustn't hurt you again. Not now. Not yet.

'Emma, I've risked everything for you. You will do what I say.'

107

Emma

'You will do what I say.'

Your face darkens.

'So you're threatening to destroy my life if I don't obey. As if it's a line of command, not a relationship. You must be mad.'

'That's not fair. You know I love you, Emma.'

Do you really believe that might somehow smooth everything over? Are you crazy? You must be. I really need to tread carefully.

I take a deep breath. 'And I loved you. But I was unsettled by the speed you were moving. And then you tore us apart with your violence,' I reply.

'It was a mistake, Emma. You need to forgive me,' you insist.

In that moment, I reach a decision. I know what men like you need to hear. I know how to play the game, you foolish man. I take a deep breath.

'I understand that I need to forgive your violence. It only happened because I had upset you, and you were afraid of losing me. I can see we need to heal and move forwards. But Alastair, you didn't need to threaten me to do that.' I pause. 'I will marry you.'

Your body eases at once. Your shoulders relax, your head and neck become less strained. Your face softens. You look at me and smile. Body trembling, I force myself to smile back. You fumble in your pockets and pull out the jewellery box. Black leather gold clasp and letters. How did you have the nerve to bring this with you? You are so dangerous. So presumptuous. I must keep calmer than calm, to play along with you. You pull the ring from its box, take my left hand in yours and push it onto my finger. It's so tight, it cuts into my skin, reminding me of the pain you have caused me. You stand up, pull me towards you and kiss me hard on the mouth.

I kiss you back, but I want to bite you. Maim you. Kill you. Are you stupid? Do you really think I'll put up with this pantomime of a relationship, after what I have been through with my father? With Colin? Do you really think I'm willing to be a passive victim?

108

Jade

Visiting time. A real visitor today. So far, since I have been incarcerated, the only people who come to see me are duty-bound professionals who will then fill in their time sheets: my barrister, my psychiatrist, my psychiatric nurse, my appropriate adult, my psychotherapist.

For the first time, I walk past the guards into the visiting room, drinking in the air of excitement. The opportunity to brush with someone leading a normal life.

I walk towards a grey plastic table in the middle of the room and sit and wait. The guards are standing at the side, backs to the wall, watching us like hawks. My visitor walks towards me. Your lover, Tomas. The Stereotype. The one who killed you. She is wearing a black miniskirt, showing off her slender, suntanned legs. And a crisp white blouse. Shaking her blonde hair so that it ripples across her shoulders. Smiling at me with glossy dark-pink lips. She is wearing rather a lot of make-up and her right eye is bloodshot. She sits down opposite me. She has put on too much perfume. The heady scent catches in my throat.

'To what do I owe the pleasure?' I ask.

'I need your help,' she says.

'What with?'

'It's Alastair. He's become a danger to me – but also the solution to both of our problems. We need to talk.' A pause. 'If you help me, I can get you out of here. All I need from you is some advice.'

Memories

Despite everything he had done, my subconscious carried me home to confront Colin. My conscious mind told me to contact the police, and run. But somewhere deep inside, after everything that had happened to my mother, I knew I had to deal with this myself.

I walked out of the café, noise from passing traffic crashing like waves against my eardrums. I turned right along the high street, then right again into our loosely tarmacked private road. Past the neighbours' houses. The neighbours we had never met. Ghost neighbours, not friends we ever saw. Let's put it this way, it wasn't a road for a street party. It was a road stuffed with 'look at me' houses for entertaining, to impress your guests. Since Colin and I never invited anyone around, its ethos was rather lost on us. At least it had a lot of space for us to ignore one another in. If our house hadn't been so large our marriage would have been even harder to bear.

Walking through our gilded gates, crunching across gravel. I had my front door key in my bag, so I let myself in. As soon as I stepped into the hallway I could see him through our walls of glass; lying on the sofa watching a snooker match on our outlandishly large pub-sized TV. Two men in dinner suits were circling the table, taking it in turn to shoot. One was wearing a burgundy velvet jacket and a yellow bow-tie with dots on. He had curly hair touching his shoulders, dripping with grease. The other man, who appeared to be losing, although less unsavoury, was less smartly dressed. Waistcoat. Bow-tie. No jacket.

Colin seemed to be having a duvet day. He was still in his striped dressing gown and UGG slippers. He hadn't heard or seen me. I marched into the drawing room and hijacked the controller, snapping the TV off.

A slow smile. Artificial. 'So the wanderer returns.'

'We need to talk.'

'We do indeed.'

I sat on the sofa opposite him, wondering what I had ever seen in him. He was thin and wiry and hairy. Hair like a werewolf on his chest and legs. Mean, diminished eyes.

'I only came back to tell you I want a divorce.'

His face didn't move. He crossed his legs. He folded his arms. 'Just try it,' he spat.

'I'll try what I want. What do you mean?' I asked.

He shrugged his shoulders. 'If you attempt to leave me your career will be finished. I've just been elected to the board of the General Dental Council. You'll be discredited.'

I went cold inside. The General Dental Council. The regulatory body for dentists. A position of power and influence. But I put my head back and laughed, as convincingly as I could muster.

'Not if I tell people what you did to me. Beat me up. Locked me in my bedroom.'

I shuddered inside as I thought about what he had done to me. He smiled a snake-like smile. 'Well, we have actually had a complaint against you already. So telling stories like that might just seem like a pathetic attempt to avoid trouble.'

'What? Who?'

'That would be telling.'

My jaw and mind clenched. 'Why wasn't I informed about it?'

He leant his head to one side and lifted his right eyebrow a few millimetres. 'Oh dear. Didn't you receive the letter? It must have gone missing in the post.' The fragmented smile he always used when he was being superior. 'I can forward it to you, but if you're staying with me, maintaining the status quo, maybe we should forget about it for now?' There was a pause. 'What do you think?'

Trembling inside, I nodded my head. I loved my job. My career was everything to me back then. Still is.

109

Alastair

I open the door with my key. You walk into the hallway and kiss me. I step away from you to feast my eyes. Looking good, Emma Stockton – soon to be Emma Brown. Seriously good. Very pleasing to me. Your miniskirt and extravagant blouse really show you off to best advantage. Simple elegance. Shapely legs. Your face is healing well, too. I haven't done any permanent damage. You no longer look like a boxer who has lost a fight.

'How was your day?' I ask.

'Interesting,' you reply, hands on hips, head to one side.

'Interesting how?' I ask, as you turn and I follow you down the hallway.

'I had a chat with someone I never used to get on with. It seems we can work together now.'

I frown, not sure who you are talking about. 'What do you mean?' I ask.

'Well, you know, she has an expertise I think I can tap into.'

My frown deepens. That doesn't explain anything. 'Is she a patient?'

You don't reply, but ask with a seemingly curious smile, 'What about you? How was your day?'

'The usual. Swabs and meetings.'

I follow you into the kitchen. I'm pleased to see that the table is laid for supper. A casserole simmering on the hob. The aroma of oregano and basil wafts around the room. A good prequel to the family home that I want us to create. Soon Stephen will be welcome, I will make sure of that. You walk across and stir the food. My stomach rumbles.

'I know it's a bore, but I need your help, Alastair. The damn sink is leaking.'

I look across to the open cupboard beneath the sink. Water is leaking from the joint around the pipe, and a wrench lies on some kitchen roll beside it, as if you have abandoned your own attempt to fix it.

'I've been trying to tighten it, but I'm just not strong enough.'

'I'll do it. It's simple.'

I pick up the wrench. It takes me longer than I expected to stop the leak. The joint is really, really stiff. Eventually, after a lot of effort, I manage to twist it and stop the water pouring out. I stand up, wrench in hand, and try to pass it to you.

'Thanks, darling. Put it just there on the kitchen roll. I'll tidy up later. It's time for some wine right now.'

You are pulling a bottle of Chablis from the fridge and opening it. Things are looking up. You never used to allow me here midweek; never mind offering me expensive wine. I smile to myself. Sometimes a firm hand does a woman good. You pour us a large glass each, and hand me mine. We clink glasses.

'To us.'

'When are you putting this house on the market?' I ask.

You smile your Julia Roberts smile. 'The estate agent is coming to value it in a few days' time. I'm taking the day out of the surgery.'

My heart jumps in my chest. Things are definitely working out.

110

Emma

I'm taking the day out of the surgery. I have rearranged all my appointments. Paid for Tania and Andrea to go on a computer course.

But it's not the estate agent, but DS Miranda Jupiter and her sidekick, who are here. In my home. In my elegant drawing room. Her sidekick today is a young man with deep-blue eyes and blond hair. Good-looking. Neat-featured enough to be a member of a boy band. Stylish haircut, every strand blow-dried and aligned. Miranda is brandishing her dark eyes and sultry good looks, running her fingers through her black shiny hair. Straightening her downturned mouth. The boy-band sidekick is sitting watching her.

She crosses her legs. 'What did you want to see me about?' she asks.

'I need to tell you something.'

She almost smiles. Her lips quiver and then straighten. 'Then maybe you should come to the station and make a statement.'

'Too dangerous.' I shake my head. 'Alastair Brown might see me.'

'Alastair Brown?' Taken off-guard, she frowns. 'Our senior forensic scientist?'

'Yes.'

'What has it got to do with him?' she asks.

'I'm in a relationship with him.'

She flinches, then shakes her head. 'That is very serious. I don't know where this is going, Ms Stockton, but it may have serious ramifications. I need to record this.' She leans forwards. 'Do I have your permission?'

I nod my head.

'Good.'

She reaches for her iPhone and presses record.

'What would you like to tell us, Ms Stockton?' she asks.

I stir in my chair and swallow. 'I have not told the whole truth.'

She does not react. The consummate professional. My words hang heavily in the air between us. The silence pressures me to continue.

Eventually, 'Go on,' Miranda says.

I look into her large brown eyes. Keep calm. Stay steady, I tell myself, sitting on my hands to disguise the fact they are shaking. I can play the game as well as she can. 'I was in a relationship with Tomas Covington.' A deep breath. 'I lied about that initially as I was also sleeping with Alastair Brown, and I didn't want him to know I'd been unfaithful.'

Her face stiffens. 'I see. So why are you telling us now?'

I lean forwards. 'Alastair and I had an argument. He was angry with me and he admitted he knew Tomas and I had slept together. Things got very heated. He admitted he killed Tomas. He said he'd kill me too unless I married him, so I said I would. He thinks we're engaged.'

I stretch my left hand towards her and show her my ring. 'But he's a murderer and I'm terrified of him.'

I close my eyes and remember. I see your thunderous face as you walk towards me. I feel your hand rise, and move towards me. I feel your heat. Taste your breath. Then your face contorts to become Colin's. Do you understand, Alastair, that no one is allowed to treat me like this again?

'Are you prepared to make a written statement and testify in court?' DS Miranda Jupiter asks.

'Yes. As long as he's locked up before he finds out.'

Miranda taps her fingers on the coffee table. 'That depends on many other factors.' She thinks for a moment. 'There is a lot that doesn't check out. Why was your and Jade's DNA on the wrench then?'

I shake my head. 'I don't think the wrench you found in my shed was the murder weapon.'

Miranda's lips flicker at the edges. She says nothing, pushing me to continue.

'Alastair was setting us both up as the potential killers, to protect himself. Me first, because he was so distressed I'd been unfaithful and he wanted to punish me. Then Jade when he decided he still loved me and wanted to spend the rest of his life with me.'

Miranda Jupiter nods and frowns. 'What about the bedsheets?'

I wince and move my body from side to side, in what I hope looks like embarrassment. 'Actually, I swapped the sheets.'

'Why did you do that?'

I look at my feet. 'We made love in Tomas' bed but I didn't like doing it on Jade's sheets. Tomas liked the smell of me. It turned him on. So I brought my own bedsheets over.' I looked up at her. 'Tomas got Jade to buy some similar sheets, gold ones from Debenhams, so that we could do this. I took those home and left mine for Tomas.'

DS Miranda shakes her head. Tears well in my eyes. I look into her chocolate-drop eyes, and pray silently that she has believed me.

'This information will be treated in confidence for now,' she assures me. 'But you need to understand the personal consequences of what you have just told me. I will arrange for you to come to a station in the area later.' She shakes her head. 'Alastair will be suspended whilst we investigate these allegations.' There is a pause. 'You'll be arrested and charged for perverting the course of justice. But you'll be given police bail, pending investigation. Your charge is procedural. As long as what you have said is true, it will all come to nothing.'

'Thank you for listening.' I pause. 'I can assure you Jade is innocent. There's been a serious miscarriage of justice.'

Miranda Jupiter nods her head and stands up to leave. Her sidekick copies her.

That evening, as soon as you return from work, Alastair, you pull me towards you and hold my body against yours. You bend your head, lean down and kiss me. I force myself to kiss you back. Your kiss becomes urgent. More insistent. I break off and step back.

'How did it go today?' you ask, staring into my face.

'The estate agent didn't show.'

A frown brushes across your forehead. 'Oh God. After you'd taken the day off from the surgery, and everything.' There is a pause. 'How annoying.' Your voice sounds forced. Artificial. Are you suspicious that I'm stalling on moving house? Are you thinking of attacking me again?

Memories

After Colin threatened to end my career and told me there had been a complaint against me, I was so frightened of being struck off the dental register when I had fought so hard to train, I tried to appease him for a while.

I tried to be his perfect woman and not annoy him. Perfect home. Perfect cooking. Perfect looks. I never had a minute to myself. I worked hard at my job. I tidied the house. I cooked Ottolenghi recipes that took hours even to find the ingredients for, never mind how long it took to prepare the vegetables, herbs and nuts. I went to the gym to keep my figure toned, took great care of my skin and hair, I even had a routine of pelvic floor exercises.

During that relatively peaceful period, which lasted about six months, he only hit me twice. Once when I dropped a wine glass on the kitchen floor and it smashed.

'You clumsy woman,' he said, pulling back his arm and slapping his right palm across my left cheek. It stung like acid.

On the second occasion I put too much milk in his tea. It wasn't an easy time. I had no freedom. I felt tired and flat. My life, except for my plan to escape, wasn't worth living. But I was just biding my time.

111

Alastair

First thing in the morning, on the way to the lab, my line manager, Sarah Dickinson, is walking towards me. Everything about Sarah Dickinson is usually enthusiastic. Her wavy hair. Her hammering smile. But today she looks cross.

'Alastair, I need to see you in my office.' There is a pause. 'Now.'

She strides along the corridor, shoulders raised. Even her buttocks appear stiff as I follow her into her office. She closes the door. She sits behind her desk frowning at me. I sit opposite her.

'You're suspended.'

'What . . . ?' I splutter. 'Why . . . ? How . . . ?'

She clasps her hands together, in front of her. 'For nondisclosure of your relationship with a suspect, which precluded you from working on a case.' There is a pause. 'In fact, suspension is the least of your problems. You'll probably be charged with perverting the course of justice.'

I go cold inside. 'Who told you?'

'I'm not at liberty to discuss that with you.'

I sit looking at her. Her face is stone. Expressionless. Her usually friendly eyes are cold and distant. Not the Sarah Dickinson I have known for so long. A new person has stepped out from inside her.

The telephone on her desk rings. She picks up.

'Hello.' Frowning. Silence. Looking up at me. 'That's fine, I'll tell him.'

Phone back in its cradle. 'That was Miranda Jupiter. She wants to talk to you. Clear out your personal belongings and go straight to her office.'

Sarah's words cut into me like a knife. Clear out your personal belongings. An elastic band tightens in my head. I close my eyes. I imagine I'm walking through a field of lavender. I inhale. Its musky scent rises in my nostrils and soothes me. I open my eyes, look at Sarah and compose myself.

I nod my head. A nod of obedience, of assent. Slowly, slowly, I walk away. Out of Sarah's office, along the corridor, back to my locker. My hands tremble as I unlock it and take out my coat and bag. I do not have any other possessions. Everything else belongs to the lab. I sign out at the exit. People I know are coming and going. Eyes burning into me as the porter takes my locker keys and my entry pass.

Into the police area, feeling numb, anaesthetised, as if I'm moving through a dream. A life that isn't real. Before I have come to terms with what is happening, I find myself in an interview room with Miranda Jupiter and a nervous sidekick. A young boy with blond hair, flashing his eyes towards her, watching her every move. Flashing his eyes towards me, weighing me up. I try to look relaxed to flummox them; shoulders low and broad, hands together on my lap. No fidgeting. But I'm feeling hot, feeling cold, feeling sick. I take a deep breath in an attempt to push my nausea away. I smile a wide, stretched smile.

Miranda crosses her legs and smiles back. It is the first time I have ever seen her do that. It is seriously discomfiting. Is she trying to trap me into a confession?

'Would you mind being interviewed to help us with our enquiry?' she asks.

'That's fine. Of course. That's what I'm here for. Sarah Dickinson explained.'

Her smile fades. 'OK then. I'll start.' She snaps the recorder on, and tells it our names.

'Why didn't you disclose your relationship with a key suspect?'

I look at the floor. I do not know what to say. Silence festers. DS Miranda Jupiter moves on.

'Where were you the night Tomas Covington died?' she snaps.

My mind goes blank. I can't remember.

'I don't know,' I reply. 'It was a long time ago. It wasn't significant to me at the time.'

The questions twist. The questions turn. I try to remember what you told me you'd said, Emma. I try to be consistent. True to our cause. The questions run on. It feels like forever.

'Thank you, Mr Brown,' Miranda says at last, switching the machine off. 'One final thing – we have a warrant to search your flat and car. Someone is at your property with your mother right now.'

Searching my flat. Police with a warrant. My mother and Stephen will be aghast, terrified. I picture Mother opening the door, her mouth drooping open, lower lip sagging as it does when she is shocked and upset. Police barging into our home and rifling through our possessions as if we were thieves. It shouldn't be happening to people like Stephen and Mother and me.

'And I need the keys for your car,' Miranda continues, stretching her hand out to receive them. 'And then you can take public transport home.'

This is ridiculous. They won't find anything. I'm clean. I didn't kill Tomas.

112

Emma

Back home after a long day in the surgery; Botox and fillers in the morning, a difficult wisdom tooth extraction after lunch. Alastair, I'm relieved you are not coming over tonight. You are working late and going back to your own flat, so I'm really looking forward to a light supper and an early night; reading a romantic novel, snuggling up with Casper in bed. Wading through constant deceit is exhausting. I need to be alone to rejuvenate.

I step into the hallway and Casper appears from nowhere, purring like a tractor engine, wrapping his body around my legs, headbutting my calves to get my attention. My stomach twists. The TV is blasting from the drawing room. I open the door. You are here. Again. Midweek. Draped across my sofa watching TV, wearing jeans and a checked shirt, your casual woodcutter look.

'What's up?' I ask.

You sit up, face like stone. 'I've been suspended from work. It's really serious. I think I'm going to lose my job.'

I walk towards you, feigning surprise. 'Why? What's happened?'

You push your snarling eyes into mine. 'My manager knows about our relationship.' You pause. 'Did you tell her, Emma?'

'No. Of course not. I would never betray you. Surely you know that.' Trying to look as if I'm about to cry. 'It must have been Jade, or Heather. They both know about us.'

I sit down next to you and wrap my arms around you. 'How awful. I'm so sorry, Alastair.'

You pull away. I watch your fingers clench. Your jawline tense. 'And they're searching my car. Searching my flat,' you continue. 'I mean, they won't find anything. But it's a shock.'

I smile inside. Not long now.

113

Alastair

After being suspended from work a few days ago, I'm beginning to relax. Watching *A Place in the Sun* on Channel 4, at your house, Emma. The TV crew are in Spain on the Costa Blanca. Laura Hamilton, the presenter, is particularly bright and breezy, extra chirpy today. What a lovely job floating about showing people houses in front of a TV camera. Becoming a minor celebrity. I lie across your sofa, Emma, daydreaming of sunshine and sandcastles. You have plenty of money. Perhaps we will be able to afford a home in the sun together one day. Maybe being suspended will have its advantages. I can be a house husband now. Look after your life full time. Co-ordinate our move to Marlow.

The doorbell rings. I do not feel like answering. If it's something important, the caller will come back. It's probably an ex-prisoner selling expensive dusters, or one of those annoying salesmen with a big white tray of smelly fish, lying about how fresh it is. They seem to call here far too often. They pick on well-heeled areas like this.

The bell rings again. Louder, more insistent. Is it a Jehovah's Witness? I sigh as I pull myself away from the comfort of the sofa. I go upstairs and peer down from behind the bedroom curtain. Panic stabs into me. A police car is slung across the driveway. Have you had an accident, Emma? I see DS Jupiter and a sidekick standing on the doorstep. DS Miranda Jupiter is frowning and pressing the bell again. It reverberates through the house. Shell–shocked, I stand, feet rooted to the ground, listening to it. She bends down and shouts through the letter box.

'Alastair Brown, we know you're in there. Let us in or we'll break the door down.'

Alastair Brown. It's me they want. Break the door down? Someone as slender as Miranda Jupiter? She must have back-up. Panic explodes inside me. Can I hide in the closet? In the loft? Can I escape via the back door and run? No. No. Running will make things worse.

I walk downstairs, breathing deeply to calm myself. I open the door. The sidekick, a man with a piggy face, small eyes and puffy skin, pushes against me. He clamps my hands behind my back and cuffs me.

'Alastair Brown, I am arresting you on suspicion of murdering Tomas Covington, and perverting the course of justice by providing false evidence. You do not have to say anything, but it may harm your defence if you do not mention when questioned something which you later rely on in court. Anything you do say may be given in evidence,' DS Miranda Jupiter spouts.

I'm stupefied. This cannot be happening. I must be having a bad dream. Hallucinating. Pig Face with his invisible cheekbones pushes me into the police car, and sits in the back with me. Too close, breathing my air. Miranda drives, whipping the siren and lights on. The siren lacerates my mind. What evidence have they got? Emma, love of my life, did you do this to me? Did you set me up?

We arrive at the police station. My pockets are searched and my personal effects recorded and confiscated: my wallet, my loose change, my phone, house keys and belt. Then Pig Face escorts me to an interview room. A room with rubbery floors and walls. A room with no windows. It contains a plastic table, four plastic chairs and a recording machine. Pig Face sits on one side of the table and folds his arms. I sit opposite him.

'I need a lawyer,' I tell him. He looks through me, as if I'm invisible. 'I know I'm entitled to one.'

'I'm waiting for DS Miranda Jupiter,' he says, staring into the air in front of him.

Obviously not bright enough to think for himself. I grit my teeth and try to be patient.

Miranda Jupiter sweeps in eventually, head held high. Imperious.

'I want a lawyer,' I shout.

Lips in a line. 'That'll slow things down, if you want to go home today.'

'Are you trying to deny me my rights?' I ask.

She tosses her silken black hair. 'I'm just warning you. Duty solicitors are very overworked. There is quite a queue for one at the moment.' She pauses. 'Do you want me to request one, or do you have a private solicitor in mind?'

'Request one, please,' I tell her through gritted teeth.

'OK. I'll call one. Come on Brian,' she says to Pig Face. 'This will take time. Let's get on with something else while we wait.'

Pig Face follows his sullen mentor. And I'm left alone, hands and mind trembling. What has happened here? How can I have been arrested for the murder of Tomas Covington? I need Miranda and her sidekick to come back and tell me what has happened. What evidence they have.

Time stops. I sit at the table, simmering with dread. Dread of the future, fear of the past. After what seems like forever, the interview room door opens. A middle-aged woman, wearing a dark suit and carrying a briefcase, enters. She has strawberry-blonde hair and freckles. A wide face. Broad nose. Large round eyes.

'I'm Hazel Brannighan, your duty solicitor. How do you do?' She pulls out the chair next to me and sits down. 'Can you run me through what has happened so far?'

I tell her everything. Well, almost. Not about punching you, Emma.

'I agree with you. It does sound as if you've been set up by your girlfriend. But what would motivate her to do that?'

I don't reply.

'My main advice to you,' she continues, 'is to tell the truth. Truth always triumphs in the end.'

And Miranda and Pig Face are here. Sidling into the interview room. Settling themselves opposite us. Miranda turns on the tape recorder and announces her presence. We all announce our presence.

'Now,' I say. 'You tell me why we're here.'

'It's normal for the police, not the accused, to lead the interview,' Miranda scowls.

I shrug my shoulders. 'Sorry. But I'm very confused about what I'm supposed to have done wrong. I would like that to be recorded.'

Miranda Jupiter leans forwards. 'We have found a wrench with your DNA and the deceased, Tomas Covington's, blood and hair on it, in the boot of your car.'

A wrench. My heart stops. I know the only wrench I have used was the one I mended your sink with, Emma. But blood and hair? What the fuck? You have set me up. My body screams with the pain of your deceit. My darling, what have you done to me?

'Do you have any explanation?' DS Miranda Jupiter asks.

Miranda's questions twist and turn, again and again. I answer carefully, as before. This time I'm thinking about myself, not you, Emma. My love for you has flowed into a river of hate.

Miranda falls silent for a moment. The interview must be over.

'Alastair Brown, I am charging you with the murder of Tomas Covington, and for perverting the course of justice,' Miranda Jupiter says. I can hardly breathe. I gasp for air. 'You do not have to say anything, but it may harm your defence if you do not mention when questioned something which you later rely on in court. Anything you do say may be given in evidence,' she continues.

272

114

Emma

I'm in my surgery, where I feel safe, where I feel in control, where I am the alpha female. In between patients. An overdose of fillings today, and a few too many difficult children. Actually it's not the children who are difficult, it is the parents – the way they react to their offspring. I am so glad not to have kids. Standing, looking out of the window, admiring my garden, my roses, my clematis, my fuchsia, my hydrangeas, when my mobile rings.

'Miranda Jupiter here. Just to inform you, Alastair Brown has been charged with the murder of Tomas Covington. He has been imprisoned and I'm sure bail will be denied in a case as serious as this.'

Relief floods through me. I'm safe.

'As we discussed, we'll need to call you as a witness in due course. I hope that's still acceptable?'

'Yes, of course.'

The call ends. I put my mobile in my pocket. Freedom dances in front of me. The flowers in my beautiful garden fade before my eyes and I'm back remembering what I have done. Back using the spare key to Jade's house. Wearing latex gloves as instructed. Rampaging through Jade's freezer, looking for Tomas' blood. It was exactly where she said it was. Between the ice cream and the cheesecake, in the container marked 'Gravy'. The blood she told me she kept in case she needed to do more to set me up. Back defrosting Tomas' DNA. Rubbing it on the wrench you used to mend my plumbing.

I smile inside. You didn't suspect, did you Alastair? You didn't know I borrowed your car keys before I spoke to Miranda Jupiter. Putting the bloodied wrench in the car boot was so simple.

Alastair Brown, you will never hurt me again.

115

Alastair

Incarcerated. Doors locking behind me as two guards escort me to my cell. Two substantial young men with brick walls for shoulders. One with a shaved head, a neck tattoo and an earring. One with long wavy brown hair. Pulling me along as if I'm a sack of potatoes; dead with no feeling. Winding along a corridor painted white. The corridor is empty apart from us. No other inmates are being moved right now.

They stop outside a cell, unlock it and push me in. Almost into the arms of my cell-mate, a man of about forty, with thin legs and a long face. Pale skin. Blond hair. The door grinds and clicks.

'Hey,' he says as I hold on to the bed to stop myself careering into him. 'Name's Fred. Who are you?'

'Alastair.'

We stand by the bunks. Pinprick brown eyes bore into mine. He blinks. He shrugs his slender shoulders, and gesticulates with his right hand to introduce me to the cell.

'Well, make yourself at home, mate. As you can see I've hogged the top bunk. I find the bottom claustrophobic.'

'I find everything about being here claustrophobic.'

He grins. 'You'll get used to it.'

I look around. Not much to see. The bunks. Two easy chairs. A small TV. A chest of drawers for our clothes. I pad across and open the bathroom door. Cold air and the stench of damp blast into my face, making me catch my breath. The bathroom has a shower cubicle with a white plastic shower curtain peppered with mould, a toilet and a basin. White tiling with mouldy grouting, spreading up the walls. I shiver and step back into the cell.

'What are you in for?' Fred asks.

'Murder.'

He raises his eyebrows as if impressed.

'You?'

'The same.'

There is a pause.

'I didn't do it,' I tell him. 'I was stitched up by my girlfriend.'

He puts his head back and cackles. 'I wish I could say the same. But my trial's coming up in a few months and, despite all the odds against us, my QC is hopeful she'll get me off. Not that much evidence against me, it seems.'

I don't like to ask him what he did. I'm not sure I want to know. I close my eyes and imagine a knife crime, sudden pain, spurting blood. Or a strangulation, plastic cord tightening around a pretty neck. I open them to find his thin weasel of a face still watching me intently. He looks a bit like Paul Hogan in his heyday. Good-looking and wiry.

'How long have you been inside?' I ask.

'A few weeks, but it's not my first time.'

'Can you show me the ropes?'

'Sure can, mate. But for now I'm watching TV. Watching TV is the only way I can relax in here.'

He flicks it on, with the remote. And sits engrossed in *Coronation Street*. I have nothing to do. Nothing to read. Nothing to unpack. No possessions with me, only the prison clothing I have been allocated and a few toiletries they gave me when I signed in. So I sit and join him. I'll have to get Emma to bring me some of the things I'm allowed. My stomach tightens. No. No. Not Emma. My body fragments in pain. Aching as if she has been cut away from me by a knife. Stephen and my mother will have to help.

Coronation Street drones on. A serious issue; a young girl with dark skin buying whitening powder behind her family's back. The actor playing her father has an empathetic voice.

I close my eyes and turn my mind in on itself. Emma, Emma, how could you do this?

Memories

Back in my swimming pool in Esher, trying to whip up some adrenalin to relax me. Colin arrived home. I heard the patio doors sliding open as I carried on timing my swim. He walked to the poolside, took off his clothes, and entered by climbing down a ladder at the shallow end. He swam up behind me, grabbed me, and pushed me under.

'Next time, whatever you're doing when I come home, please have the manners to come and greet me.'

He ducked me again, for longer this time. When he released me, my lungs felt as if they were spitting blood.

116

Alastair

My brief is here, in the meeting room with me. And my solicitor. My brief, Crispin Ward, is a crusty old man with more hairs in his nasal cavity than on his head. Whenever I look at him I think about tortoises. Today as I sit opposite him I realise why. His mouth is straight, cutting a line through his wrinkles, just like the mouth of the tortoise my grandfather used to own. A crack through scaly creviced skin.

My solicitor, Jane Perkins, is a young woman with her hair cut in a bob so severe it doesn't move when she turns her head. She has large bulging eyes and rosebud lips. The sandy-haired, curvy woman I had to begin with has disappeared.

'I've been stitched up by my fiancée, Emma Stockton. I'm sure she planted the wrench in my car. A week or so earlier she asked me to mend her sink with a wrench, which she wouldn't touch when I handed it back to her. She asked me to leave it on some kitchen roll. I'm serious. The woman is dangerous.'

My brief and my solicitor exchange glances.

'What would be her motive to do this? It would help if we could explain why she wanted you incarcerated. Juries and judges like motives. Had you and Emma fallen out?'

'Nope. I just think she's a psychopath who is frightened of men.'

'And you didn't frighten her?'

'Of course not, no.'

I lean forwards and meet Crispin Ward QC's grey eyes. 'I think she's the murderer. All the evidence pointed towards that in the first place. She killed Tomas Covington, not me. I knew she did. Like Jade said, she was furious that Tomas had finished with her. I just covered up her crime because I was infatuated with her.'

Crispin Ward QC shakes his head slowly.

'No. You can't argue that. You are clutching at straws. The evidence against her is inadmissible because you tampered with it. And anyway, she now has an alibi for the night of the murder. If I were you, Alastair, I would concentrate on telling the truth.'

I clench my fingers together. 'An alibi? Who from?'

'Your ex-wife, Heather.'

I exhale quickly. The sound of air rushing from my windpipe slices across the room.

'What?' I ask.

'Yes. She was hiding in the garden all evening, hoping to speak to you. She saw Emma come home at seven thirty, switch the lights on, and says she didn't leave the house. Heather left at about ten forty-five p.m. apparently.'

Heather. Emma. Jade. A female conspiracy. A trio of bitches. And Emma, you are the biggest bitch of all.

117

Jade

It is so good to be home. The golden colours of autumn forming a fresco along the river, tumbling beauty pushing into my life as I walk my new golden retriever puppy, Monty. He is adorable. Easier to love than a man. He never says anything to upset me. Never answers me back. I stroke him for hours, his fur is as soft as silk.

The Stereotype is still pretending to be my friend, not my enemy. But I know what she really is; and she's admitted it now. A whore who was shagging my husband.

118

Alastair

Fred has lent me the mobile phone that his wife smuggled in for him. The wife he showed me pictures of, with her large eyes and simpering blonde curls. Fred, my champion in here.

I'm standing in our shower room calling you, Emma. Watching a spider crawl across the mouldy grouting, across the shower tray, and disappearing between the cluster of hairs lining the plughole. The bathroom stinks of urine however much we clean it, as the toilet is leaking. We've reported it but no one has come to mend it yet.

The phone is ringing. Pick up. Pick up, you bitch. Twenty rings. Your answer machine clicks in. Your honeyed voice melts down the phone line towards me. So sweet and sycophantic, it makes me feel sick. I do not leave a message.

An hour later, I try again.

'Emma speaking.' It is really you this time.

'Alastair here.'

A wall of silence. I know you are there, and after all I have done to help you, you are still ignoring me. Still in your home of privilege, surrounded by crystal and marble and silk, not body odour, locked doors and violence.

'What do you want, Alastair?' you eventually stutter.

'An explanation. Why did you stitch me up, you bitch?'

I imagine you standing by your kitchen counter picking

up the phone from the wall socket, and then looking through the window, at your professionally tended flower beds as we talk.

'I didn't stitch you up,' you tell me, voice sharp.

'Who did then?' I growl.

'Jade.'

Your emerald-green cat's eyes will be narrowing as you lie.

My throat tightens. 'Why should I believe you? You haven't come to see me. You don't care about me.'

The line goes quiet. No crackling. No breathing. For a second I think we've been cut off.

'Are you still there, Emma?' I ask.

'Yes. Yes. I was just wondering how to explain.' There is a pause. 'You've just been so cross and violent lately. You know what you did to me. I was frightened.' Another pause. Longer this time. 'It was Jade. I can assure you.'

'Oh Emma, how do you expect me to take this bullshit? You must have helped her. Otherwise how did she get the keys to my car? How did the police know where I was staying?'

I hear you breathing down the phone line. 'She must have paid someone from in prison. It's easy enough to break into a car. She's dangerous. You know she is.'

'How did she get my DNA?' I snarl.

'Maybe she kept some from when we went for dinner.'

This is so pathetic, I laugh inside. 'Get real Emma. You made me use a wrench to mend your sink.'

'I just wanted you to help fix the sink, I promise you.'

'You promise, and I'm supposed to believe you. How touching.' There is a pause. 'I know what you said to the police. My barrister told me.'

'I'm frightened of her, Alastair. She threatened to kill us both if I didn't give evidence against you.'

I clench my fists and grind my back molars. 'I don't believe

283

you. I hate you, Emma, for what you've done to me. It's me you should be frightened of now. Watch your step. I've got connections in here.'

119

Emma

Saturday morning, walking along the Thames path towards Temple Island, living for the moment, with the sun on my back. The Temple sits in front of me in the middle of the river, like a beacon. So early that not many people are about. An eight practising the regatta course glide past. I hear the edges of the cox's voice shouting at her crew. I strain my ears but I cannot make out exactly what she is saying.

I stand on the bank watching the river birds; swans and ducks, moorhens, grebes, terns and coots, listening to their cooing and chattering. As I turn to walk on I see a tall woman with dark hair walking towards me with a dog. She comes closer. A woman wearing jeans and trainers, and a baggy jacket with a fur-lined hood. Closer still and I see it is Jade, a puppy lolloping at her heels. Floppy gait, legs too big for its body.

We meet on the towpath. She stops in front of me. The puppy lies at her feet, panting. I bend down and stroke his head. He licks my hand and slobbers on it. I think of Casper's elegance. I have never been a dog person. I wipe his saliva away with my handkerchief.

'Hey, how's it going?' she asks, her masculine, make-up-free face squinting in the sun as she speaks.

I look at the lines on her brow and around her eyes. At the crevices each side of her lips. I know exactly where I would inject Botox and fillers if she was one of my patients.

'Life's ticking on,' I reply.

She smiles and the lines around her eyes deepen. 'Not seducing anyone's husband right now? I've not seen any strange cars outside the house.'

I press my eyes into hers. My lips tighten. 'I never seduced your husband.'

'Did he seduce you?' she asks.

'Jade, we didn't have an affair.'

She laughs. 'I believe you. Thousands wouldn't.'

I stand glowering at her by the riverbank. She glowers back. So unattractive. So unbalanced. How did someone as handsome as Tomas ever marry a woman like that? She still really believes I slept with her husband. Whatever I say, she will always think that. She is unbalanced and I have used her. A loose cannon, loaded and dangerous.

'How's your social life now?' she pushes.

I stir uncomfortably from foot to foot. 'Quiet. Just keeping myself to myself.'

'You should come to mine for a drink sometime.'

And drink Cherry Bomb again and wake up with no memory? Do you think I'm stupid?

But I manage to crack my lips into a saccharine smile. 'That would be lovely, yes.'

'Come on, Monty,' she says to the dog. 'We can't stand chatting by the river all day, can we?'

She walks away with a cheery wave. 'This way, Monty. This way.'

The dog pulls himself up to standing, tail wagging, and follows her. A few minutes later he is running ahead of her along the path, tail raised.

I turn and continue walking towards Temple Island, shuddering inside. A clusterfuck is always a clusterfuck, however much you help them out. My mobile phone trills in my pocket. I pull it out. My heart sinks. Alastair. I press reject and switch it to silent. One difficult conversation is enough for today.

Back home, sitting in my kitchen drinking coffee. Breakfasting on cranberries and muesli. I look at my phone. Twenty missed calls from Alastair. One voicemail. I brace myself to listen to it. He might have something important to say.

I fucking hate you. You fucking bitch.

How childish, Alastair. When will you stop behaving like this?

120

Alastair

Visiting time. The buzzer sounds. The guards open the doors and allow us to rush in. The prisoners' eyes are bright, shoulders squared, smiles playing on lips, as we wait for our families to arrive. I find a table near the entrance to make it easier for my mother. I sit and wait for her to arrive, riddled with a combination of longing and dread. Longing to see her. Heavy with guilt as to how my incarceration has affected her. Having to bring up my son alone at her age is not a joke.

She is here. Standing by the entrance, waving across at me. Wearing her maroon raincoat. The one she bought in a sale at a posh department store many years ago. A designer make that she is proud to own. She makes her way towards me, walking as she always walks, stooped, head down to make sure she doesn't trip up on anything.

I stand up when she reaches my table and we hug. She clamps her body against mine and says my name, 'Alastair,' as if it is the most precious name in the universe. I'm her only son, so I suppose it is to her. I inhale her scent of lily of the valley. The talc and cologne that she has worn ever since I can remember. Her love and familiarity engulf me. And for a second the world of pain I live in now stops moving around me. All that matters is this moment.

The moment moves on.

'That's enough,' a gruff voice barks behind me.

I know it is the guard standing by the wall behind us. Mother and I have hugged for too long. She doesn't hear him. I try to pull away but she clamps on to me more tightly. The guard is here, ripping me away from her as if I'm dangerous. Pushing us apart.

'That's enough,' he growls again.

'How dare you stop me touching my son, young man,' Mother says, staring at him over the top of her half-moon reading glasses.

The beast of a man, with a shaved head and a tattoo dancing across half of his face, stares back. 'Prison rules. Not me who makes them, love. I'm only doing my job.'

'Sit down, Mum,' I instruct.

She does as I ask, stiff with anger. She reaches across the table to take my hand. I pull my hand back.

'Maybe later, when the guard's not looking. We're only allowed brief body contact at the start of the visit.'

Eyes wide. 'Why?' she asks.

'They minimise body contact so visitors can't pass prisoners contraband; drugs, knives, mobile phones. Things we're not allowed.'

'But they've already searched us. X-rayed our bags, made us walk through a machine.' She shakes her head, slowly. 'It took me ages to get through security. There was a long queue. I would have thought they would trust me now.'

'It's not about you, Mum. It's prison, remember. There are a lot of bad people in here.'

Her eyes fill with tears. 'But you're not one of them.'

I shrug my shoulders. 'The guards don't know that. They can't take any risks.' I lean forwards. 'Come on, let's not waste time talking about prison procedure. How are you? How's Stephen?'

Her face closes. 'Fine,' she replies, voice clipped.

'Come on, spill the beans. How is he really?'

'They're teasing him at school.'

'About me being in prison?'

She bites her lip and nods her head.

'Do you mean bullying him?'

Her eyes hold mine. She doesn't reply.

'You've explained to him that I didn't do it, that I'm innocent?'

'Yes. And he believes that. He loves you. He trusts you.'

My eyes are filling with tears. I swallow hard to try and push them back. But one escapes and trickles down my cheek. I brush it away with the back of my hand. 'Just keep reminding him. Tell him to ignore what people say.'

Mother pulls a large handkerchief from her pocket and blows her nose. She is trying to stop tears too.

'When is he coming to see me?' I ask.

She sniffs and grimaces. 'Do you think he's old enough to cope with it?'

'Children are more resilient than we think.'

'Only if they need to be.'

'Don't say that, Mum, it hurts.'

Her face crumples into her handkerchief, and she weeps now. Full-blown shoulder-heaving sobs. Guilt for the pain I'm causing her by being in here clamps in a band around my head, around my chest. She looks up, breathing deeply, pushing the tears back, red-faced and gasping. She shakes her head. 'I'm sorry. I didn't mean to hurt you. I'm doing my best.' There is a pause. 'I just wasn't sure whether you wanted him to see you, in here, like this.'

'The thing is, I want to see him.'

'OK, OK. I'll bring him next week.'

I look around. The nearest guard is staring out of the window. I reach across and take Mother's hand in mine.

'I'm so sorry about what's happened. I'll make it up to you one day, I promise.'

121

Emma

My patient, Emelie Rose Cirencester, is lying on my dental chair, eyes closed, hair scraped from her forehead in a white towelling hairband, Vivaldi's *Four Seasons* serenading her from my sound system. A lavender-scented candle burns on the windowsill as I massage her forehead with anaesthetic cream. Pummelling. Pressing. Telling her to relax.

'Lie there and rest for ten minutes while the cream starts to numb your skin,' I instruct.

Her lips curl at the edges. She is almost asleep. I step away, tiptoeing across my consulting room, not wanting to wake her. I go to the fridge, pull out the Botox and dilute it to the right strength with saline. By the time I return to the consulting area, brandishing the needle, she is fast asleep, Tania is standing by the chair watching her.

'Oh, to be so relaxed when you're about to be punctured by needles,' she says when she sees me.

'Let's wake her up. We've got a lot of patients to see. I need to crack on with the day.'

Tania leans across and shakes her right arm gently. 'Emelie, Emelie, it's time for your injections.'

Emelie stirs in the chair, stretching her arms above her head. She opens her cornflower-blue eyes and smiles. I hover over her face, needle ready.

'Please frown, as tightly as possible,' I instruct.

She pulls her neat little face into an evil grimace. Like an ugly gargoyle.

'OK, OK,' I laugh. 'That's enough.'

I inject the soft skin at the top of her nose, between her eyes. I press a tissue across the puncture marks and hold them down, to prevent bleeding.

'Are you all right?' I ask.

She nods her head. Now I'm ready to attack her frown lines. I stand above her, needle poised, planning where to inject. Her pale face contorts to the darker, stronger face of Jade. Jade's taunting eyes. Jade putting her head back, laughing. 'I believe you. Thousands wouldn't.' Her laugh turns to a frown. 'You shagged my husband, didn't you? I saw you. Heard you climax.'

Her face changes shape and becomes Alastair's. He is pushing his dark hair from his eyes with his right hand. 'I fucking hate you,' he spits.

I stand above him, brandishing my needle. Stomach constricting, anger rising. Pulling my arm back, lifting the needle back, ready to stab him. I close my eyes and open them. Alastair has disappeared. My patient, Emelie Rose Cirencester, is lying in front of me, face still, eyes closed again, humming to Vivaldi.

Breathe, breathe, hold steady. It is time to inject Emelie's forehead. I lean forward and puncture her skin, gently, so gently, just as I did three months ago. I press down on the pinpricks with a tissue.

'All done. Sleep on an extra pillow tonight.'

She pulls herself up to sitting, shaking her head sleepily.

'Thank you so much Emma,' she beams as she leaves.

Tania nips out to buy a sandwich for lunch. I sit on a stool by the window, hands trembling. I nearly harmed a patient because I was hallucinating about Jade and Alastair. I need to do something about this.

122

Alastair

Stephen is here, in the visitors' room, sitting opposite me. Wearing blue jeans, shiny blue trainers and his favourite red shirt. Eyes wide and staring. At the guards. At the other prisoners.

Mum has gone to buy coffee and chocolate: Mars Bars and Maltesers, Stephen's favourites. I know she has sidled off deliberately to make sure Stephen and I have some time alone together. I know her so well. She will be gone for as long as possible.

He leans across the table. 'Tell me about the villains you've met.'

'They're people, not villains to me. People I have to live with.' There is a pause. 'Some of them are quite kind, actually.' I lean back and cross my arms. 'And some of them are innocent, like me.'

'Innocent until proved guilty,' Stephen chants.

I nod my head. 'Exactly.'

'OK,' he says, turning to look at the chubby middle-aged man sitting at the next table, wearing a pink polo shirt and black jeans, waiting for his visitors to arrive, 'what's he done?'

'He robbed a bank. Held the cashier up at gunpoint, and stole her necklace too.'

'Wow.'

I shake my head. 'It's not wow, it's crime. Let me remind you of the important saying – crime doesn't pay.'

I sigh inside. Maybe I shouldn't have encouraged Mum to

bring him. Not if he is going to use my incarceration as an excuse to hero-worship criminals. Especially the man he has just pointed out, who has an anger management problem worse than mine.

'Who's that?' he asks, pointing at Fred.

Fred is sitting at the back of the room, wearing a tracksuit and flip-flops. Blond and angular. Keeping slim by running in the gym three times a week. Talking to his slim, curly-haired wife. Her twisted curls bubble around her face, falling past her shoulders. They make an attractive pair. Always chatting happily at visiting times. He seems so relaxed. He must truly believe his barrister is going to get him off the hook. He sees us watching him, looks across and waves.

'That's my cell-mate Fred.'

'What's he in for?'

'Murder.' I pause. 'His trial is coming up soon. He hopes his barrister will get him off. He's my best friend in here. He would do anything to help me.'

Stephen wriggles in his chair. 'Why are so many people who shouldn't be locked up, locked up in here?'

I shrug. 'I don't know. I guess no system is perfect.' I take a deep breath and continue. 'Grandma says someone's bullying you at school. Who is it?'

'No one.'

'No one. What sort of a name is that? Grandma says the person is called Francis Hudson. She says he's the ringleader.'

Stephen's face stiffens. He holds his head up, shoulders wide. 'He teases me a bit sometimes.'

I lean forward. 'What does he say? Does he talk about me?' I can see from his eyes that he wants to tell me, but he hesitates. I smile. 'Don't worry. Whatever it is I can handle it.' He takes a deep breath and moves his weight from buttock to buttock. 'Come on Stephen. Tell your dad. Isn't that what dads are for?'

Another deep breath. 'He says you're a low-life, and it's genetic. Low-life is my nickname at school now.'

My jaws clamp together, my fist clenches. Soon Francis Hudson will find out how a low-life operates. A low-life who has nothing left to lose.

123

Jade

Standing in our bedroom, determined to throw your belongings out now. Six months after your body has been burnt to bone-fragments and ash, and scattered among the roses at the crematorium, it is time for the last remnant of yours to leave this house. Having this constant reminder of you near me is too painful.

I have a roll of plastic bin bags waiting on the bed. Once I wrapped your dead body in plastic. Now I will wrap anything else of yours that is left. Ready to dump at the tip or a charity shop. Nearly all the dead people's clothing in this country goes to charity shops. Charity shops that smell of dust and death.

I open your wardrobe. Your hangers point in random directions. The sign of an untidy mind. Weird that you were so good at maths and earnt so much in the City. This wardrobe contains all your favourite clothes. Your smart designer jackets. Dior. Givenchy. Your Gant chinos, hanging in a row; cream, caramel and navy. Your Hugo Boss shirts. Pink stripes. Fancy collars. Your Crew Clothing polos. Tasteful shades of blue and cream. I pull them off the hangers, fold them and lay them in the bin bags.

Shoes: Loakes, Churches, Dubarry, Sebago, UGG slippers. Charity bin bags again.

I open the drawers where you kept your smalls. Underpants and socks, into the bin bag for the tip. Even the morbid people who hang around in charity shops like gannets, looking for the clothes of the dead, do not want their underwear.

Your bedside drawer: cufflinks, watch. Do I want to keep them? No. Why would I want mementoes of an unfaithful man?

I open the drawer beneath. Two letters. I pull them out and sit on the bed to look at them. Of all the letters that come and go in a lifetime, these are the only ones you've kept. A letter I sent you shortly after we first met. I remember writing it. I was so enamoured with you. You were so beautiful, weren't you, Tomas? I stand, tears rolling down my face. I howl, silently inside, and wipe my tears away. How could I have been so short-sighted as to fall in love with your looks? I can't bear to read the letter and remind myself of my stupidity.

And an unopened letter in a sealed envelope. Addressed to me. A letter you never gave me. Two hidden letters. One from me. One from you. I open yours to me, and read it.

Dear Jade,

I know you are unwell, prone to paranoia. I just wanted to write this letter in case things ever become so difficult between us that we cannot communicate because of your illness.

I love you Jade, always have. Always will. I have never been unfaithful to you. Not once. All the women you have accused me of sleeping with have been platonic friends. Jane Halliday, Sally Smith, Josephine Reynolds, Amber Trecastle. Friends I've worked with. People I've met dog walking. Just to pass the time of day with for a random chat. The woman you said I kissed at a party never even existed. And recently Emma Stockton. She has simply been treating my teeth. Root canal pain is devastating and she relieved me of it. That's all. You decided her looks were the sort of looks I like, and made up a story in your mind.

Jade, your looks are the ones I love.

I have always tolerated your moods, your accusations, because I know you can't help it and because in between times, no one is more fun, more intelligent.

I love you my darling Jade. Thank you for being my wife. I will love you forever.
Tomas

I know you didn't write it. The Stereotype copied your hand-writing and planted it here to try and fool me. To cover up your relationship. I know you were unfaithful, whatever this letter says.

124

Alastair

Fred and I are watching TV. The early evening news. Knife crime in London is rocketing. Frightening. I know there are knives in here. If you have money you can get hold of one. Money makes the world go round even when you are incarcerated. I zone out, stop focusing on the screen in front of me and think about my visit from Stephen.

My son with his wistful expression, grey eyes turning to stone as he tells me they call him low-life at school. Low-life. Because I'm in here. Because of you, Emma.

I know your name, Francis Hudson, you little prick. If my son is such a low-life, do you really think you will get away with this?

125

Jade

The wood burner is roaring like an engine. Flames as hot as flamenco dancers, twisting and gyrating. Intertwined – stretching, kicking, reaching. I open the door to the wood burner and throw in the letter. The one the Stereotype forged. Blue flames lick its edges. Dancing orange tongues engulf it. The paper turns black. It fragments into ash, and collapses to the base of the wood burner. Ash like your body. Is this how your body went in the oven at the crematorium, so many months ago? Black and fragmented? Collapsing to dust.

Next up, your passport. The flames diminish as they try to engulf the leather cover. I throw in a firelighter and the passport takes. Your birth certificate. It ignites and burns in seconds. And your death certificate. No proof you ever lived.

Your memory still hurts me. You damage me, even from the rose garden in the cemetery. When everything you touched or owned is gone, will I be able to forget about you? Will I stop talking to you? Stop feeling your arms around me?

126

Alastair

Visiting time. You are here, sitting in front of me. A vision of perfection, in your camel coat, and designer boots. With your carefully blow-dried hair. Gold jewellery that matches your skin tone.

'Why did you want to see me, Emma?' I ask, voice clipped.

You swallow and take a deep breath. 'Please stop phoning me.'

I smile a long, slow smile. 'I'm only being friendly.'

'Friendly? Harassing me, threatening me, calling me a bitch?'

Your usually sweet voice sounds whining and plaintive. Good. I must be getting to you.

'Why should I stop harassing you?' I hiss. 'Look at where I am. Look at what you've done to me.'

You shake your head. You bite your lip. 'I told you. It wasn't me. It was Jade.'

This Jade excuse is so pathetic I'm not sure whether it makes me want to cry or laugh.

'You didn't need to go along with it,' I snap. 'And how come Heather is your sudden alibi for the night of Tomas' murder? Is it three bitches working together?'

'Heather was harassing you, remember? She came to my house to try and find you. She was there that night.'

'How convenient.'

You raise your chin, your shoulders. 'If you carry on ringing me and being abusive I will make a formal complaint. You'll have your room searched. Your mobile will be removed. If you ring from a prison landline your calls will be monitored and abusive language will not be tolerated.'

Now, I cannot help it, I laugh. 'Listen to yourself, Miss Hoity-Toity.' I pause. 'I know you won't complain to the authorities. You won't want to do anything to draw attention to yourself after the flimsy way you have set me up.' I push my eyes into yours. 'Two can play stupid games, Emma.'

There is a pause. I sit looking at you as you clasp your hands together on your lap, clicking tastefully tapered nails against one another. Nails painted to match your shiny lip-gloss. I lean across and take your hand. I pull you towards me, inhaling your scent of musk and vanilla. The scent I once so loved, that now makes me want to vomit. The woman I once thought was so much kinder than Heather, who has turned to her and used her against me.

'Come on Emma, the onus is on you to make things right between us.'

Tears well in your eyes. 'I wish I could, Alastair. Why don't you try and see what will happen when you stop bullying me.'

I squeeze your wrist tight. Chinese-burn tight.

You wince in pain and pull your hand away. 'Hurting me won't help. It'll only make things worse for you,' you hiss.

Memories

Colin was good at Chinese burns, too. One snowy winter's day — sun streaking through bare trees — walking in the woods behind our house, Colin reached for my arm and twisted his hand around it until I yelped in pain.

'Why are you hurting me? What have I done to annoy you now?' I asked, tears streaming down my face.

'You're dawdling behind me. I want you to keep up.'

'Let go and I will.'

He released his grip. My bruises lasted past Christmas. I covered them with a false smile and a long-sleeved lacy dress.

127

Jade

The Stereotype's navy-blue Mercedes pulls up in her drive at the same time as mine. I hear her car door open as I slide out of my Porsche. I see her wearing her cashmere coat, and a fancy blow-dry, walking slowly towards her front door. Head heavy. Mouth in a line.

'Hey,' I shout over the hedge. 'What's up, Emma?'

Surprised to see me, her body jumps a little. She must have been in a daydream. 'Where've you been?' I ask.

'To see Alastair,' she shouts back.

I pad down my drive and onto hers, feet crunching across gravel. She turns to face me. I stand looking into her emerald eyes.

'Why did you go to see him?' I ask. 'I thought we were going to keep our distance.'

Her eyes darken. 'He keeps sending me unpleasant texts and messages. I went to tell him to stop.'

'And is he going to?'

She shakes her head. 'I don't think so.'

Unpleasant texts and messages? Visiting him to ask him to stop? Are you and Alastair about to stitch me up for the second time? I can't trust you further than I can throw you. I will watch you more closely from now on.

128

Alastair

Lockdown. Fred is glued to *Hollyoaks* this evening. I close my eyes, pretending I'm sleeping. But I'm not. I just want some privacy. I'm lying on my bunk, thinking. Always thinking. About you, Emma, and what you have done to me. About Stephen, the haunted look in his eyes when he came to visit me. About my mother, holding his hand, hobbling into the visiting area.

'Don't worry, I'll look after him,' she promised when I was first charged.

She shouldn't have needed to do that. It should have been you and me, Emma.

The image of your face rotates in front of me. Your blonde hair soft as silk. Your deep-green eyes. Your little nose, so perfectly shaped. The tasteful clothes you were wearing when you came to visit me. Your designer boots. Your camel coat. You always dress perfectly, don't you? Your smile moves towards me, your soft, sweet lips moving to kiss me. Then your lips change shape. They begin to snarl. Your hair begins to spread out around your head, thinner and thinner strands, spinning into a spider's web. I reach out to touch it. My hand is stuck. My body is sucked in. Surrounded by threads. Threads that tighten around me. I'm curled into a ball. The threads are squashing me. Trying to kill me. I begin to scream.

Fred is leaning over me, shaking me. 'Stop it, mate.'

I cling on to him, and even though the scream is still in my head, no sound comes out. 'Calm down. Calm down. Take a breath,' he says.

Calm down. Calm down. Take a breath. The scream is diminishing.

'I need you to help me sort things out,' I beg.

129

Jade

One last check around my house to make sure none of your possessions are here to remind me of you. To hurt me with your memory. I'm pretty sure everything has gone. I have even poured your remaining aftershave down the sink and taken the empty bottles to the bottle bank.

Just going through your drawers, one last time. The drawer in your bedside table. A piece of paper sticks out past the lining. I pull it gently. A photograph. Our wedding day. I am wearing a floaty white dress, and a headdress of white roses. You are resplendent in top and tails. Did you cherish this photograph?

Hands trembling, I take it downstairs. One last look at our young faces, before you broke my heart. I open the door to the wood burner. I fling it in. It melts and bends in the heat. Then the flames take, and cut across our images.

You and I are over, Tomas. Once and for all.

Memories

A crisp spring day. Trying to keep away from Colin. In my garden planting aconite. Acontium carmichaelii. Arendsii kelmscott. Royal flush. Planting in the large south-facing border I had dug out behind the tennis court, breath condensing in the air as I worked.

Working in the garden relaxed and soothed me. Apart from my work, gardening had become my main interest. Aconite, aka monkshood, aka wolfsbane, was my favourite plant. The medieval soulmate of vagabonds and witches.

130

Alastair

Visiting day again. That tinge of excitement in my toes, in my stomach. A tingling, a vibration when I know that Stephen and Mother are coming. The buzzer goes. Fred smiles his craggy smile at me as the door opens and we rush to take our seats. His wife arrives and his face lightens.

They hug, and as they hug I envy them. My hatred for Emma rises up inside me again.

I watch the door as the visitors move through it. Mothers. Wives. Children. Faces all brushed with a strange combination of anticipation and sadness. Mother and Stephen are here, standing in the entrance, looking across at me.

They walk towards me. I hug Stephen first, then Mother. Then Stephen again. Missing physical contact is one of the worst things about being in here. Touching my mother, my son, is so precious I feel like weeping. I force my body to pull away. We sit down.

'How's it going?' I ask.

They exchange glances.

'What's up?' I ask.

'There's been an incident at school.'

I lean across the table, closer to Stephen, to listen.

'It's Francis Hudson,' Stephen explains. 'He's been badly beaten up. The police were called. They questioned everyone in our class. Asked us if we knew anything about it.'

'What happened to him?' I ask, as if I don't know.

Stephen's eyes widen. 'He was walking home from school, when a man jumped out from behind a tree and punched him so hard he fell to the ground.' There is a pause. 'He broke his nose.' A shake of the head. 'He's had to have an operation to straighten it.'

Mother grimaces. 'It was awful. Such a frightening thing to happen to a young child. The whole school is in shock. The head is advising children not to walk home without an adult.'

I smile inside. 'I suppose if someone is always mean like him though, they're asking for trouble. Imagine how many people must despise a little shit like that.'

'People have been very upset for him.' There is a pause. 'Even me,' Stephen says.

'Did he recognise the attacker? Has he been able to assist the police?'

'Not much. He said the guy was tall. But he was wearing a black balaclava, so he couldn't say anything about hair and face.'

I sit shaking my head.

'Anyway, he's back in school now. I took him a cake that Grandma had baked, to cheer him up. He smiled and said thank you and forgot to call me low-life.'

I smile inside. A little bit of violence seems to have worked.

131

Emma

A wad of post thumps through the letter box and lands on the hall mat. I step into the hallway and bend to pick it up. The usual. Adverts for local estate agents. For gardeners. For cleaners. A free glossy magazine – adverts again, no real articles. No substance. My credit card bill. My bank statement. And one more thing. A jiffy bag. I inhale sharply when I see it has prison franking and my address written in your handwriting, Alastair.

I step into the kitchen, and sit down. I rip the bag open. It contains a series of photographs of us, together. Walking along the river. Drinking at the Angel. Our day out at Oxford. With Stephen the weekend he came to stay: eating pizza, eating eggy bread, playing cricket. An envelope with my name on it is tucked between the photographs. I open it and pull out a note.

How could you, you bitch?

132

Alastair

Mum is here, without Stephen. He is on a school trip today to the science museum. I took him there last year. His favourite part was the friction slides in the Forces Zone. He spent almost the whole afternoon sliding down them. I wish I was there with him again. Hearing his laughter. Buying him pizza and ice cream.

I'm holding Mum's warmth against me as I hug her. As I inhale her scent of lilies. Reluctantly I let her go. We sit down at opposite sides of the grey plastic table. She looks at me with dark worried eyes. The lines on her face have deepened since I last saw her. Darker panda bags have formed beneath her eyes. It is getting closer to my trial and I know she won't be sleeping. After Dad died she had to go to a sleep clinic. It took months and months to sort her problems out.

She leans across the grey plastic table to take my hand.

'No touching,' a guard barks through his microphone. The guard with the widest chest; nicknamed 'The Wardrobe'. There is a rumour going around the prison that he weighs twenty stone.

Our limbs jump apart.

'First things first,' she says. 'The kids at school have stopped calling Stephen a low-life, since the mugging. I wouldn't have wished for such an awful thing to have happened to that boy, but . . .' She trails off and smiles. A slow sad smile. 'How are you dear?' she asks.

I daren't tell her the only thing that keeps me going is retribution. Against arrogant pricks like Francis Hudson. Against Emma. She would disapprove so strongly if she knew.

I look into her eyes and try to smile, but my lips don't move. 'I'm OK.' I pause. 'Bearing up.'

'You're low. I can tell from your voice.' She leans forward. 'Tell a warden. Try and get some help.'

'I'm fine.'

Her eyes narrow. 'Are you eating?'

'Yes.'

A short, clipped smile. 'That's a good sign.'

'Is it?'

'Yes. People who are *really* low don't even want to eat.'

I shake my head, unsure as to when my mother became an expert on depression. 'Look, I'm not depressed, Mother.'

'Is anyone bullying you?' she continues.

'No. No one is bullying me. Fred is protecting me. He is well respected both inside and outside this prison.'

She folds her arms over her ample bosom. 'Is your barrister any good?'

'Are we playing twenty questions?'

'Don't be sarcastic – just tell me, is your barrister any use?'

I shrug. 'How do I know? I've got no choice but to trust him. He's the lawyer, the QC I was allocated. He can't be that bad, he's a Silk.'

'When you explain what happened to the court the jury will believe you.'

My lips tighten. 'I wish I could share your optimism. My brief thinks it's fifty–fifty.'

My brief, with his truncated vowels and nasal hair, who came to see me last week and stayed ten minutes. I'm almost in tears looking at my mother, brandishing her over-cheery smile, and false optimism. Wearing the ruby-red woollen dress I bought her for her birthday. How could life take me away from her

313

when we need each other so much? Anger solidifies in my heart, in my stomach, when I remember it isn't life that has done this to us, it is you, Emma. My fingers tighten as I think of you. As I imagine the satisfaction I would have if I could crush your flesh with my fist again. Did you enjoy looking at the photographs I sent you?

I lean towards my mother. 'I need you to do me a favour.'

Her eyes soften. 'Anything to help, Alastair.'

'I need you to pay four thousand pounds into a bank account. I owe someone some money.' I fumble in my pocket and pull out a piece of paper. I hand it to her. 'Here's the account number and the sort code.'

She frowns. 'Have you got yourself into a mess, Alastair?'

'No, Mother. Don't ask questions. Just do it please.'

The buzzer goes. She waves the paper at me and nods her head as she leaves. I pull my body up from the plastic chair and join the throng of prisoners walking back to their cells. Doors locking behind us. Doors and locks and revenge. That is all my life is now.

133

Jade

I park my Porsche at the crematorium, slip out and slam the door. A dull November day, rain hovering in the atmosphere waiting to fall, making the air feel damp. A swathe of mourners skulk in the car park, waiting to enter a chapel and pay their last respects. A constant flow of grief and pain moving through these buildings. You know what they say: nothing is certain except death and taxes.

I march towards the memorial rose garden armed with my map, a spade hidden in my rucksack. I enter through the arched bower, and concentric circles of rose beds interspersed with paving and benches open up before me. A peppering of people are paying their respects. A middle-aged couple, walking hand in hand, heads bent. A young woman sitting on a bench in the middle, glaring into the distance.

I whip out my map and stare at it; confused. I hold it up and turn it around, trying to get my bearings. Suddenly it pushes into my perspective and I understand where your bush is. Pitch A23. I walk towards your memorial rose, Tomas. The one I paid for to commemorate your life. I stand in front of it and think of you. I picture you lying naked next to the Stereotype. Kissing her. I picture your blood pooling beneath the cling film when I unwrapped it from your head. It stinks as I rub it across my fingers. As I put it in my mouth, taste its salt and cry.

The image of your dead body fades and I am back standing

in front of your rose bush. It is young, and thin and spiky. Not a great specimen. When it flowered it was bright yellow. The colour of cowardice. Chosen specially for you.

I look around. The couple are still walking, heads down. The young woman is still staring into space. I detach my rucksack, pull out a trowel and dig the rose out as quickly as I can. Thorns pricking into my hand as I work. I shove it in a plastic bag and struggle against it to force it into my backpack.

I march towards the car park, wanting to get away from here as quickly as possible. Footsteps behind me fall in synch with mine. A tap on the shoulder. I turn around. A man with sandy hair and freckles, wearing a dog collar and a kind expression. A minister of a Christian church.

'Did I see you remove a bush from the rose garden?' he asks.

I screw my eyes up, as if I'm about to cry. 'It's six months since my husband died.' I look at the ground and make my lips quiver. 'I'm missing him so much I decided I would plant his memorial rose in my own garden, near the kitchen window so that I could look at it every day.'

His soft hazel eyes grow softer. He smiles. 'I see. Well technically you should have informed the crematorium staff. But I won't tell if you won't.'

'Thanks.' I smile back.

I turn away from him and continue walking to my car.

Back home, I build a bonfire with all the fallen twigs and branches from the garden. Your rose, Tomas, is the centre of my funeral pyre. I rejoice as I light it. The flames from the fire twist and dance. Now your body, all your possessions, and your memorial rose, are well and truly gone, I can pay more attention to your bint.

134

Emma

Wednesday evening. The Angel on the Bridge. My favourite pub. Back in my old routine, sitting in the corner with Andrea who is drinking a double gin and tonic. Andrea, smart in her mock Chanel suit – giant collar, square shape, flamboyant buttons. I think she is overdoing it a bit with her grooming at the moment. She has acquired that modern look. Artificial eyebrows, artificial talons so long she has to pick up her drink carefully. An orange glow from fake tan. But as she pads to the toilet and back, she turns heads, so what do I know?

'How's your love life?' she asks.

I splutter into my white wine. 'It's stalled right now.' Andrea sits, right shoe-horn eyebrow slightly raised, waiting for me to continue. 'I mean, I'm not interested in a relationship at the moment after my relationship with Colin, and this debacle with Alastair. It has been such a shock that he was charged with Tomas' murder.' I take a large gulp of wine. 'What about your love life?' I ask. Looking at her extravagant fingernails, wondering how she manages to caress someone in bed.

'I'm still braving Tinder,' she announces. 'I've got a date tomorrow night. Meeting someone who looks quite hot, so I'm hopeful.'

'I use Tinder when I'm in the mood for dating. I met Colin and Alastair on it.' I shrug my shoulders. 'But I'm sorting my life out right now. I don't want any distractions.'

She taps her talons on the table. 'What are you doing in your leisure time exactly?'

I shake my head. 'Not much. I'm just clearing my mind at the moment.'

Andrea leans towards me and puts her hand on my arm. 'It must have been so difficult for you to go to prison unnecessarily and then to find out Alastair was guilty.'

I put my hand on hers. 'It was.' I pause. I bite my lip. 'Maybe when the trial is over I'll date again. I mean, I miss having a man around. I get lonely.'

Andrea raises her gin and tonic into the air. 'Let's drink to new relationships.' We clink glasses. I take a sip and drain mine. 'Another one?' she asks.

'Yes please.'

After our drinks I meander over the bridge, and turn left to walk along the footpath by the river. Darkness presses against me, enveloping me in privacy. The moon is just a sliver. I stop by the riverbank to look up at the stars dappling the sky.

Breath on my neck. Someone is behind me. I try to turn, but cannot. An arm tightens across my chest, pulling me back against a hard torso. A cord is tightening around my neck, cutting through my skin. I'm choking, spluttering. I bend forwards. The cord slices further into me. I feel light-headed. I cannot see. I push through the pain and bend further. The cord constricts again. I bend down far enough to grab my attacker's knee. I pull his leg between mine. He falls over and the cord loosens. I turn around. A large man wearing black jeans, a black jumper and a balaclava is lying on his back on the ground in front of me.

I kick him in the groin and run, panic bubbling inside. Pushing my body, every tissue, every sinew. Gasping for air. Gasping for breath. I look back. He is standing up. He is running towards me. I turn. I run back towards him. Faster. Faster. You bastard, I think. No man is hurting me again and getting away with it.

I run straight into him. I headbutt him in the nose. Bones crack. Blood spurts. He staggers backwards. I pull my leg back and throw my foot forward to kick him in the groin again. He bends in pain. I pick up a rock from the path and bash him on the head. He sinks to the ground.

Heart thumping, I run again. Back to my house. I fumble in my handbag for my keys. Sighing with relief when I find them. Turning the key so quickly I bump my hand on the doorframe. Inside the hallway, double locking the door. I slump to the ground and wait for my heart to slow.

When my body has calmed, I close all the blinds and curtains. I double lock the doors. When everything is secure I throw my coat and shoes off and pour myself a whisky. In my drawing room, sinking into the sofa, sipping my Chivas Regal, I determine that I do not want to draw attention to myself. I will not call the police. I will sort this out alone.

135

Jade

The Stereotype is home later than usual on a Wednesday night. What has she been up to? Where has she been? Has she been plotting against me? Trying to get me incarcerated again? I hear her running up the drive. I open my window and put my head out to get a good look at her. She is panting heavily. Her hair and clothes are dishevelled. Has she had a sexual rendezvous on the towpath? Probably, knowing her sexual appetite. Her penchant for men. I need to keep more of an eye on her. I don't want anyone else to be hurt like me. She's a marriage wrecker who needs containing.

136

Emma

It's late when I arrive home from work on Friday night. Darkness is burying my garden like a shroud. I snap on the house and garden lights from inside the car, using a control on my phone. The world lights up around me. I step out of the car, press the key fob to lock it and slowly walk towards the door, all senses enhanced. Listening. Watching. On tiptoe, ready to pounce if I'm attacked. I know the thug was here. I saw him on the doorbell app on my phone, this morning, when I had just arrived at work. My phone has all the gadgets. He spoke into the answer machine, pretending he had a delivery for me. But I could see him. No parcel. No van. Putting on a balaclava. I couldn't deal with him then. I had to stay at work. If he is still here I will deal with him now.

I unlock the door, pull it open and immediately know something is wrong. The doors of the hallway dresser have been pulled open. The lamp that usually sits on top of it has smashed across the hall floor. Casper appears from nowhere, pressing his head and back against my legs, vibrating as he purrs. I bend down and stroke his head. At least he seems to be all right.

Heart sinking, I walk around the house, Casper following me. Into the kitchen. My herb and spice rack has been ripped off the wall, tearing the wallpaper behind it. Herbs, spices and broken glass scattered across my stone floor. Glass from the spice jars pricking the rug. Smashed wine glasses. Smashed mugs and plates. Everything that was in the dishwasher pulled out and destroyed.

Bracing myself, I step out of the kitchen and enter the dining room. The words 'Beware Bitch' are scratched across my mahogany table. *Beware bitch.* I tremble inside. Two of my antique dining chairs have been smashed to smithereens. That hurts. They were hard to find and very expensive. My curtains have been pulled off their rails. So childish. So pointless.

The drawing room stinks of urine. He has peed across my Axminster carpet. The ornaments from the mantlepiece have been swept off and broken. My paintings are slashed. I hardly dare go upstairs but I force myself.

The guest rooms are clear. I take a deep breath and enter the master bedroom. All my clothes have been flung from the wardrobe onto the bedroom floor. My favourite blue silk dress lies at the top of the pile. I pick it up to inspect it. Ripped from neckline to hemline. My Chanel perfumes are empty. My blushers, lipsticks and eyeshadows trampled across the floor.

Alastair Brown, you must have paid the thug to do this. This is war.

Memories

Back to my kitchen in Esher. My blue and white kitchen with patterned blue and white Amtico flooring. Preparing the lamb rogan josh that Colin had requested, or rather demanded, before we went to bed the previous night. Frying the chillies, onions, garlic, ginger and meat. Adding the fresh tomatoes, dried spices and fresh coriander. He arrived home. I heard the click of his key in the door. My stomach tightened. Footsteps padded along the hallway.

He stood behind me.

'Good evening.'

I turned around slowly.

He pulled me towards him and kissed me, pushing his tongue into my mouth. He tasted of beer. He must have been for a drink before he came home from work. He pressed my body against the counter.

'I'm cooking, Colin. The curry you asked for.'

'I'm hungry for something else right now, my beautiful girl.'

137

Alastair

'The trial is set for next month. I've been going through the papers in detail,' my brief Crispin Ward QC announces, tapping his papers on the table. 'And I've got a few comments.'

My heart hammers in my chest. I lean forward to listen.

'We still need to do some work to try and find out where you were on the night Tomas was murdered. I know you can't remember. But it would be extremely beneficial if we could find out.'

'You could ask my mother. My colleagues.'

'What about receipts? Bank statements?' My solicitor, Jane Perkins asks. 'They might jog your memory.'

'They're all at home with my mum.' Almost in tears, I shake my head. 'I admit I doctored the evidence to free Emma, but I can assure you, I did not do this. I'm sure Jade and Emma got together to set me up.'

Crispin Ward QC leans back in his chair and folds his arms. 'It's all so complicated. The DNA. The re-analysis. Two possible murder weapons.'

He looks across the meeting room table at me.

'You mentioned Emma Stockton has asked to visit you again,' he continues. 'I think the best thing you can do is to beg her to refuse to give evidence.'

'Would that help at this late stage?'

'Yes. As you know, Emma has told the police, and is willing

to testify in court, that you admitted to the murder. If she refuses to testify there will be no evidence of your admission. It could get you off the hook. The supposed murder weapon was the second one found and we have a strong argument that it was planted. Why would someone as forensically knowledge-able as you leave the murder weapon in his boot splattered with DNA evidence?' There is a pause. 'So you see, Emma could make a big difference, even at this late stage. She's pivotal to your case.'

138

Emma

I'm at my surgery, after a long morning treating patients. A difficult wisdom tooth extraction today that I barely had the strength for. A patient who had refused to have it removed in hospital as she was terrified of general anaesthesia. It took me an hour and a half to crack it out under local. I almost chipped some bone off her jaw. I should never have said yes.

I have just closed up shop and given Andrea and Tania the afternoon off. I pad to the fridge and open the door. I pull out a large vial of Botox. Botox, a drug that no autopsy will be looking for. No one will expect this. I calculate the dose I need, and mix it with sterile saline. Then I decant it into a tapered plastic bottle. A plastic bottle whose shape has been very carefully considered. A plastic bottle I wrap in cling film and coat with lubricant.

I lie on my dentist's chair, pull off my black lace knickers, and open my legs. Slowly, carefully, I push the bottle up into my vagina. I close my legs and pull up my knickers. This is the way to do it. This is the way to smuggle into Her Majesty's Prisons.

139

Alastair

I'm sitting next to Fred in the canteen at lunchtime, eating bangers and mash. Mash that tastes like wallpaper glue. Sausages that smell of chicory.

'Are you all right?' Fred asks.

'No. My brief says my only hope is to beg Emma to refuse to give evidence, when she comes to visit me this afternoon. Not that there will be much chance of her wanting to help me. I expect she's guessed I had something to do with her being mugged, and the damage to her house.'

'Coming to visit you this afternoon? What's she up to now?' he asks as he lifts some wallpaper glue to his mouth.

I shrug my shoulders. 'I don't know. But I want to find out. As I said, my brief seems to think it might be a good idea to speak to her, to try and convince her not to give evidence.'

'He's deluded.' There is a pause. 'You need to be careful; she's dangerous. My guy got beaten up by her. And he's quite an expert. Never failed to do a job for me before.' He pours himself a glass of water and tosses it back.

'I know she can be a bit of a ballbreaker, but I've decided to take my brief's advice. Wait until I give the word before you carry on.'

140

Emma

I arrive at the prison and sling my car into the first parking space I see. Walking to the prison entrance feeling as if bricks of lead are pushing on my undercarriage. Into the entrance. Queuing for my bag and coat to be X-rayed. Holding my upper body back, so that I look relaxed. My bag and coat are through their check. I step into the body scanner. Feet apart. Arms raised. The machine rotates and clicks. An Amazonian female guard asks me to step to the side. She pats me down. She waves a metal stick near my groin and allows it to hover, inside my upper thigh.

Just as my heart rate is creeping up and I'm beginning to panic, 'Fine go through,' she snaps.

I grab my bag and coat, and soldier on into the entrance of the prison. I look at my watch. Half an hour to visiting time. I have mistimed this. Every second is excruciating. Half an hour seems like a lifetime. I need to sit and relax.

I sit on a plastic chair in the waiting area, close my eyes and concentrate on my breathing. Inhale. Exhale. Breathe. Breathe. Imagining I'm on my back, floating in the sea. The water is lapping my body, soothing me. I hear footsteps moving across the hard flooring. Other people are beginning to arrive. I open my eyes and begin to watch them to pass the time. A young woman wearing blue jeans and a black leather jacket. Her hair needs combing. Her eyes dart. Her nails are bitten to the quick. Is she visiting her father?

Her brother? Her lover? The anxiety in her eyes makes me guess it is her lover. A middle-aged couple in tracksuits with grey hair and pot bellies. Holding hands. Staring into the distance. Old enough to be visiting an offspring. An offspring I guess they didn't bring up properly. A man with razor-blade cheekbones, emblazoned with tattoos. He looks moody and edgy.

I look at my watch. Five minutes to go. I stand up. I straighten my back. Head high, I walk across the room, to the vending machine, looking for the CCTV cameras. There is one directly above me. That's fine. It isn't illegal to buy a remand prisoner chocolate and a bottle of Diet Pepsi. I fumble for change. I fumble to press for Diet Pepsi and Cadbury's Fruit and Nut; Alastair's favourite bar. I slip the chocolate and Pepsi into my handbag and drag myself to the toilet.

No cameras in the toilet. A sigh of relief. I let myself into a cubicle and lock the door. I open the Pepsi and pour half of it down the loo. My fingers shake as I pull my knickers down and sit on the toilet seat. Breathing deeply, I retrieve the plastic bottle I've smuggled. Slowly, carefully, I pour the contents of the tapered plastic bottle into the Pepsi, and screw the lid up tightly. I put the Pepsi in my handbag, with the chocolate. Then I push the bottle back inside me. I smile to myself. Nearly over. No external evidence if I get stopped.

Out of the cubicle. Washing my hands. Walking carefully back to the bench where I was sitting. Not long now.

The buzzer sounds. Time to go in. I stand up and walk into the visiting room, biting my lip to distract myself. You are sitting at a table in the middle looking out for me. Thinner. Paler. Hair too short for your usual look. I sit at the table, opposite you.

'To what do I owe this pleasure, Emma,' you ask, voice clipped.

'I wanted to see you. Before the trial.'

'Emma. We need to call a truce. I need to ask you not to give evidence. In return I promise to stop harassing you and calling you a bitch.'

You look around to check the guards are looking the other way, and then reach across and take my hand in yours.

'Please Emma. We were close once. I need to get out of here to look after Stephen.'

You are almost in tears.

'Yep. Well, I have been thinking about it. I came to tell you I *have* decided not to give evidence against you. I've taken legal advice. If they subpoena me I'll just change my story. Tell them the truth: that Jade forced me to lie.'

Your eyes soften. You smile. 'Thank you, Emma.'

'I've brought you some Pepsi and some chocolate, as a peace offering,' I say, pulling them out of my bag and putting them on the table in front of you.

'Thanks.'

You open the Pepsi, and slug it back. A quarter of the bottle is gone.

'But I'm confused. Why did you do it in the first place, Emma?' you ask. 'It's been hell for me.'

'I know. I'm sorry.' I shake my head. 'We've been through this. How many times do I have to tell you? It's all because of Jade.'

My heart thumps as I watch you. You haven't had any more Pepsi. You open the chocolate wrapper and break off a piece. You lift it to your mouth. Still no more interest in the Pepsi. Panic rises inside me. I breathe deeply to suppress it. Then you slowly reach across towards the bottle, lift it to your lips, put your head back and down it in one. You put the bottle on the table.

'That was nice. Thanks.'

You eat the rest of the chocolate. Your eyes darken. 'What about your witness statements? What you said to the police. You said you were having an affair with Tomas and I was jealous. Giving me a motive. It was you who said that to the police, not Jade.'

'How many times do I have to tell you? She made me, Alastair. Threatened me. She said she'd kill us both if I didn't. She sent letters, messages on my phone. Someone to frighten me. A man who attacked me when I arrived at work,' I lie.

You push your eyes into mine. 'Did you have an affair with him?'

'No. It was all a lie that Jade made me make up.' I bite my lower lip. 'I'm still scared, Alastair. Someone's been trying to frighten me. Roughing me up. I was attacked on the towpath. But I miss you. I still love you Alastair. I've decided to take the risk.'

You take my hands in yours and look at me as if you believe me. The buzzer sounds. 'Goodbye Alastair.' I reach across and kiss you hard on the lips. 'This nightmare will end for you soon. I'll make sure of that.'

'Goodbye Emma, my love.'

I take the empty Pepsi bottle and I walk out of the prison. Past the X-ray machines. Past the guards. Longing to pull the container from my body. Longing to get back home.

141

Alastair

I have eaten my evening meal without bumping into Fred. Ignoring the men I was sitting near, not in the mood to talk to them. The food was worse than ever; an omelette with the consistency of plastic foam. I feel a bit sick. It must be the egg. I move through corridors towards my cell for lockdown, pushing nausea away.

I've been dwelling on everything you told me. Is it true? Did Jade force you to set me up? How did she do that from prison? My stomach tightens. I have been harming you and threatening you from in here. Anything seems possible while I'm incarcerated, except buying my freedom. Do I love you? Do I hate you? There is a fine line between love and hate. I have felt both towards you, Emma, my darling, my love. It is a tribute to how much you have meant to me. And now I need to decide whether to love you or kill you. Whether to trust you. Whether to call off the hit.

I stumble back into my cell. Love you or kill you? Fred is here. Sitting in front of the TV, about to switch it on. I feel a little strange, woozy and light-headed. But I know I love you, Emma.

'How did it go?' he asks.

Love not hate. Trust and love.

'You need to call off the hit. She's helping me. She says she still loves me.'

'Are you sure, mate?'

'Call off the hit.'

I see two of him. Everything is blurring. I'm having to concentrate to breathe.

Somewhere through the mist in my head, I see two Freds using their thumbs to send a text. I want to thank him for stopping the hit, but I can't speak. I need the toilet. I need to get to the bathroom.

Into the bathroom. Closing the door. My face is losing feeling. I must be having a stroke. I try to shout for help, but my lips won't move. I collapse on the floor, gasping for air, wheezing, grunting. The world turns grey and bleeds slowly into black.

142

Emma

DS Miranda Jupiter stands in front of me on my doorstep.

'Can I come in?' she asks.

Heart pounding, I open the door wide, and nod my head. 'Of course. Come into the drawing room.'

She follows me and we sit in the armchairs either side of my white marble fireplace. Her face is like stone. She leans forward.

'Alastair Brown died this morning.'

A sharp intake of breath. 'What? How?' I ask.

She crosses her legs. 'The doctors aren't sure what was wrong. His body closed down. He stopped breathing. There'll be an autopsy to find out.'

I shake my head. 'That's dreadful. I'm so sorry he has died. His poor family.'

'I want to offer you my condolences. The whole situation is awful for you. And I can't tell you how much it upsets my colleagues and me when someone dies in custody.' She pauses. She shakes her head sadly. 'I'm so very sorry for you, especially as you were in a relationship with him, before you suspected he'd committed murder. It can't be easy to lose him.' Her dark eyes harden. 'Did you notice anything unusual about him when you saw him, just before he became ill?'

'He seemed fine.' I pause. 'So fine, it's hard to believe what's happened.'

'Well everyone is very shocked, including his cell-mate.'

I put my head in my hands, and heave my shoulders. After a while I lift my head. Large almond-shaped eyes are watching me.

DS Miranda Jupiter stands up. 'Obviously, it all needs to be investigated carefully. Post mortem, coroner's inquest; any death in prison attracts the works.' She pauses and sighs. 'But again, so very sorry for your loss,' she says as she steps towards the door to leave.

143

Jade

Death follows you around, Emma. Do you kill everyone you touch?

Memories

Looking back. Back to the beautiful garden, in the house in Esher I shared with my husband, Colin. A border of monks-hood, purple- and cream-hooded flowers, tumbling and trumpeting with their brightly coloured lips. Back picking them on a hot summer evening; an August heatwave, solid heat pressing against my skin. Standing in the kitchen, grinding up the roots and stems with my pestle and mortar. Spending hours cooking lamb rogan josh, Colin's favourite curry. Mixing monkshood into half of it, and chopping in a few extra chillies. Colin always liked his curry extra hot. Preparing homemade naan bread, okra and pilau rice.

A key rattled in the front door lock and he was home, standing in front of me, smartly dressed in grey flannel trousers and a blue blazer. A flamboyant yellow tie. He had been lecturing on dental implants at the university. He moved towards me and kissed me. Holding my arms so tightly I feared he would bruise me. I forced myself to kiss him back.

'Supper's ready. Are you hungry? It's curry night.'

I laid the kitchen table. He sat watching me and drinking beer. I served the food, carefully, from two separate casserole dishes. We didn't converse. We rarely did back then. I didn't want to say anything to displease him. He flicked the remote at the TV and a documentary about submarines lit up the screen. I picked at my food. He sat watching TV, relishing his curry, using the end of the naan bread to wipe his plate clean.

'That was delicious, thank you.'

I cleared the table, grinding the remains of the curry down the waste disposal. Starting the dishwasher. Colin helped himself to another beer and we moved from the kitchen to the informal sitting room. We sat glued to the TV.

At the end of the evening, just as we were about to go up to bed, he rushed to the downstairs cloakroom, feeling sick. I hovered by the door, listening.

'Is there anything I can do to help?' I asked as I heard him retch.

'Leave me alone. Go away.'

I sat by the door, waiting. Waiting as he repeatedly vomited. At last he fumbled with the lock. The door opened. He tumbled through the doorway and lay on the carpet in front of me, clutching his stomach. Groaning in pain as I checked his pulse. So weak I could hardly feel it. I dialled 999 to request an ambulance. His breathing was laboured. He vomited again. More and more laboured. He was struggling to live.

The paramedics arrived, accompanied by a wailing siren and flashing lights. They lifted him onto a stretcher and carried him into the ambulance. I followed the ambulance to the hospital. By the time I arrived at the hospital he was dead.

144

Emma

Miranda Jupiter's words pierce into my head. *Obviously, it all needs to be investigated carefully. Post mortem, coroner's inquest. So very sorry for your loss.*

The words run together and contort into a chorus of sound bites. They echo in my mind and stop me sleeping. I toss and turn. I throw my duvet off because I'm too hot, and then I shiver. I pull it back over me and find myself lying in a lake of sweat. I get up to go to the toilet and as I stand up I feel sweat pooling between my breasts. In the bathroom I dry myself with a hand towel. I look at my watch. Four a.m.

I lie on my side. My foot develops cramp. I lie on my stomach, my breasts are crushed. I roll onto my back and press my back into the mattress to relieve the tension in it. I see Alastair's pleading eyes as he asked me to help him. I see him drinking the Pepsi. I imagine him going back to his cell and collapsing. Will death by respiratory failure seem natural enough?

With Colin it was easy. The coroner's report said he died of multiple organ failure due to a virus. No one ever questioned a thing. Can I get away with it again?

145

Jade

I'm watching you, Emma, every day. All you ever do is drive to work, spend the day at your surgery and drive home again. On Wednesday evenings you have a drink with your receptionist Andrea, at the Angel on the Bridge. One Wednesday night you were dishevelled and late, but that isn't much for a whore like you. What are you up to, Emma? Is this the calm before the storm?

I'm wading through a nightmare. Being shouted at by Miranda Jupiter, about to jump off a high building. She is on the ground below with a loudhailer.

'The post mortem results show you did it. We're coming to arrest you. You're going to jail.' There is a pause. 'You poisoned him, didn't you?' *Didn't you? Didn't you?*

I wake up, trembling. My bedroom comes into focus. My cream and yellow curtains. My bedroom suite. Casper is lying on top of me, purring. My mind comes into focus. It is the coroner's inquest today.

Why does the coroner want to interview me? I have been waking up at 4 a.m. every morning for weeks, mind on fire, not able to drop back to sleep. I look at my watch. It's 5 a.m. I've had a lie-in. I drag my permanently exhausted body out of bed and run a bath. Hot water and lavender oil to help me relax.

I slide into the bath. The hot water caresses my body and makes me feel comfortable. I hear a mew. Casper jumps onto the side of the bath, and stretches his right paw into the water. He pats it and purrs. His loud buzzing purr. I lean my neck back onto the side of the bath and sleep comes now.

I wake up. The bathwater is cold. Casper is still by my side sleeping and purring on the lip of the tub. My fingers are pink and crinkly. I pull myself out of the water and dry myself. I pull the plug out and the water moans as it drains. What will the coroner ask me? Will the coroner's decision lead to a criminal trial?

I dress carefully. Smart but subtle. Unostentatious designer clothes. Expensive but no one will guess how expensive. A black suit, the skirt well below the knee, with a crisp white blouse. Shiny black heels.

I drive to Oxford and park in the centre, at the back of St John's College. My stomach twists as I remember the day out we had here. Our walk along the river. Lunch at The Perch. Squeezing your hand, saying, *This is what we need, isn't it? A bit more fun. A bit more time out.*

Before you hurt me, Alastair. Before I hurt you back.

I walk into The Randolph Hotel. Heather is here, sitting in the Morse Bar, drinking coffee as she waits for me. She is dressed smartly for once, in a black dress with gold buttons. An office look suitable for a coroner's inquest, no doubt not designer like mine, but at least she's made an effort for a change. Hair blow-dried. Make-up carefully applied. As soon as she sees me she waves and smiles.

'How are you feeling?' she asks, as I approach.

'Nervous,' I reply as I sit down next to her. 'Worried as to why I've been called as a witness.'

'It'll be because you were one of the last people to see him alive.'

'Is that supposed to reassure me?'

She smiles. 'Don't be paranoid.' There's a pause. 'Should I order you a coffee from the bar?' she asks.

I look at my watch. 'No thanks. We haven't much time. I'll just wait while you finish yours.' I take a deep breath. 'Are you sorry he's dead?' I ask.

Silence lies awkwardly between us as Heather sips her drink.

After a while, she replies, 'I'm trying to be. I mean, he was the father of my child.'

'How's it going?'

'I'm renting a house near Mary, visiting Stephen every weekend, and applying to the court for custody.'

I lean across and take her hand. 'I'm sorry I didn't believe you.'

Her eyes soften. 'I understand. I know he could be very convincing to begin with.'

'Thank you for your alibi.'

'Well I was there that night, waiting to talk to him, thinking he was living with you midweek. I saw you come home at seven thirty. My eyes were glued to your house. I know you didn't leave.' She pauses and shakes her head. 'I would have spoken out earlier but I was frightened I might be implicated. Later on when I realised, thanks to you, that Alastair had committed the murder, and was even more dangerous than I thought, I knew I had to speak out.'

She takes a sip of her coffee, 'Are you relieved he's dead?' she asks.

'I'm numb. Not glad or sad. Just accepting. Hoping my life will move on after today.'

As we walk to the Coroner's Court, I try to ignore the attractions of Oxford. Its spires and quads, pubs and tearooms. The beauty of its soft, yellow sun-baked colleges. Not wanting to think about my time here with you, Alastair. Trying to push away your memory. The way you tried to control me.

The Coroner's Court is situated in a building which is modern and brutalist. A blot on Oxford's historical landscape. I step inside and shudder. As I pass through security I feel as if I'm entering prison again.

The woman at the information desk informs us, with a shake of her grey curls, the inquest into your death will be held in court two, second floor.

A clerk ushers us into an anteroom to wait 'in peace and privacy', as he explains. It is a small room with coffee in an urn, and rich tea biscuits and Jaffa cakes, laid out on a table in the corner. Heather and I are the only people here. I pour myself a coffee and stand sipping it. It tastes bitter. Heather takes a biscuit.

Mary, your mother, Alastair, enters looking as if she has aged twenty years. Frailer than ever. She hobbles towards us, head down, leaning hard on her walking stick. She walks past us without noticing us and heads towards the refreshments. I step behind her.

'Hello Mary,' I say. 'Can I help you? Can I pour you a coffee?'

She turns around, almost swiping me with her stick, and losing her balance. Heather rushes towards her and takes her arm. Her eyes are red and puffy, as if she has been crying. Black bags beneath them as if she hasn't been sleeping.

'The only way anyone could help me would be to bring back my son.'

The clerk is here.

'It's time to enter the courtroom,' she announces, opening a door on the opposite side of the anteroom to the one we came through.

Heather guides Mary and I follow. Slowly, so slowly. Into the courtroom. A room with a table at the front and four rows of chairs facing it. A man – the coroner, presumably – is sitting behind the table, nodding at us as we enter. He is wearing a silver-grey suit, with a white shirt and yellow tie. His smooth grey hair tones with the grey of the suit. He has a square face and square shoulders.

We sit down, Mary and Heather on either side of me. In the corner of my eye I see DS Jupiter and a sidekick. My stomach rotates. Does she know something I don't? Today's sidekick is a young woman I haven't seen before. She has a long nose and small eyes. Blonde hair. Dark roots.

Other people are arriving. Other people I don't recognise. Doctors? Pathologists? Prison wardens? A prisoner is here, sitting cuffed at the back, a uniformed guard on either side of him.

The prisoner is a skinny man. Heroin-addict thin with a craggy face.

And Jade. Dressed in a baggy black dress. Moving towards me. Sitting behind me. Tapping me on the shoulder. I turn round. She smiles at me with her mouth but not her face. Her lips are drawn and tense. Eyes thunderous. I smile back, a short clipped smile, sit on my hands to disguise their tremor and turn my head back to the front.

'Good morning,' the coroner begins, 'I am opening the inquest into the death of Alastair Brown.' There is a pause. 'First I would like to call Emma Stockton, who visited him in prison just hours before he fell ill.'

First. I didn't realise I would be first. Shocked, I stand up and have a head rush. I hold on to my chair to stop myself from falling. Eyes burn into me. Everyone is staring at the woman who visited you just before you fell ill. The woman who will soon be accused of murdering you. My heart is beating like a dying bird's wings.

'Please come to the front, Emma.'

I walk in slow motion. The room moves around me like a film montage.

'I have read your statement carefully and I just want to double-check you haven't remembered anything more since you made it?'

'No.'

'Just to reiterate, did Alastair say or do anything to insinuate he felt unwell during your visit?'

'No.'

'That's all. Thank you.'

That's all. Relief floods through me so quickly, I feel weak and light-headed again. Spots form in front of my eyes. But I hold on to the coroner's table, on to consciousness, take a deep breath and walk back to my chair. Mary's eyes push into mine like daggers. I push back with mine. *Your son was aggressive to women. You didn't bring him up properly.* I sit down and begin to breathe.

'And now I call Fred Suggs, Alastair's cell-mate,' the coroner continues.

The prisoner I saw sitting at the back earlier steps forwards, uncuffed now. His guard walks with him and stands next to him at the front. Your cell-mate. The man DS Miranda Jupiter said was devastated by your death. He doesn't look well. So thin. So wizened.

'How did Alastair seem to you just before he died?' the coroner asks, glancing at his notes and frowning. 'You were one of the last few people who saw him alive.'

He looks down at the ground in front of him. He swallows. He looks up again, tears welling in his eyes. Mary's face is buried in her handkerchief. She is sobbing gently.

'Something had happened between him and that woman, Emma Stockton.' He points at me. 'She had just visited him and, despite all the trouble she had caused him, she told him she still loved him.'

The coroner's frown deepens. 'Mr Suggs, please, we are just here to ascertain medical facts. We need to keep emotion out of it.' He pauses. 'Did he appear unwell?'

Fred Suggs' face reddens. He bites his lip and continues.

'He said he felt strange. I was about to watch TV. I thought he just meant because of Emma's visit. I didn't realise he was ill. He went to the toilet and I watched *EastEnders*. When *EastEnders* was over I realised he'd been in the bathroom for ages. I went across and knocked on the door. He didn't reply. I turned the door handle. He hadn't locked it so I . . . so I . . .'

He stops speaking. Silence rings around the courtroom, louder than sound.

'Please continue, Mr Suggs,' the coroner prompts.

'So I opened the door and found him. Lying face down on the floor, hardly breathing.'

'Did you touch him? Move the body?'

'No. I just called for help immediately.'

'Thank you, Mr Suggs. That's all.'

The prison guards cuff Mr Suggs and lead him out of court.

The coroner flicks through the pile of papers in front of him. 'Moving on, I would like to call Dr Wilson. The first doctor who examined him in prison.'

A man who looks as if he has just stepped off a golf course steps forward. Chinos. Polo shirt. Unseasonal suntan. Over-whitened teeth.

'How was Alastair when you examined him?'

'Moments off dying. He simply couldn't breathe. He appeared to die of respiratory failure. He died before I could call an ambulance.'

'Thank you, Dr Wilson. Your statement is very clear. Do you have anything to add?'

He shakes his head. 'No, sir.'

'You may sit down,' the coroner instructs. 'Finally I would like to inform those present that the post mortem shows that Alastair Brown did indeed die of acute respiratory failure. No contamination of the body with drugs or chemicals was detected by blood tests. So the verdict of this inquest is death by natural causes. A viral infection is the probable cause.'

I sigh inside with relief that they didn't suspect foul play. Mary's sobbing increases beside me.

147

Emma

Miranda Jupiter is here sitting in my drawing room with the same sidekick she had at the inquest. The long-nosed woman with the bad hairdresser.

Miranda Jupiter looks at me, mouth in a line. 'I'm just curious Emma, is what Fred Suggs said true: that despite everything, you told Alastair you loved him just before he died?'

I take a deep breath. 'Yes. After all, we had been very close once. Even though I was shocked by what he'd done, I missed him. I still had feelings for him.'

She raises her eyebrows. 'Despite the threat to kill you?'

'Despite everything. I'm devastated he has died.'

'Life isn't always straightforward, is it?' There is a pause. 'Anyway, we just popped in to tell you that the CPS have closed the case.' She pauses again. 'Their suspect has died. The Coroner's Court found no suspicious circumstances. The evidence against both you and Jade is too weak to consider reopening.'

The sidekick smiles at me. Champagne corks explode in my head as they stand up to leave.

148

Jade

Standing on your doorstep looking at you. 'I need to talk to you. Can I come in?'

You put your head on one side, considering. You want to say no. I see it in your eyes. But slowly, reluctantly, 'Yes of course,' slips from your mouth.

We step into your drawing room. Your room that boasts of money with its sumptuous fabrics and valuable antiques. Is this where you seduced my husband? Did you do it here, by the fireplace on the deep-pile carpet? Did you burn your buttocks on thousands of pounds' worth of Axminster as you fucked? We sit in the armchairs by the fireplace, looking at each other.

'Is it time to celebrate, now we know the CPS are dropping the case?' I ask.

'I think we can afford to do that.' You smile your whore's smile. The one you used on Tomas. On Alastair.

'Not so fast,' I say, leaning across and putting my hand on your arm. 'Your husband died unexpectedly, like Alastair. I wasn't born yesterday. I'm not stupid like the police.'

Your green eyes darken to emerald. 'Jade, it was you who killed your husband, not me.'

149

Emma

So, I killed my husband. But no one will ever be able to prove it. And I most certainly will never admit it to you, a paranoid woman who thinks I shagged her husband. Let me tell you, Jade Covington: Colin Stockton and Alastair Brown deserved their fates. You are the maverick. Tomas was innocent. Simply a man with toothache. A man who should have been allowed to live.

150

Jade

I lift the carpet in the corner of the hallway, and then the floorboard. I press my right hand into the cavity beneath, feeling for the plastic container. My fingers touch it and I know my stash of Rohypnol is safe. I pick the container off the ground to feel its weight. It's heavy. Plenty left. Operation Emma Stockton on track.

I'm standing, watching your house from my bedroom window, waiting for you to leave. Your Mercedes pulls out of the drive. I wait five minutes and walk from my drive into yours. Past rhododendrons and crinodendrons; pink and red and purple. Past tulips and late daffodils.

I take my hands out of my pockets and ring the front doorbell. No reply. I take the key from my pocket and open the door. You don't know I have copied your house keys, do you? When we had lunch together, and you were ordering your sandwich, you left your bag open. I 'borrowed' your keys and took them to Timpson's. I handed them back to your receptionist who didn't know who I was, telling her I found them on the pavement outside the surgery. I don't suppose you remember, do you Emma? It was almost a year ago now.

So, I'm in your hallway now, burglar alarm buzzing. I found the code in your diary last time. I haven't forgotten it. A tap of the fingers and it shows 'Welcome', allowing me into the core of your house.

Casper pads towards me, tail raised. I kick him away. He flies back towards me, hissing and snarling. Back arched. Hackles raised. Is he a cat or a guard dog? I shout at him and kick him again. This time he runs away.

I dash upstairs into your bedroom. Unmade bed. Yesterday's underwear still on the floor. Not as perfect in private as you like to make yourself look in public. Into your bathroom. I open the cabinet door and plant a large, unmarked tub of Valium.

Then I stand still in the middle of your bedroom, close my eyes, and inhale your scent. I will get my revenge, you perfume-loving whore.

151

Emma

You rang my doorbell, Jade. I see you from my consulting room at the surgery, through my iPhone app attached to my doorbell camera. You are standing ringing the bell, wearing latex gloves. Shifting your weight from side to side, impatiently, as you wait. No reply. I can reply remotely by speaking into my iPhone. But I choose not to. I want to watch you, without you knowing. I need to find out what you are up to. No one will infiltrate my house again without being recorded. After my visit from the thug I have carefully placed internal cameras, all linked to my iPhone.

You ring the bell again, count to ten under your breath, pull some keys from your handbag, unlock my door and step into the hallway. How did you get those keys? Tomorrow I will change my locks.

Casper rushes to greet you. He is a friendly cat who welcomes anyone who comes to the house. You kick him twice. He yowls and runs away to hide behind the sofa in the lounge. I'll be home to kick you, if you go near him again.

You move up the stairs to my bedroom, straight into my bathroom. You open the cabinet and pop a bottle of something in there. I will find out what as soon as I get home.

I thought you would leave after planting something in my bathroom cabinet, but no. You walk back into my bedroom and stand still in the middle of it, eyes closed, inhaling deeply. Inhaling the karma of my house.

I wade through the day at work, longing to get home to check Casper is OK. To see what you have done. As soon as I open the front door he comes to greet me. Rubbing his head against my legs, purring like a rattlesnake.

I race upstairs to see what you have planted in my cabinet. Valium. And I know what you are up to, Jade. You are going to poison me with a concoction of Rohypnol and Valium, and make it look like an overdose. Two can play that game. You killed Tomas in cold blood. You hate me. You are unstable. There is only one way forward for us both.

152

Jade

I ring your doorbell. The door opens and you stand in front of me wearing a pink and purple silk dressing gown. Hair tousled. No make-up. What's happening, Emma? Have you got a new man upstairs? Have you replaced Alastair and Tomas already?

You blink and push your untidy hair from your eyes. 'Hi Jade. What's up, so early on a Saturday morning?'

I frown and look down at my watch: 8:15 a.m. I couldn't sleep. I have been up since 5 a.m. It feels like midday to me.

'Sorry. I didn't realise how early it was. I just wanted to invite you to come around for a drink this evening.'

You hesitate. The thought of any one-to-one time with me always makes you hesitate.

'Please,' I beg. 'I know I upset you last time we spoke. But I think we need to bond together, not argue. I want to be your friend. I want to make it up to you.'

You smile, a wide stretched smile. 'That would be perfect Jade, I've nothing on tonight. What time?'

'About eight p.m.?'

153

Emma

Eight p.m. This is it. The moment I have been waiting for. My invitation to your house for a drink. It's your trap, isn't it, Jade? The way you plan to kill me. Do you really think I trust you after what you did to me before? After what you did to Tomas? After you have planted Valium in my house? I leave my mobile phone at home, on the sofa in the drawing room. I put Netflix on – *Ozarks*, my favourite programme. The one I know off by heart. My new cameras are in the hallway, so I climb out of the side window to visit you.

154

Jade

Everything is ready. Crushed Valium and Rohypnol powder taken from capsules, waiting to slip into your drink. Any drink you choose. Last time it was Cherry Bomb, my special recipe. But I thought you would be suspicious if I tried that again.

You arrive, wearing a dress of cream and lace. You kiss me on both cheeks and surround me with your scent of vanilla and musk.

'Do come into the sitting room,' I say.

You follow me, across my hallway.

'Sit down, make yourself comfortable. What would you like to drink?'

'Red wine please.'

I pad back into the kitchen. Hands trembling, I open a bottle of Cabernet Sauvignon; deliberately chosen because of its strong tasting notes – blackcurrant and tobacco leaf. I know you love red wine. I busy myself decanting half of it into my wine carafe, adding the Valium and the Rohypnol. As I stir the mixture together, it goes a bit cloudy.

I pour the cloudy wine into a black designer glass, from the new set of coloured wine glasses I bought in Debenhams last week. I pour myself a glass from the bottle. My glass is red. Red and black. No confusion. Red for me. Black for you. Soon your world will be black too.

I take the glasses into the sitting room. You are inspecting my flower arrangement. Bent down, sniffing the spring flowers. Pretty as a picture standing next to tulips and daffodils. A powerful combination. Tomas would have had a hard-on looking at you. I hand you your glass and place mine on the table.

Then I remember, I forgot to put out the crisps and nuts. Salty snacks to make you drink more. That's what they do in nightclubs and casinos, isn't it? Hand out the free salty snacks to make people sink more alcohol.

'I'll just be a minute,' I tell you as I dash off. 'Back to get the nibbles.'

You smile. So relaxed and unsuspecting. So far, so good. Everything is going to plan.

155

Emma

As soon as you leave the sitting room, I open the window, pick up your wine glass and tip its contents into the flower bed beneath. I pour the contents of my glass, which I guess you have poisoned, into yours. Drink my chalice and that will test your integrity, you bitch. My generous Mulberry bag contains everything I need to keep myself safe, water to rinse out my glass, tissues to dry it. A small M&S plastic bottle of wine to replace the poison you have given me. As you return with crisps and nuts, I sit sipping my favourite Côtes du Rhône, smiling to myself.

'Would you like some?' you ask, pushing them towards me.

Jade. I know what you are doing, trying to get me to eat salty things.

'No thanks.'

You can't fool me again. I'm not taking any risks.

156

Jade

I watch you take a large gulp of your wine. Good. Good. It is slipping down easily. You look relaxed. As if you are enjoying it. To encourage you to drink I match you, gulp by gulp.

Sipping my wine; heavy and syrupy. Rather pungent taste. I'll avoid labels with 'tobacco leaf' tasting notes next time. But I force myself to drink it to help me relax. You are sitting looking out of the window at my rhododendron bush in full bloom, running your fingers through your silken hair as my plan for you mulches in my head.

You will take your last breath on my sofa. Then I will carry you home under cover of darkness, like I did last time, but I'll make sure I don't drop you. I don't want any evidence to suggest you weren't at home. You will be found dead in bed after taking an overdose. Valium pills planted in your bathroom cabinet. Valium pills scattered around your body. Dying on Saturday night. Such an isolated bitch these days, no one will miss you until Monday when you should be at work.

You are speaking to me but I can't hear what you are saying. I lean towards you. I don't know why but I am slipping off my chair. You help me up.

'Can I get you something, a glass of water perhaps?' you ask.

'No. No, I'm fine,' I try to say, but my words run together, indistinguishable. Incomprehensible. They don't sound anything like what I thought I just said.

You smile at me. Your smile seems to twist and turn in front of me. Faster and faster. As if you are smiling at me from a roundabout that can't stop. Faster and faster. The sky is going darker and darker.

'I need to go home,' you say. 'I've got a lot of paperwork to catch up on tomorrow morning.'

No. No. You can't go. *You won't be able to walk*, I try to warn you. But my words are stuck inside my head.

'Thank you for a lovely evening.'

You stand up. You walk towards the door. I try to stand up too, to follow you. To stop you. But my limbs are like lead, I cannot move. The front door opens and closes.

The world is spinning and then fading around me. Spinning into the distance like a tornado. Darkness swirling around me. Darkness enveloping me. I cannot see. I cannot think.

157

Emma

I'm watching your house, through binoculars, from my bedroom window. I think you must have passed away where you sat. No lights went on upstairs last night.

A car arrives. A pale-blue Mini Cooper. A woman with sandy-coloured shoulder-length hair steps out. I've seen her before. Your chiropodist, I think. She is carrying a large shoulder bag. And her car number plate would spell 'feet', if the letters weren't interrupted by numbers.

She rings the doorbell. No reply. She rings it again. She frowns, and rummages in her handbag for her phone. The person she is calling doesn't pick up. She dials three times. I watch her walking around the house, peering through windows. Into the sitting room. On tiptoes to check the kitchen. She disappears around the back. I hold my breath and wait.

About ten minutes later, sirens begin to whine in the distance. Louder. Closer. Nearer. First an ambulance and then a police car spew across your drive. I put my binoculars away. I need to sit and wait. When you have committed murder, life is a waiting game. Waiting to be discovered, every second of every day.

Two hours later, as I expected, my doorbell rings. I answer the door to find DS Miranda Jupiter and her large-nosed sidekick, standing in front of me.

'Can we come in?' she asks.

'Yes. Of course. What's happened?'

She follows me into the sitting room. She stands in front of the fireplace as if she has a rod up her back. Her sidekick hovers next to her, head down, looking uncomfortable. Casper is here, mewing, pushing his head against my feet.

'Jade is dead. Her body was found in her sitting room. So many substances in the house, it looks as if she committed suicide. But we didn't find a note,' Miranda Jupiter says.

'Oh, how dreadful,' I say, looking down at the strands in my shag-pile carpet.

She moves closer and stands in front of me.

'So much death around you, Emma.' There is a pause. 'This will be taken very seriously by the coroner and by the police. I would like you to come to the station with me now, and make a statement.'

I sit in the back of the police car with the sidekick, who introduces herself as PC Newton. She gives me half a smile as she slips into the seat next to me. I smile back. Close to, she looks so young. Skin so plump and fresh a plastic surgeon could bottle it, and make a fortune. DS Miranda Jupiter starts the car.

I look out of the window as the world that I live in flashes by. High hedges. Well-maintained houses, large enough for twenty people to live in. We turn left onto the main road, and drive through Shiplake towards Reading. Half an hour later we arrive at Loddon Valley Police Station, where I'm escorted to an interview room by DS Jupiter and PC Newton.

Grim-faced, they sit down opposite me. DS Jupiter's eyes are hard. Her body is hard. Everything about Miranda Jupiter is hard.

'Do I need a solicitor?' I ask.

'I don't know, do you?' Miranda Jupiter snaps. 'It depends how defensive you feel.'

'I don't feel defensive. Why should I?'

'Everyone around you seems to die.'

I put my head in my hands. 'I'm going through a difficult time. Some empathy would be nice.'

'This is an interview, not an arrest. We can get it over with now, or wait for a solicitor to arrive. You know the ropes. You've been through it before.'

I look up at her. 'Let's just do it.'

Miranda Jupiter nods at PC Newton, who snaps the recording machine on. She announces the date and time. We all confirm our presence.

Miranda Jupiter puts her arms on the table and leans forwards. 'Where were you last night?' she asks.

'At home.'

Leaning further towards me. 'With anyone?'

'No.' I shake my head. 'Home alone, with my cat.'

'And what time did you get home?'

I frown. I hesitate. 'About seven thirty p.m.'

'What do you mean, "about"? Aren't you not sure?' Voice snappish.

I shrug a little. 'I just finished off at the surgery and then came straight home. I didn't look at my watch at the end of the day. I just got through what I needed to do.' I pause. 'Tania, my dental assistant, left at the same time as me. You can check with her and with the surgery CCTV.' I pause. I make a show of considering. 'Actually, you can see what time I came back on my doorphone camera. It keeps the recordings for five days.'

I open the app and pass my phone to her.

'Seven thirty-four p.m.,' she announces, mouth straight. Her lips twitch as she hands me the phone back. 'Did you leave the house at any time during the evening?'

I shake my head. 'No.'

'What were you doing?' Her mouth turns downwards.

'Watching Netflix – *Ozarks*.'

'Tell me about it. What happened?' she pushes, trying to catch me out, not even knowing what it's about.

'I just watched the first few episodes. The main character, played by Jason Bateman, is in a difficult fix. He has been threatened by a drug baron and has to launder money for him, otherwise he and his family will be murdered. The drug baron has already murdered his business partner.' I pause. 'Actually that's how it starts – with the murder of his business partner, which is why Jason Bateman's character is so terrified. It's a bit like *Breaking Bad* except . . .'

Miranda Jupiter puts her hand in the air. 'OK, OK. That's enough.' Her eyes darken. 'Let's just clarify, as you were home alone, you cannot actually prove you were there? You could have watched *Ozarks* and remembered the plot, any other night.'

'Oh yes, I can prove I was there. My house has cameras; not just the door camera.'

She widens her eyes, as if she doesn't believe me. 'Can you show me?'

I open the app on my phone and show her the rest of the evening's footage. Of me entering the hallway. Grabbing a sandwich in the kitchen. Moving to the drawing room to switch on the TV. A perfectly angled camera. I can't be seen climbing out of the window, and back in again. My absence isn't noted. The film moves on. Eleven p.m. I switch off the TV and go up to bed, followed by my purring cat. A perfect night in.

Miranda Jupiter snaps the recording of our interview off. 'You're free to leave.'

Your house has police tape around it. Forensics are crawling all over it. I can see them from the landing window, in their white suits, searching and swabbing. They will not find the cup I was drinking from. I brought it home with me. They will find my DNA in the house. So what? We were friends. I visited you from time to time.

Your body is in the morgue waiting for autopsy. I picture you on a table waiting for the pathologist to cut you open. Your shiny skin will have a pale-grey hue. The stiffness of death making you hard to recognise; a stone sarcophagus that is no longer you.

What will happen to your beautiful house, Jade? Did you die intestate? Will your money be taken by the government? Or have you left it to charity?

I continue my daily routine, time stagnating around me as I wait for your post mortem. Until the coroner's report is through. Until I know I am safe.

I'm in the surgery, reading my next patient Grace Preston's notes, when I see a police car pull into the car park rather too quickly, screeching to brake beneath my willow tree. Miranda Jupiter steps out with PC Newton. My heart races. Is this it? Are they going to arrest me? I can no longer concentrate on Grace Preston's fillings and the poor state of her dental hygiene. Her receding gums and dental implants. I close my mind to my surroundings, and sit and wait. I hear Miranda Jupiter and PC Newton's voices in reception talking to Andrea.

A knock on the door and they are here, walking towards me. Standing in front of me. I stand up, hands shaking.

'Can I help you?' I ask.

Miranda Jupiter straightens her mouth. 'I just wanted you to know that we've received the coroner's report on Jade Covington.' There is a pause. 'It was suicide. Her body was full of Valium, Rohypnol and alcohol. All drugs she had at home. Also she had mental health issues, and had attempted to kill herself several times before.'

I shake my head. 'That's so sad. Poor Jade.'

'We got in touch with some old friends of hers who are organising the funeral. I'll email you their details.'

'Thanks.'

Silence, except for the hum of traffic moving past.

'I just want to apologise for treating you with such suspicion when you came in for your interview.'

I smile, relief flooding through me. 'That's your job, isn't it?'

A half smile back. Be careful, Miranda, if you smile too much you might strain your facial muscles.

'Goodbye then. I expect you've seen the back of me.'

'I don't mean to be rude, but I hope so.'

'No offence taken.'

And my nemesis for over a year leaves, walking out of my surgery with her young sidekick. I watch the police car pull away. And my body is embalmed with a calming sense of peace.

160

Jade's funeral. Up early to swathe myself in black. At our local crematorium, on a dull April day. Wispy grey clouds frothing across a steely sky, pan scrub and metallic. Walking from the car park to the low-slung red-brick modern building. People standing outside waiting to go in. Huddled together in small groups, heads down, voices low and appropriate. As I approach the entrance of the left-hand chapel, where Jade's funeral is to be held, I see only three people waiting. I recognise the freckled face and sandy hair of her chiropodist, standing a few yards away, vaping. The scent of cherry vape wafts over me, making me feel sick. I step towards the other mourners, a middle-aged couple, with muted smiles, walking towards me. The man's black suit is thin and shiny, accompanied by chunky brown boots. Not City smart. The woman is wearing a black cotton dress splattered with red flowers. Very Laura Ashley.

'Hello, I'm Sam,' he says. 'And this is my wife Tina.' He gesticulates towards the woman standing next to him and she nods.

'Are you here for Jade's funeral?' Tina asks.

'Yes.'

'We met her years ago when we were at college. The college helped us organise a mutual support group, where we mentored one another. That's how I met Tina. That's how we both met Jade.' There is a pause. 'How do you know her?' he asks.

'I'm her neighbour, Emma.'

'A sad day,' Sam says, eyes filling with tears. 'We hadn't seen her for years. Suicide. How tragic. The police got in contact with us after the coroner had made the report, a woman called Miranda Jupiter. She told us that Jade had no living relatives, she was the single child of two single children. Parents and grandparents deceased. They found my name at the top of her contacts list. They needed someone to organise her funeral. So we stepped in for old times' sake. Didn't we, Tina?'

Tina nods her head. 'Even though we were out of touch, we thought it was the least we could do to help an old friend.'

'Did you know her well? And Tomas?' Sam asks.

I hesitated and bit my lip. 'They moved in a year ago January.'

For a second I am back in her kitchen looking at an extravagant arrangement of black and white orchids, her gravelly voice spitting towards me, telling me her husband has a wandering eye. Jade, thanks to you, the last year and a half of my life has been hell.

Sam's eyes well with tears again. 'Really, really tragic.'

It's time to enter the chapel. We step inside together, Sam and Tina and me. It is cooler inside than outside. I shiver and wish I was wearing a heavier coat. The chapel has pale oak pews and white-painted walls. A crucifix rises above Jade's white cardboard environmentally friendly coffin. Like a large cake box with rope handles. The vicar arrives, feet slapping on the floor as he marches to the front. A portly young man with round eyes, round glasses and a grizzly beard. I look at it and wonder how male facial hair managed to come back in style. I thought fashion had moved on from Victorian times.

'Welcome,' he says beaming at us. 'We are not here today to mourn Jade's passing but to celebrate her life.'

Celebrate the life of a woman who killed a man for no reason and set me up for doing it. No. I'm here to celebrate her death. Tina sniffs and Sam passes her a large white hankie.

'We are here to pay our last respects to Jade Covington, a respected member of the community . . .'

I stop listening to him. He obviously didn't know her. Respected member of the community, indeed. Lying to stitch me up. Poisoning me with Cherry Bomb. Attempting to poison me again.

The congregation kneels for the Lord's Prayer. I don't believe it, so I don't join in the chant. I remain seated with my eyes tightly shut and place my hands beneath my buttocks to disguise their tremor. The incantation finishes. Everyone sits up.

'And now it's time for the committal. Please pray for her soul, that she may be happy in heaven with Tomas, forever.'

A recording of classical harp music resonates around the chapel. As the casket moves backwards and the curtains begin to close, my body exhales with relief. The Tomas Covington case is finally over.

I drive home feeling invigorated, restless. So I park my car and go for a walk along the sun-dappled river, towards Temple Island. The grey sky and wispy clouds of earlier have evaporated. I see a woman in jeans and a pink jumper walking towards me on the towpath. Long dark hair. Large brown eyes. As we grow closer I see that it is someone who looks a bit like Miranda Jupiter. But this woman is loose-limbed and smiling. She stops in front of me.

'Hello Emma, how are you doing?'

I recognise the voice. The eyes. It is Miranda Jupiter. More relaxed when not at work.

'I'm OK. Just got back from Jade Covington's funeral.'

Her eyes moisten. 'What a sad case.' She puts her hand on my arm. 'I hope you can move on from your grief, and enjoy the rest of your life.'

161

Miranda Jupiter, thank you for your good wishes. I'm moving on with my life. Big time. I'm sitting at my computer searching for men on Tinder again. The first man I look at is far too old for me. I do not want to become a nursemaid. I swipe left. The next one – a bit like Matt Damon. I swipe right.

Left. Right. Right. Left.

Then a demi–god appears in front of me, beaming at me from the computer screen. A cross between Channing Tatum and Jude Law, with pale-brown hair and toffee eyes. I swipe right, desire rising, starting in my stomach and throbbing through my body. I will definitely contact him first.

I hope I find a good relationship now. Men can be so controlling at times.

Acknowledgements

A long list this time. First, the team at Avon HarperCollins with thanks to Sabah Khan and Phoebe Morgan. And my inspirational new editor, Tilda McDonald, whose guidance with this tricky, forensically challenging novel has been invaluable. My agent, Ger Nicholl of The Book Bureau, who is so supportive. A good agent is a friend indeed.

This novel has required a lot of scientific research and input. I would like to thank Dave Sivers, Clare Heron – a senior crime scene investigator – and my police adviser, Charles Owens. My medical adviser Lindsay Parr. Joanna Tempowski and Carol Robson, my scientific advisers. Don't blame any of them if you find a fault. This is a story, not a scientific exposition – and I do sometimes bend their advice.

Let me mention the Psych Thriller Killers: Caroline England, Sam Carrington and Libby Carpenter. My fun-loving writer friends who liven up my life.

Special mention to my close family and friends, they know who they are. They are the pivot my world swings around.

And last, but by no means least, my husband, my first reader, without whose judgement and support over the years I would never have become a published writer.

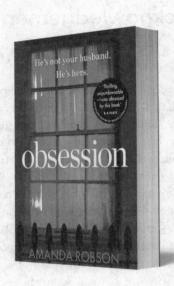

The claustrophobic, compulsive thriller about the murder of a twin sister

'I read it over one weekend, completely enthralled'
Emma Curtis, author of
The Night You Left

A stalker. A secret.
Someone will pay . . .

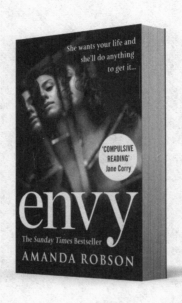

'Captivated me from the unsettling opening until the breath-taking finale'
Sam Carrington, author of
Bad Sister